Valissa's Home

Valissa Prescott stared at Milton Bower. What did the solicitor say? She must have heard him wrong. There was no way her half-brother Kyle could have been so careless. He couldn't have gambled away everything they owned, including her home. He just couldn't have. Or could he?

Milton said everything the Prescott siblings owned was gone. Even the house. The beautiful pink-brick structure in one of Galveston's most desirable neighborhoods. The estate where three generations of Prescotts had lived. The home her grandfather had built for his wife and named 'Heartsong' when the shipping business had become prosperous. The home where her mother was born, and had been the mistress until she died of a fever when Valissa was ten years old. The home where her father bled to death from a bullet wound from an angry rival when Valissa was fourteen. The home her half-brother was to hold in trust for her until she married or until her twenty-fifth birthday if she remained single. If she were married between the ages of nineteen and twenty-five, she and her new husband would get Heartsong immediately. Valissa would celebrate her nineteenth birthday in November.

According to her grandfather's friend and solicitor, the stipulation no longer mattered. Heartsong didn't belong to the Prescott family any longer. It was owned by a stranger. Someone who had no connection with the family at all. Someone who wouldn't care about the history of how the beloved mansion had always sheltered the Prescott family.

How could Kyle have been so irresponsible?

VALISSA'S HOME

by

Agnes Alexander

A Wings ePress, Inc.

Western Historical Novel

Wings ePress, Inc.

Edited by: Jeanne Smith
Copy Edited by: Leslie Hodges
Senior Editor: Jeanne Smith
Executive Editor: Marilyn Kapp
Cover Artist: Pat Evans

Wings ePress Books
http://www.wings-press.com

Copyright © 2011 by Lynette Hampton
ISBN 978-1-61309-850-9

Published In the United States Of America

September 2013

Wings ePress Inc.
403 Wallace Court
Richmond, KY 40475

Dedication

To the memory of my dear friend, Vera Brewer, who attended many book signings with me.

One

Valissa Prescott stared at Milton Bower. What did the solicitor say? She must have heard him wrong. There was no way her half-brother Kyle could have been so careless. He couldn't have gambled away everything they owned, including her home. He just couldn't have. Or could he?

Milton said everything the Prescott siblings owned was gone. Even the house. The beautiful pink-brick structure in one of Galveston's most desirable neighborhoods. The estate where three generations of Prescotts had lived. The home her grandfather had built for his wife and named 'Heartsong' when the shipping business had become prosperous. The home where her mother was born, and had been the mistress until she died of a fever when Valissa was ten years old. The home where her father bled to death from a bullet wound from an angry rival when Valissa was fourteen. The home her half-brother was to hold in trust for her until she married or until her twenty-fifth birthday if she remained single. If she were married between the ages of nineteen and twenty-five, she and her new husband would get Heartsong immediately. Valissa would celebrate her nineteenth birthday in November.

According to her grandfather's friend and solicitor, the stipulation no longer mattered. Heartsong didn't belong to the Prescott family any longer. It was owned by a stranger. Someone who had no connection with the family at all. Someone who wouldn't care about the history of how the beloved mansion had always sheltered the Prescott family.

How could Kyle have been so irresponsible? He was twelve years older than Valissa; therefore their father probably considered him capable and responsible enough to take care of his younger sister. The will had been written while Edward Prescott was dying, so there was no disputing it. Kyle received the shipping business, which he promptly sold, and Valissa was to receive the estate with an allowance her brother was to provide through Milton Bower as banker and solicitor to keep the place running.

Mr. Bower insisted that, at the time, no one had known about Kyle's gambling and drinking habits. No one had ever guessed that his trips out of town were spent losing money in gambling houses, bordellos, and saloons.

He informed her that, when it began to dawn on the bank that Kyle Prescott had depleted the large account in his name and had begun to dip into Valissa's inheritance, they tried to stop him from leaving his little sister in dire straits. It was no use. They could do nothing. Little by little, Kyle had let all their inheritance slip away. Of course no one informed Valissa of any of this until this meeting with Milton Bower.

"Why didn't someone tell me?" Valissa looked at him with her big aqua-blue eyes that were misting in spite of her resolve not to cry.

"I'm so sorry, my dear. We all thought it best if we didn't bother you with the details until we had to. We actually thought maybe Kyle would come around with some answer." Mr. Bower's soft voice seemed to try to sooth her. "As I was about to explain, Valissa, the new owner of Heartsong has given you three weeks to vacate the premises."

"Three weeks?" she stammered.

"I'm afraid so." He cleared his throat. "Of course you're to take nothing with you with the exception of your clothes and your personal items. The contents and the house belong to him now."

"But what about my mother's silver collection? It was handed down to her by her great-grandmother. Everyone knew it was supposed to be mine one day."

"I'm sorry, Valissa. The silver has to go with the house." He had a strange look in his eyes. He had to be embarrassed, since he'd been one of the people in the bank appointed to keep an eye on her and Kyle. As least, she knew he must want to get this meeting over with as soon as possible.

Again biting back tears, she asked, "How about money, Mr. Bower? Surely my brother made provisions for me to have some money to resettle someplace else."

Again he said, "I'm so sorry, my dear, there's no cash. Kyle depleted all of the accounts."

"But my monthly allowance…"

"There will be no more allowance. You got the last one in September."

"But the servants? How will I pay the servants?" Valissa began to feel desperate.

"I think you should tell them the situation and let them seek other employment. Everyone in town knows what good employees they are and there is simply no more money left for you to pay them."

Valissa felt as if she were in the midst of a nightmare, one she hoped to wake from at any minute. She closed her eyes. Maybe if she could get in touch with Kyle, he'd tell her it was all a big mistake. That some mixup had caused the money to be put someplace else and he would straighten it out. "Do you know where my brother is, Mr. Bower?"

He looked away. "The last the bank heard from him he was withdrawing the last of the money. Someone told me later he said he was heading to California. Said he was sure his luck would change in San Francisco."

Valissa's heart sank. If he were that far away, she probably would never hear from him again. She took a deep breath and stood. "Then, I guess there's nothing else we have to talk about."

He rose from behind the mahogany desk and came to put his arm around her shoulder. "I'm so sorry about this, Valissa, my dear. I know if your father had ever guessed this would happen, he would've done things differently."

Valissa was a little uncomfortable and she moved away from the man. "I'm sure he would have."

"My best advice to you is to find yourself a husband as quickly as you can."

"What man would want to marry a penniless heiress, Mr. Bower?" She looked at him, again her eyes misting.

He patted her arm and gave her a wry smile. "I bet a lot of men would jump at the chance. You're a beautiful girl. Why, if I didn't have a wife and wasn't old enough to be your grandfather, I'd marry you myself."

She forced a smile. "Thank you, Mr. Bower."

"Shall I send for a buggy for you, Miss Prescott?" He placed his hand in the center of her back, ushered her out his office door and across the lobby of the bank.

She started to tell him to do that, then she remembered the small amount of money she had in her reticule. Though it was several blocks home, she said, "No, thank you. It's a lovely day. I think I'll walk."

"Please call on me if I can be of any help to you," he whispered. "I will try to do all I can to make this as painless for you as possible."

Valissa nodded, but knew there was nothing more to say. She let him open the front door and she left the office with her head held high, though her spirits sank as low as some of those lost pirate ships out in the Gulf.

The wind whistled around the corners, making it hard walking. It took Valissa almost thirty minutes to reach the house. Though the streets were cobblestone, dust raised by the wind had settled in the folds of her worn deep green velvet skirt and on the sleeves of her jacket. Her matching hat was askew and sported a sprinkling of slender maple leaves. Her raven hair fell around her neck and her ears. If this weren't enough, when she reached home she saw Wilbur Colbert's buggy parked at the walk leading to the front door.

Valissa sighed. Hadn't she been humiliated enough today? Now she had to face Wilbur Colbert, the most annoying man she knew. He'd been calling on her for several weeks. She was sure he knew she was soon to reach her nineteenth birthday and would be the owner of Heartsong if she married. He had actually told her he wanted to be first in line to ask her for her hand. She had fluffed it off because she knew she'd never marry him. Now she wondered what he'd say when she informed him she was penniless and the grand estate that was supposed to be hers belonged to a stranger.

"Well, I might as well get it over with," she muttered and climbed the steps to the double carved wooden front doors with their leaded glass panels.

The door opened. The tall thin maid, with a neat silver ball of hair on the top of her head said, "Miss Valissa, Mr. Colbert is here to see you. I put him in the parlor."

"Thank you, Flo."

Valissa knew Flo noticed her unkempt condition when she asked, "Would you like to freshen up before you go in, Miss?"

"No. I'll see him now." She turned around. "After he leaves, I need to talk with you, Flo."

"Yes, Miss."

Valissa crossed the marble entrance and slid the parlor doors open. "Hello, Wilbur."

He hopped up from his seat on the blue crushed-velvet settee. "My dear, you look tired and your hair is windblown. Were you walking in this terrible weather?"

Valissa couldn't help noticing he was not much taller than her five feet and six inches. She reined her thoughts in and answered him. "I had some business at the bank and I decided to walk home."

"Oh, my. You foolish girl. You should have never done that. I'm sorry I wasn't at the bank to help you, then I would have gladly sent my carriage to bring you home."

She reached up and removed her hat. She stuck the long stick pin in it and placed it on the harpsichord. "I enjoy walking during this lovely time of year. I like looking at the leaves as they begin to dress in their fall colors."

"But, my dear, don't you realize that a delicate lady such as yourself should never be on the streets alone, even in daylight hours? I don't care if you think it is lovely outside, it's still dangerous."

She ignored his statement. "Would you like some tea, Wilbur?"

"No, thank you, my sweet. I can't stay long. I need to get back to the bank. I only came by to invite you to attend Mrs. Eugenia

Maxmillion's party next month. You know it will be the event of the fall season. Many important people will be attending." He straightened his tie. "The man who owns my uncle's bank, along with several other businesses, is coming to town and we hope he'll be here in time for the event. I hear Mrs. Maxmillion has decided she wants her daughter to marry this wealthy bachelor."

"Wouldn't somebody that rich be too old for Candice Maxmillion?"

Wilbur shrugged. "You know how homely Candice Maxmillion is. Maybe her mother thinks an old man won't be picky when it comes to a wife."

"That isn't nice, Wilbur. Candice can't help… "

"Come now, dear. You know good and well Candice is tall for a woman and she has the face of…"

"I thought the Maxmillions were friends of your uncle's family."

"They're very good friends. I think for a while after I came to live with them, Mrs. Maxmillion wanted Candice to set her cap for me." He sighed. "Even for all their money, I couldn't see myself married to such a woman. Now you, on the other hand…"

Valissa shook her head.

He sighed. "Well, at least we're good friends."

"Are we, Wilbur?"

"What?"

"Are we good friends?"

"Of course we are, my dear. You know how I feel about you. You're going to need a level-headed man to help you manage this estate…"

"I'm sure Heartsong will continue to be well managed." She wondered if she should tell him the place he was dreaming about owning through marrying her belonged to some stranger.

"That's something we can discuss later." He moved closer to her. "Now will you please accept my invitation to this important social event? It'll be a good excuse for you to have Mrs. Dupree-Fontaine design a beautiful new gown for you."

Valissa knew it could never happen. Even if she went to the dance, there was no way she could have a new dress designed, but she said anyway, "A new gown would be nice."

"See. I know what ladies such as you care about. All you have to do is relax and let me take care of you."

"I can take care of myself, Wilbur."

"Of course, you think you can, but you're wrong. What in the world would have happened to you if your dear brother hadn't been taking care of your inheritance these last few years?"

She felt a stab in her heart and couldn't keep the sharpness out of her voice. "I assure you, I wouldn't be in the condition I'm in now."

Wilbur completely misunderstood her statement. He smiled as he reached for his hat. "At least you understand men always know the best thing to do when it comes to business. Now, are you going to tell me you'll go to the party with me?"

"I'll tell you this, Wilbur. If I'm still here on that Saturday next month, I'll go to Mrs. Maxmillion's party with you."

"Where else would you be, my dear?"

"I could be anywhere."

"You silly girl." He took her hand and lifted it to his lips. "I'm so glad you accepted my invitation. I was afraid there were others who might plan to invite you to the event because you'll soon inherit Heartsong, but now they'll be too late." He gave her a silly grin. "They won't have a chance, because I know you won't be changing your mind about who your escort will be."

She ignored his statement about Heartsong. He'd find out soon enough that she wouldn't be inheriting anything. "Thank you for the invitation, Wilbur."

"Thank you for accepting. Of course I'll see you before then, but I'm dearly looking forward to our first dance at that party." He was still grinning. "Why, we may even have an announcement to make that night."

Without giving her time to answer, he strode to the door. Then he turned and blew her a kiss.

When the front door closed, she shook her head. The thought crossed her mind that she might be able to talk Wilbur into eloping before it became known she was no longer a marriageable young society lady. Would he…? "Don't be ridiculous," she muttered. "Being married to Wilbur Colbert would be a worse future than being penniless."

~ * ~

The enclosed black carriage pulled by two handsome black geldings clopped its way down the cobblestone street. Pulling back the shade with his large calloused hand, Nathan Stone looked out. The sun had gone down and dusk was settling over the city. He was a little tired and hungry, but they should be there in the next few minutes. As soon as he arrived, he'd get the staff to prepare a quick supper, if they were still there.

It was too bad he hadn't had time to send a message that he was coming to check out his property, but he had to get away from Stone Ranch. Things had become tense between him and his stepmother. He knew he'd given the former owner of this estate three weeks to move, but he had taken all he could from his stepmother without saying something he would regret.

Since he'd heard the fool who lost this place in a poker game had already headed to California to try his luck with the gaming there, Nathan figured he might as well take possession today instead of going to a hotel. There should be no problem. He only hoped the staff was still in residence and was reliable. He'd keep them in place if they were. That would be simpler than having to find a new team for this house. Certainly he wanted to keep his faithful employees at the ranch because they offered all the peace he found there. Though when he was in Galveston, he knew he'd miss Rosita's cooking and Carlos's instructions of how things should be run, he didn't want them moving here. He'd only use this house when he had to be in town or when he had to get away for some peace and quiet. Because of the work there, he'd still have to spend most of his time at the ranch in spite of Ada Stone's constant bickering.

The carriage turned onto the street where his new purchase sat and Nathan looked at the surroundings of his new estate. *Not bad. I should be able to make out fine when I'm here. If I decide to marry her, Maurine should like it, too. She's always talking about buying a big house in town. Of course she means Fort Worth, but this will have to do.*

He had his driver, Phillips, circle the block and noticed the large stables and the guest house on the back section of the property. The gardens were beautiful if a little unkempt. This surprised him. He didn't think a gambler would bother with gardens in the first place. Maybe the fool had a few redeeming qualities.

Phillips stopped at the front of the mansion when they came back around. Without waiting for his driver to climb down and open the door, Nathan jumped out. "Go ahead and put the horses in the stable, Phillips, then come to the house. I'm sure you're hungry, too. If nobody's here, I'm sure we can rustle up something." He bounded up the front steps. Not wanting to scare the servants if they were there, he didn't use the key to go inside. He paused and banged the big brass knocker.

In a few minutes a tall, slender woman with a severe gray bun on the top of her head opened the door. "Yes, sir?"

"Ma'am, I'm Nathan Stone, the new owner of this house and I'm moving in."

~ * ~

Like everyone else at the dinner table, Rowena Colbert was stunned when Milton Bower related the story of Valissa Prescott's destitute status. She was having a hard time believing it. After all, she'd grown up with Valissa, the two had been friends since they were little girls and the families had been close through the years. Since the girls were the same age and got along so well, their mothers insisted they attend the same finishing school in Virginia. And unbeknownst to anyone, Rowena had always had a secret crush on Kyle Prescott, though he was twelve years older than the girls.

She dabbed her mouth with her napkin to hide her surprise and continued to listen to the conversation.

"Oh, Milton, you must be mistaken." Beverly Colbert placed her hand on her breast and looked across the dinner table at the solicitor. "I can't believe this."

"I'm afraid he's telling the truth, Beverly. He came home all upset about it." Thelma Bower answered for her husband, which she often did. Though she didn't know it, everyone in their circle of friends talked about it behind her back.

"Anyone would have been upset. The poor girl was devastated. She never dreamed her brother would run through their fortune in such a way." Milton accepted the coffee the maid poured him. "I wanted to take her home and take care of her, she looked so alone and distraught."

"What will she do now?" Lyman Colbert asked as he served the huge beef roast the servant had placed before him.

"I told her she should find a husband before too many people found out about her state of affairs." Milton looked pleased with himself.

"As if anyone she knows would marry her, knowing she'd lost everything." Thelma stuck her nose in the air. "I don't know why Milton feels so sorry for her. She should have managed her money better."

"I'm sure you're right that no man in our circle will marry her now. It would be too humiliating for everyone," Beverly muttered. "I know Wilbur won't be going there again."

"It's a pity. I thought he'd marry Miss Prescott and be able to own Heartsong someday." His uncle shook his head. "It's a beautiful place. Would've been a fine place for Wilbur to live."

A still-stunned Wilbur spoke for the first time. "I thought I would one day own it, too. I even went by there this afternoon and invited Valissa to Mrs. Maxmillion's party."

"What did she say?" Rowena muttered.

"She accepted, of course."

"Oh, Wilbur, you can't escort her to that party. People will know all about her losing Heartsong by then. Why, you'd be the laughing stock of the community. Isn't that right, Beverly?" Thelma Bower asked.

His aunt nodded and looked at him. "There's no way we can let that happen. I'm sorry, but you'll just have to tell the poor girl you can't take her to the party. Don't you agree, Lyman?"

"Yes, I agree with your aunt, Wilbur. As I told you, the owner of the bank is coming into town and I don't want you to embarrass us. You can't let a man like him know you're escorting a penniless nobody around town. It would be a bad reflection on all of us. Especially you and me."

"I think that's a little harsh, Lyman." Milton looked at him. "Miss Prescott is still a beautiful young woman. A lot of men may still find her intriguing. She could end up some rich man's mistress before it's all over."

The women all gasped and Lyman said, "Maybe so, Milton, but you know how things work. If I let my nephew spend his time with a disinherited heiress before she gets her life straight, it wouldn't be long until people began to wonder how I run things at the bank. Even the owner might have questions." He grinned. "I hear the man is not married and I intend for him to meet my daughter."

"Oh, Daddy. You can't be serious." Rowena couldn't help the frown, not only because of her father's remark, but at the idea Milton suggested about Valissa becoming someone's mistress.

Before he could answer, Beverly said, "We must protect our children from this mistake. That means you have to give up your friendship with Valissa Prescott, Rowena. Since she'll no longer be accepted in our circle, I can't have my daughter being her friend."

"Valissa and I have been friends since we were little girls," Rowena protested. "I don't want to give up our friendship."

"Your mother's right, dear girl," Thelma said. "Your actions always reflect on the family, whether you want them to or not."

Her father must have noticed that Rowena was becoming upset. "Listen, sweetheart, I know it's hard to accept, but the women are right. You have to be careful of who you are friends with. Why don't you concentrate on becoming better friends with the Maxmillion girl?"

Rowena bit her lip, but she didn't answer. What could she say? She'd always listened to her parents and tried to be the daughter they wanted. But this was asking too much. How was she supposed to give up a friendship as old and as deep as the one she had with Valissa?

"Tell me about the man who's coming to town, Lyman." Milton Bower changed the subject and all eyes turned to him. "Have you met him before?"

"No. He's some rich rancher who has invested his money in a lot of businesses around the state. He'll arrive in a few days, I'm sure."

"Lyman invited him to stay with us, but he wired back that he had other plans." Beverly wiped her mouth with the white linen napkin. "It would have been nice to have him here. Rowena could have gotten to know him and you never know what could have happened."

"I guess that would be all right, since you and Lyman are here to chaperone, but isn't he too old for Rowena?" Thelma asked.

"Lyman isn't sure how old he is, but a lot of older men like pretty young wives and I'm sure he would be more attracted to my Rowena than poor Candice Maxmillion."

Thelma grinned, but hid it behind her napkin.

"That's for sure," Milton said, but nobody contradicted him.

After the maid served dessert, the men excused themselves and said they were going into the den for brandy and one of the expensive new cigars Lyman had been able to import.

The women retired to the sitting room with tea. Rowena's mind still reeled with the news about Valissa and she was content to sit quietly and let her mother and Thelma Bower do most of the talking. Of course the conversation centered mostly on Valissa's terrible ordeal and the shame it would bring on the Prescott name.

Two

Valissa was exhausted. She'd had a heart-wrenching talk with Flo and her husband, Alvin, after Wilbur left. The wonderful couple had insisted that they were not going anywhere as long as their mistress was still at Heartsong. With grateful tears in her eyes, Valissa accepted their gracious faithfulness and hugged them both.

She then escaped to her room and wondered if she could find some way to pay her faithful servants a small amount. After some deliberation, she remembered she'd heard some society women sold their used gowns at the docks for quick money. Women on the fringe of society, who couldn't afford to have dresses designed and made, were eager to buy the ones those of the upper class didn't want or need any more. Of course most of Valissa's ball gowns were old. She'd even had some of them made over and redesigned a few times and now they were beginning to show some age.

As she surveyed her clothes, it dawned on her she didn't become poor in one day. She'd been headed in this direction for a while. Though she'd spent little money on clothes and other things women needed, most of what she had went for necessities. Her monthly allowance had barely paid the servants and other essential household expenses.

"I'm not a stupid person. Why wasn't I more aware of what was happening?" she said aloud and dropped to the side of the bed with a dress in her hand. "If I'd known what Kyle was up to, maybe I could have stopped him. Oh, I could just shake him. How could he do this to me? To us? What has he done with all the money? How could he have gambled it all away?"

The sound of the knocker on the front door interrupted her thoughts. She dropped the dress she was holding and went to the window. "Lord, I hope Wilbur hasn't come back."

She saw a carriage heading down the drive toward the stables. She frowned. The sight of the black carriage drawn by those beautiful black horses gave her a strange feeling. Who could it be? And who would have the audacity to stable their horses before being invited inside as an overnight guest?

She put the dress back in her wardrobe and decided she'd go downstairs and find out who had arrived. Before she could there was a tap on her door.

"Yes?"

"Miss Valissa, there's a man downstairs who says he's the new owner of Heartsong and wants me to fix him some supper. I put him in the study."

"But Mr. Bower said I had three weeks to get out of the house."

Flo looked helpless. "I didn't know what to do except let him in. Supper is almost ready and there's enough for him."

"You did the right thing letting him in, Flo, but I don't know about feeding him. Maybe I can get him out of here before we eat." Valissa followed the servant down the stairs.

The study door was closed. "Would you like me to bring some tea, Miss Valissa?"

"Make it coffee, Flo. From the looks of this man's carriage, I don't think he's the tea type."

"Yes, Miss." She headed toward the kitchen.

Valissa started to knock on the door, but changed her mind. After all, until her allotted three weeks were up, this was still her house. Mr. Bower had said so and she was counting on him being right.

She pushed the door open and stepped inside. A man stood with his back to her looking out the window. He was the biggest man she'd ever seen. Not fat, just massive. He was at least six feet and five or six inches tall. He had wide shoulders that seemed to have muscles on muscles. His waist tapered to powerful hips and his thighs, which were encased in tight black breeches, were almost as big around as her waist. His rusty brown hair curled around the collar of his white linen shirt. He wore a black vest and there was a holster hanging low from his waist. The pistol it held boasted a pearl handle.

Valissa's heart raced. This was no ordinary man. Even from behind he looked as if he could kill a man without a second thought. She didn't know whether to run or to make her presence known.

Before she could make up her mind, he turned. His brown eyes bored into hers when he asked in a deep voice, "Who the hell are you?"

Valissa couldn't speak. She wasn't sure if it was from fright or from being mesmerized by this giant of a man.

"Well, speak up. You can talk, can't you?"

She nodded.

He dropped his right hand to the butt of his gun. "Then I suggest you say something before I shoot you for trespassing. Now, who are you?"

Finally she blinked back her stunned expression and whispered, "Valissa Prescott."

His brow wrinkled. "So the scoundrel was married. I wasn't informed of that."

When she said nothing, he moved toward her.

Valissa backed against the door and held on to the knob behind her. It helped hold her up because she wasn't sure her rubbery knees would do the job.

The man was almost close enough that her nose touched one of the buttons on his white shirt. She smelled the scents of spice, tobacco and a hint of male musk. She tried to back away, but she was already against the door and couldn't go any farther.

"I must say," the giant said as he reached out and took one of her raven curls in his hand. "Prescott has good taste in women. I don't see why he left you behind. You're a looker."

"I don't understand," she muttered.

"I'm just trying to understand why your man took off to California and left you here to face me alone." He gave her an evil grin. "Well, pretty lady, maybe that wasn't a bad idea. I wouldn't mind having a pretty little woman like you around. I'm sure I'd enjoy you warming my bed while I'm at this house."

Valissa snapped to her senses and glared at him. "How dare you say such a thing to me! This is my house, at least it is until my three weeks are up."

"I don't think so. I bought this place from a gambling friend of mine. It's all legal and registered and everything. My lawyer saw to that." He grinned again. "But I must say, I didn't expect such a nice bonus to be waiting for me here."

"I was not waiting for you, sir. My solicitor told me I had three weeks to move out. He didn't say I'd be invaded by an ill-mannered, despicable oaf such as you." Valissa's chin rose ever so slightly.

He laughed out loud. "I've been called that before. But not as charmingly as you did it."

She ignored him. "What are you doing here?"

"As I said, I own the place. I felt since it belongs to me, I should come and see what my money purchased." His eyes roamed her body.

"Well, your money didn't purchase me," she snapped. "Please back away and let me catch my breath."

"If you insist, but I must say, I like taking your breath away."

He backed up.

Valissa opened the door and left it open. "I think we should talk," she said, moving to one of the brown leather wing chairs her father kept in his study for his business meetings.

As soon as she sat, he closed the door. "I agree we should talk first. But when we undress, I think we should have a little privacy."

"You…you…"

A tap at the door interrupted. "Come in," Valissa called before he could say anything.

Flo came in with a silver coffee pot and two cups on a large silver tray. She'd also placed a few sugar biscuits on a lacy linen napkin beside the pot. "Shall I put them on this table, then serve you, Miss Valissa?"

"Yes, Flo, Thank you."

The man watched them and she could see interest in his eyes. He said nothing, but took the coffee when Flo handed him a cup.

"Would you like cream or sugar, sir?"

"Black is fine."

She put cream in Valissa's coffee, then asked, "Will there be anything else, Miss?"

"Yes, Flo. Would you have your husband come to the house? I need to discuss something with him. He can wait for me in the kitchen."

"Yes, Miss." Flo looked confused, but she said nothing further.

As she scooted out of the room, the man said, "I hope you're getting that supper ready I asked for. I'm still hungry."

"I…ugh…" She looked at Valissa.

"It's all right, Flo. Let me know when supper is served."

"Yes, ma'am." This time she made it out the door.

"Well, well, Lady Prescott, I must say, you're not only beautiful, but you have some smarts in that pretty little head of yours. Sending for the maid's husband to let me know you weren't going to be taking your clothes off for me tonight was a smart move."

"That's right. I won't be taking my clothes off for you tonight or any night, Mr. …whoever you are."

"May I remedy that question for you? My name is Nathan Stone. As I said, I now own this estate. Heartsong, I believe it's called, but I'm not sure I like that name. Sounds a little feminine to me."

Valissa gasped. "You can't change the name of Heartsong."

"Listen, sweetheart." His voice boomed and she jumped. He went on without lowering his tone. "This place now belongs to me. I'll call it any damn thing I choose and I'll make any changes I damn well please to make it the home I'll be living in while I'm in Galveston."

Valissa lowered her eyes. What could she say? He was right. He owned the place and there was nothing she could do about it. At this moment, she almost hated her half-brother.

"Mr. Bower told me I had three weeks to vacate this home. I only learned today that I no longer own it."

"I didn't know anyone was living in the house. I heard the man who gambled it away had headed for California."

"I learned that today, too." She sipped her coffee as he eyed her. "I'll see about getting out as soon as I can make arrangements. I have to locate somewhere else to go."

"So, your husband left …."

"Mr. Stone, I have no husband. My brother gambled away…."

He frowned. "Your brother lost this house in a poker game and left you with no place to go?"

"Yes, Mr. Stone. That seems to be what happened."

"Damn. It takes a low down son-of-a-bitch to do that to his sister."

She had the urge to defend Kyle, but she knew she couldn't. Instead she said, "If you'll give me a couple of days, I can be out of your house, Mr. Stone."

"Where will you go, Miss Prescott? It is Miss Prescott, isn't it?"

"Yes. It's Miss Prescott and I don't see that it's any of your business where I go as long as I leave your house." She stuck her chin in the air and rose to exit. "I assume you'll go to a hotel until I'm gone."

He chuckled. "You assume wrong, my dear. This is my house. I intend to stay right here."

"But…you can't…you…"

"Don't be ridiculous. Of course I can." He gave her a slight grin. "I'll be moving into the master suite tonight."

"But it's not proper."

"If you don't think it's proper, then I suggest you go to a hotel and come back tomorrow to pack." His brown eyes raked over her body.

"I can't afford to waste what little money I have left by staying in a hotel," she snapped, then wished she'd kept quiet about her financial situation. It was none of his business.

"Then, Miss Prescott, feel free to spend what few nights you have left in this house. I have no objections." He sat his cup on the desk.

"Now, I want to see if the servant has supper ready. I've had a long trip and I'm hungry."

"Flo happens to be very efficient. I'm sure she'll be able to find you something to eat."

"I figured as much. As a matter of fact, I smelled a wonderful mixture of cooking odors when I came in."

There was a knock on the door. "Supper is ready, Miss Prescott," Flo announced.

"Good." Nathan moved across the room and took Valissa's arm in his hand. "Let's go eat. We can finish our discussion over food."

Valissa jerked her arm, but was unable to dislodge it from the powerful hand that held her. Though he wasn't hurting her at all, he still held firmly. "I can get to the dining room on my own."

"Don't be silly. A gentleman always escorts a lady to supper and you are a lady, aren't you, Miss Prescott?"

She didn't answer and he didn't lesson his grip as they went out the door.

When they entered the dining room, he walked her to the table and pulled a chair out to the right of the head of the table. Not wanting to argue any more, Valissa allowed herself to be seated. She wondered if he planned to eat across from her.

He didn't.

As if he'd always been the master here, he pulled out the chair at the head of the table and sat. Valissa was so surprised at his audacity that she didn't say anything.

Flo appeared with a platter of roast beef surrounded by carrots and potatoes. She placed it in front of Nathan. Hurrying back to the kitchen, she soon reappeared with a bowl of peas and a basket of freshly baked bread. The butter was already on the table.

"For someone in dire straits financially, I must say you eat well, Miss Prescott."

"I figured since I couldn't stay here much longer, I'd not leave the better supplies for the new owner. I decided to eat what I wanted from the pantry." She eyed him.

"Again, I admire your ingenuity." He took the carving knife and pulled the platter to him. "Hand me your plate."

She started to tell him that she wasn't hungry, but changed her mind. Why should she let him enjoy this delicious meal and she go hungry? She picked up her plate and held it out to him.

He placed a large slice of roast on it, then scooped up potatoes and carrots to go with it. While he filled his plate, she picked up the peas and added them to her meal. Without a word, she handed the bowl to him.

They ate in silence for several minutes. He broke it. "I must say, your servant is a wonderful cook. What did you say her name was?"

"I didn't say, but it's Flo. Flo Sherman. Her husband is Alvin." Valissa sighed. "I don't know what will become of them. They've worked for the Prescott family for over twenty-five years."

He raised an eyebrow. "Aren't you taking them with you?"

"I wish I could, but there's no way I can pay them and they have to make a living."

"I see." He reached for a second helping. "Would you like more?"

She shook her head. "No thank you. I'm getting full."

Flo came back into the dining room. "Miss Prescott, there's a man in the kitchen. His name is Ryan Phillips. He said I was to feed him."

"That would be my driver," Nathan said. "I'm sure he'd appreciate some of your wonderful cooking. We've had a long, hard drive."

Flo looked unsure, but when Valissa nodded, she said, "I'll see that he gets his fill."

"I noticed that Flo is devoted to you, Miss Prescott."

"As I said, she's been here a long time."

"But you're not going to be able to take her with you when you move out?"

"That's right."

By the time Flo served them peach pie and coffee, Nathan Stone seemed to be in a better mood. When he pushed back his chair, he said, "I have an idea that I think you might like, Miss Prescott. Would you come back to the study with me and we'll discuss it?"

"I want to go to my room."

"You can, but first, I need to talk over something with you."

~ * ~

Later that evening, Valissa sat before her mirror and brushed her waist-length raven hair. As she thought about the conversation with Nathan Stone, she knew there was no way she would let Flo and Alvin refuse the man's offer. He'd suggested they remain at Heartsong after she left and it would save him the trouble of having to hire a staff. He'd even said he'd give them a raise. Something they hadn't had in several years. No matter how much she wished she could be with them, it was a godsend. Now she wouldn't have to worry about putting this wonderful couple out on the street. She only hoped he would be a nice boss and treat them well. If he did, she was sure he'd soon earn their respect and their devotion.

She laid the brush down and stood. Checking to be sure the chair she'd pushed under the doorknob was still in place, she went to her four-poster feather bed and blew out the lamp on the night table. "I wonder what kind of bed I'll be sleeping in a few nights from now," she muttered as she pulled the fluffy quilt up to her chin. "I know it won't be like home, but I'll find something suitable. I have no other choice."

Valissa thought it would take her a long time to go to sleep, but she was wrong. She must have been more exhausted than she thought because within minutes she was drifting off to dreamland.

~ * ~

In the master bedroom that Flo had made up for him, Nathan couldn't help feeling troubled. He didn't understand it. He stood at the window and looked out on the lawn surrounding the Prescott mansion and wondered what was going to happen to the pretty raven-haired woman whose home he was taking away. Of course he knew it was none of his business and it was not something that should even cross him mind. He didn't really take her home away. Her good-for-nothing brother lost it in a grandstand poker game. The gambler who won it happened to be a cousin of Nathan's and when he learned Nathan was going to need a place in Galveston, he offered to sell the Prescott place to him.

Now it was his and he had no reason to feel bad about the former residents. And he hadn't felt anything until this evening. When he saw Valissa Prescott's haunted eyes and the emotion she kept trying to hide, he wanted to comfort her and tell her to forget the whole thing. She could keep her house.

But he realized that wouldn't work either. She had no money to keep the place up and to pay the servants. And from the looks of things, this had been an ongoing problem. No, she was better off going to live with some relatives or getting married.

Hell, I don't want her getting married just to have enough money to live. She's the kind of woman who needs a man who is not only capable of taking care of her, but who is able to meet her on an intellectual level. Not some city-bread bastard who wants to parade her around at parties and then slip away to enjoy his mistress.

Nathan shook his head. Where did he get the idea that Valissa wouldn't like that kind of life? He was sure if Kyle Prescott hadn't swindled his sister, she would have ended up as some slick businessman's wife, or heaven forbid, his mistress.

Disgusted with his thoughts, Nathan drank the last swallows of whiskey in his glass and sat it on the table. Forcing his mind to concentrate on the business he had to accomplish in Galveston, he blew out the lamp and flopped down on the over-sized four-poster bed. Plumping up his feather pillow, he wondered what Miss Valissa Prescott looked like with all that pretty raven hair hanging down.

"What does it matter?" he swore at himself. "I've always wanted women with pale blond or red hair. I've never been attracted to those with black hair, even if it does have shimmering highlights when she was dropping her head at the dinner table. Besides, she may be five-five or so, but she's still too little for me. I like them long and tall with legs that go on forever. Women like Maurine, who happens to be about five-ten, though she was about the same size as Miss Prescott in other areas."

Nathan was still arguing with himself when he fell asleep an hour later.

Three

The next morning, Valissa dressed in a blue day dress and twisted her braided hair around her head. She knew it wasn't the popular style for a lady of means, but it was practical, and practical was what she had to be. Besides, she chuckled, she was no longer a lady of means. She was as destitute as many of the people she met on the streets. People she wasn't able to look at without feeling a little sorry for their plight. She wondered if people would look at her in that way.

Now wasn't the time to worry about her station in life. She had to get downstairs and see what Mr. Nathan Stone was up to this morning. She wouldn't be surprised to find he'd thrown most of the furniture out and brought in some of his own.

She found Flo in the kitchen.

"Good morning, Miss Valissa."

"Good morning, Flo." She looked around, but there was nobody else in the room.

"He's outside looking over the property." She handed Valissa a cup of coffee. "I have the bacon cooked and it will only take a minute to fix your egg. I'll bring it into the dining room for you."

"Thank you, but I'll eat here in the kitchen with you." Valissa sat down at the wooden table. "If you have any free time today, I need you to do me a favor."

"Of course I will, child."

"I want you to take some of my better gowns down to the docks and sell them for me."

"Oh, no. You don't want to sell your gowns, do you?"

"I don't want to, but I have no choice. I need some money and it's all I can think of to do to raise a little."

Flo sat the egg before Valissa and patted her shoulder. "I'm so sorry."

"I know you are." Valissa sighed and took a bite of her breakfast.

"There's something I need to tell you, Miss Valissa. Mr. Stone offered Alvin and me a job here."

Valissa nodded. "He told me he was going to do it."

"What do you think?"

Valissa smiled at the woman who had helped raise her. "You know there's nothing I'd like more than for us to stay together, but you also know that's impossible. I think if you can get along with Mr. Stone, it would be a good thing for you to do. At least you wouldn't have to move away from Heartsong."

"I don't think Mr. Stone will be all that hard to handle."

Valissa couldn't help it, she laughed. "I guess if anyone can handle him, it's you, Flo."

She finished her breakfast, pushed back her plate and stood. "Thank you. That was good."

"You didn't eat much."

"I'm not very hungry." She started for the door. "I'll get the dresses sorted and have them ready for you to take this afternoon."

When Valissa got to her room, she wanted to have a good cry, but knew it wouldn't do any good. She was in this situation and the only way to cope with it was to attack her problems one at a time. At least, if she could put up with being in the same house as Nathan Stone, she had three weeks to get everything done she would have to do before she moved.

Her first task was to raise as much money as she could with her clothes and … No. She didn't want to think about selling her grandmother's emerald earrings. The ones her grandfather had given his wife when they celebrated their move into Heartsong. Some way, somehow she hoped she could manage to keep those earrings, but she knew chances were slim.

Pushing these thoughts away, she went to her wardrobe and began taking out dresses. She wouldn't let her mind linger on where she'd worn the gowns or about the good times she'd had as she jerked them from the rod.

As carefully as she could, she folded each one and placed it in the carpetbag for Flo to carry to the wharf. She was busy with her chore when there was a knock on her door.

"Miss Valissa, Mr. Wilbur Colbert is here to see you again."

Oh, my. I wonder what he wants today, she pondered silently. Aloud she said, "Thank you, Flo. I'll be right down."

Wilbur was sitting in the same chair he sat in the day before. He stood when she entered the study. "Hello, Valissa." His voice didn't sound friendly. "My, don't you look like a little peasant today."

She raised an eyebrow at him and he dropped his eyes.

After a short silence, she said, "May I ask why I have the pleasure of this visit today, Wilbur?"

He swallowed and stammered, "Well, Valissa, I don't know if you're aware of it, but my family and the Bowers are good friends."

"I believe the Bowers have a lot of friends. I've seen them at many functions I've attended."

"Of course," he muttered. When she didn't say anything more, he went on. "Milton told us a disturbing story last night at dinner. I was in hopes that it wasn't true."

"Oh?"

"Yes, and I felt compelled to check it out personally with you this morning." He cleared his throat and blurted, "I want to know if Heartsong has a new owner."

She looked him directly in the eyes. "Yes, Wilbur, that's true."

"How could this be, Valissa?" His entire countenance showed his distress. "I thought I'd be taking over this estate."

"I'm afraid it's too late for that, Wilbur."

"Why couldn't you have been more careful with your inheritance?"

"My brother was in charge of my inheritance."

Wilbur shook his head as if he didn't believe her. "I'm sorry this happened. I really liked you, Valissa. I even thought we had a future together."

She was growing weary of his condescending way and couldn't keep the sharpness out of her voice. "You thought wrong, Wilbur. Even if I still owned Heartsong, there was no future for you here."

"I don't believe that. I'm sure you're only trying to cover up if it was Kyle's mistake and not yours that lost you the mansion." When she said nothing, he went on, "You know how things work, Valissa. Now that you've lost everything, you can't continue to associate with our circle of friends. You just wouldn't fit in. Why, last night Aunt Beverly told Rowena she had to break off the friendship with you."

"I'm not surprised. I doubt any of our friendships were more than a social thing. I don't expect them to last through this." She wouldn't let him see how much it hurt to think her best friend would desert her at this time.

He glanced at the floor. "What do you plan to do, Valissa?"

"I don't think that's… "

He interrupted. "I assume you'll be moving out soon."

"As I was saying, I don't think that's any of your business, Wilbur."

He jumped up. "You're not making this easy for me, Valissa."

"Why should I? None of this is easy for me either."

"Well, my aunt wanted me to find out if you'll be living with relatives or…" He paused.

"Or what?" She snapped.

"Valissa, you know it's not seemly for a young lady to live on her own."

"What if the young lady has no choice?"

"That's beside the point. Look at yourself, Valissa. You're already dressed like an underling and you've never worn your hair the way you have it now. You know I couldn't be escorting a woman of no means around town."

She stood and straightened her back. "All right, Wilbur, get to the point."

"Mrs. Maxmillion came by this morning and Aunt Beverly told her I'd invited you to her party. As you might imagine, she was a little upset by it."

"Are you trying to say Mrs. Maxmillion doesn't want me at her party?"

"Don't be difficult, Valissa. You surely understand why she wouldn't want you there and of course, Aunt Beverly had already told me that I couldn't possibly bring you. We have to make the best impression on the important people who will be there. There's a very important man coming and…well, we must show him how things are run in Galveston."

Though she wanted to hit him, Valissa gathered her wits and kept her voice calm. "Well, Wilbur you can give your aunt her wish. I wouldn't go with you even if I were going to Mrs. Maxmillion's party. Maybe she would approve if you acted as Candice Maxmillion's escort. Now, please take your leave."

Wilbur didn't argue with her. He grabbed his hat and ran from the room and straight into Nathan Stone.

"Who the hell are you?" Nathan bellowed.

Wilbur faltered. "I'm… Let me pass, please."

Nathan took hold of Wilbur's arm. "I will not. I want to know who you are and what you're doing in my house upsetting Miss Prescott."

Wilbur stared at him. "So you're the new owner?"

Nathan ignored his question. "I'm going to ask you one more time, who are you and what are you doing here?"

"I'm Wilbur Colbert and I came to see Valissa. Now I'm ready to leave."

Nathan frowned. "Colbert. You wouldn't happen to be any relation to Lyman Colbert, would you?"

"He's my uncle."

After staring at Wilbur for a minute, Nathan dropped the man's arm and said in a low angry voice, "Then Wilbur Colbert, get the hell out of my house. Miss Prescott doesn't seem to want you here."

Wilbur stumbled through the grand entry and out the front door without another word.

Watching the entire encounter, Valissa couldn't help being pleased that Nathan Stone had arrived, but she wouldn't tell him this.

Nathan turned to her. "What dealings do you have with a man like that?"

"I have no dealings with him, Mr. Stone. Not anymore, anyway."

"What does that mean?"

She couldn't think of a reason not to tell him. "Wilbur invited me to a party when he thought I owned Heartsong. Now that I don't, he came to cancel the date."

"He's not much of a man if he cancels a party date he's already asked you to attend."

"It doesn't matter. I won't be attending the event anyway."

Nathan stared at her. "I don't see why you'd want to go with him in the first place."

"I really didn't, but he came by shortly after I was told I was destitute. It was easier to let him assume we were going to the party together than to tell him I wasn't going with him. At the time, all I wanted was to get him out of the house so I could face the situation I found myself in."

"I see."

When he said nothing else, Valissa moved toward the door. "Excuse me, Mr. Stone. I was packing."

"Then I'll let you get back to it."

~ * ~

After she disappeared up the stairs, Nathan stomped to the study and shut the door behind him. He couldn't explain the rage that he felt toward Wilbur Colbert because he didn't understand it himself. He didn't know the man.

Of course, he thought it terrible of young Colbert to treat Valissa Prescott the way he had, but why should he care? She was nothing to him. She just happened to be one of the former owners of this house and why should he feel any remorse about putting her out? Surely she knew what her brother was up to when he gambled it away. He'd bought the place in good faith, though he didn't know the circumstances of why such a find was available until after the purchase. Even when he found out, it didn't matter. He was offered the place at a good price and as the astute businessman he was, he jumped at the chance to buy it. How was he to know he was taking the home away from an innocent woman? Or was she as innocent as she seemed? Maybe she was in on the dealings of her brother?

Nathan went to the liquor cabinet and poured himself a drink of whiskey. "What the hell does it matter, anyway," he muttered. "She'll be gone in a few days and I won't have to look at her haunted aqua-blue eyes any longer."

He thought he meant these words when he said them.

It was almost noon when Valissa finished sorting and folding her gowns. She had packed five that she thought were in good enough condition for Flo to take to the docks to sell. She wasn't sure how much the dresses would bring, but because hers were somewhat worn, she wasn't expecting them to generate a lot of money. Of course any amount would be appreciated.

There was a sharp rap on her door and before she could cross the room to answer, the door burst open and Nathan Stone strode into the room.

"Why the hell are you selling your clothes?"

Thoughts of reprehending him for walking in vanished and she stared at him. "What business is it of yours?"

"None, but I want to know."

Why did he have a way of throwing her thoughts in all directions? Now she couldn't argue with him for asking her about selling her clothes. He admitted it was none of his business.

She sighed and said, "I need the money."

"I see." He turned back to the door. "It's time to eat. I'll see you in the dining room."

"I'm not hungry."

"I don't care whether you eat or not, but you will come to the dining room for the mid-day meal. If you're not there in five minutes, I'll come back and carry you down." With that, he closed the door and she heard him stomping down the hall.

Furious, Valissa slammed the carpet bag with the gowns closed. "How dare he order me to come to the dining room? Who does he think he is? I'll eat when I want to."

Determined not to join him in the dining room, she stalked across the room and locked her door. *That will show him.* She smiled as she went to her dresser and sat on the stuffed stool cushion. Picking up the brush, she touched it to the wisp of hair that had escaped from the top of her head. After she was satisfied, she dropped the brush and picked up the small jewelry box. Taking a deep breath, she opened it and stared at the emerald earrings that had belonged to her grandmother. The drop was a large emerald surrounded by glistening diamonds set in platinum. She didn't know how much they were worth. She only knew they were valuable. The only valuable things she owned.

Oh, how she hated the thoughts of selling them. She touched each one and the sadness in her heart was almost unbearable, but she couldn't let it overcome her practical mind. Deep down she knew she had no choice, so she might as well get it over with. Tomorrow, she'd take the earrings to town and see if she could sell them for enough money to sustain her for a while.

Before she could grieve over them longer, she heard heavy steps in the hall. She snapped the jewelry box shut and smiled. She knew Mr.

Stone was going to be surprised that she'd dared defy his order. She wondered what he'd do.

It didn't take her long to find out.

When he tried the door and it didn't open, he pounded on it. She smiled, but it faded when he said, "Miss Prescott, I'll give you to the count of five to open this door. If you refuse, I'll break the damn thing down. When it crashes on your floor, you'll learn that I never make idle threats. One."

Valissa's heart pounded. Was he strong enough to break down the door?

"Two."

He was certainly big enough to do it. But would he dare?

"Three."

Yes, he'd dare. Valissa stood and scurried across the room.

"Four."

She turned the lock and opened the door.

He offered her his arm. "Smart move. Now let's go down to the dining room. I'm sure Flo has a nice dinner for us."

Valissa thought it would be easier to accept his arm than to argue, but she didn't understand why she didn't choose to argue. Nathan Stone was certainly the most infuriating man she'd ever met. Even greedy Wilbur didn't rile her as much. Of course, she had to admit, even with his bad manners, Nathan Stone was more interesting than Wilbur. Or any other man in her circle of friends, for that matter. She amended the thought to, circle of *former* friends.

After Flo served them, Valissa nibbled at her fish and refused to look at Nathan.

Several minutes passed before he spoke. "I'm going into town this afternoon. Alvin and Flo will accompany me."

Her head darted up. "I've asked Flo to run an errand for me this afternoon. She'll need Alvin to go with her."

"I've heard about your errand, but it's not going to happen."

Valissa threw down her fork. "How dare you ask my servants to go…"

"Just a moment, Miss Prescott. Whose servants are we talking about?" His voice boomed.

"They're my…I mean, they were…" Her voice faltered and her blue eyes glistened.

"Now that we're clear on that issue, please pass the potatoes."

Without speaking, Valissa grabbed the bowl and set it down in front of him so hard the serving spoon fell out.

"My, my," he said with a chuckle. "For such a little woman, you sure have a big temper."

"I'm not so little," she snapped as she pushed back her chair and stood.

"Don't do it," he roared. "Our meal isn't over."

She threw her napkin down. "What difference does it make? My life might as well be over."

"Sit down and try to calm yourself, Miss Prescott. Finish your dinner." He seemed to ignore her outburst.

Valissa dropped to the chair and her shoulders slumped. "Why is it so important I eat my meals with you?"

"You're a guest in my house. I wouldn't think of sitting down to eat without you at the table. That wouldn't be hospitable at all."

She didn't feel like a guest, but she supposed he was right. As long as she stayed here, she would be a guest. She sat and reached for her fork, but she only picked at her food. She was trying to think of a place she could go and get away from this man and his idea of how a guest should be treated.

Shortly after the noon meal Valissa watched from the window of her room as Nathan Stone's black carriage pulled into the street behind the two big black horses. Flo and Alvin were inside and Valissa couldn't help wondering what he was up to. Why did he insist the couple go with him? Couldn't he take care of his business without involving them?

Shaking her head, she decided she wasn't going to think about it. Instead she turned and began sorting the things left in the room that she owned. She knew she could only take what she could carry with her. This meant anything else she owned could be sent to the docks with the gowns.

~ * ~

When Flo returned, Valissa hurried to the kitchen and found the woman preparing to cook supper. "I hate to bother you, but my curiosity has been killing me."

"I thought it might be."

"It got worse when I saw Mr. Stone bring you home, then leave again."

"He's taking Alvin to pick up things for working on the grounds. He said it had been neglected too long and there were several things that could be done this fall that will make it easier to plant in the spring."

"You know I didn't have the funds to keep the grounds up as they should have been. Besides," Valissa felt a twinge of shame, then she frowned and added, "You don't have anything to do with the grounds. Why did he take you off this afternoon?"

"He wanted me to help him pick out something."

"Flo, are you going to keep me in suspense? You know I want to know why he took you to town."

"It was really very simple, Miss Valissa. We went to Mrs. Dupree-Fontaine's Dress Designing Shop. He wanted me to help him pick out a dress for a lady friend of his to wear to Mrs. Maxmillion's party."

Valissa wrinkled her brow. "How would you know anything about his lady friend's taste in clothes?"

"I told him this, but he insisted I pick out the most expensive material and the fanciest pattern Mrs. Dupree-Fontaine had. When I told him I had no idea of her size, he told me she was about the same size as you and that her hair was black like yours, so I went from there."

"Did you choose a pretty gown?"

"I'm sure it'll be the most beautiful gown at the party. Mr. Stone told the seamstress it better be a gown that all the women would envy and one that would be different from what any other woman would wear. He also told her if she let anyone see it while it was being made, he'd not pay for it."

"Since he's gone to so much trouble, I hope his friend likes the dress." Valissa didn't realize she had snapped until Flo gave her a strange look. "I'm sorry, Flo. I didn't mean to be rude to you. I've just got a lot on my mind."

"It's fine, Miss Valissa." Flo swallowed. "Maybe I shouldn't be the one to tell you, but Mr. Stone said since the woman was the same size as you, he wanted to take you in for a fitting of the dress in a couple of days."

Valissa jumped up from the chair at the kitchen table. "I will not permit him to subject me to this humiliation. Let his friend come and try on her own dress."

"Don't fret, Miss Valissa. Maybe his friend will reach town in time to go for the fittings herself."

"Did he say when she would arrive?"

"No. He only said he wanted to be sure the dress fit the woman perfectly."

"That's his problem. He won't be trying it on me to see." Valissa turned and walked out of the room.

~ * ~

Valissa didn't see Nathan Stone for the rest of the day. He didn't come in that night until after she had retired. The next morning he was again gone when she came down for breakfast.

"Has he left already?"

"He said he had business in town this morning," Flo said. "Something about not being able to concentrate as he wanted to last night."

"What did he mean?"

"I think he had supper with the Colberts. From what I gathered, Mrs. Colbert spent most of the time trying to get him interested in her daughter."

Valissa laughed. "I can't imagine meek Rowena Colbert being interested in Mr. Stone."

"I think it was more of her mother's idea. Mr. Stone said he actually felt sorry for the girl because she seemed ill at ease with the whole situation."

Valissa shrugged. "Though I guess it's not important, I'm glad he was sensitive to Rowena's feelings. She can easily get flustered."

"When she has visited here, I've noticed that."

"Did Mr. Stone say how long he'd be gone today?"

"Not really, but he did say not to expect him for the mid-day meal."

"Good. I want to look at some things in Daddy's study and that will give me plenty of time."

"I'll be sure to let you know if he comes home earlier."

"Thank you, Flo. I know I can count on you."

In the study, Valissa pulled her household account books from the bottom drawer. Flipping to the last page, she bit her lip and wondered if this would be the last time she looked at them. She glanced back thorough some of the pages. Was there somewhere she could have been more careful with the money so she wouldn't be in the situation she found herself in now?

After carefully going over the figures, she realized she'd done a good job with the money she had to deal with. Had she bought the things she'd wanted to, but didn't really need, she'd probably have lost the house sooner.

With a sigh, she put the books back in the desk and looked around the room. Would Nathan Stone notice if she took something from this room to sell? Maybe the candlesticks on the mantle. They were a wedding gift to her parents from her mother's grandmother. They should stay in her mother's family.

Valissa walked to the fireplace and reached for one of the ornate candleholders. It was heavy. Probably solid silver. Too heavy to put in her luggage. Besides, that would be stealing and that went against her nature. She'd have to forget about the possessions she'd grown up with and loved all her life. She was broke and destitute. The last thing she wanted to do was turn into a thief. Besides, knowing Nathan Stone, she was sure he'd have her arrested and put in jail without a second thought. If being destitute was humiliating, being thrown in jail would be a worse disgrace.

The tears came without warning. Swiping her eyes, she ran out of the study, up the stairs and fell across her bed. In a short time, she cried herself to sleep.

When she opened her eyes again, the sun had risen high in the sky. She jumped off the bed, washed her face and hurried to the kitchen.

"Has Mr. Stone come home yet, Flo?"

"No, Miss Valissa, but he did say he might not make dinner. He did say to make extra supper because he was bringing company."

"Must be that woman he's having the dress made for."

"He didn't say who it was."

"Then I think it's a good time to take the gowns to the dock. You should be able to sell them and get back before he returns."

"I …uh… "

"What is it, Flo?"

Flo dropped her head. "I hate to tell you this, child, but Mr. Stone told me I was not to take your dresses to the docks."

"He has no right to do that. Of course, you'll not obey him."

"I'm sorry, but I have to, Miss Valissa. He said he'd fire me if I didn't listen to him. I believe he'd do it, too."

Valissa's temper flared. "How dare him! Who does he think he is?"

Flo didn't answer and Valissa went on. "I'll take them myself. Alvin will go with me."

Flo shook her head. "He told Alvin the same thing."

"That man is the most exasperating human being I've ever met. What makes him think he can come in and dictate what I do with my clothes?" She swallowed the threatening sob. "I hate him and I don't even know the man. How can he treat me this way?"

Flo moved over and put her arm around Valissa's shoulder. "Please don't cry, child. Things will work out."

"I hope so, Flo. I really do."

"Let me fix you something to eat. That'll make you feel better."

Valissa pulled away. "Thank you. Would you put it on a tray? I think I'll take it to my room."

"That's a good idea, Miss Valissa. You eat, then take a nap. You'll feel better after you're rested."

Valissa didn't tell her she had just awakened from a nap. "I think you're right. I've been racking my brain about how to get out of the mess Kyle left me in. Maybe I need to forget it for a while." She started for the door. "Please wake me before supper, Flo. I don't want the tyrant to come bursting in and dragging me to the table."

Flo chuckled. "I won't let him do that, Miss Valissa."

Four

Valissa had no intention of taking another nap, but she didn't let Flo know that. Instead, when she got to her room, she hurried and ate the food on the tray. She knew she'd need the strength it would give her for carrying out her plans.

As soon as she finished eating, she grabbed the valise she'd packed the dresses in to sell. Slipping out the door and down the front stairs, she eased the door open and stepped onto the wide-columned front porch. She paused long enough to make sure Flo hadn't heard her leave.

Satisfied she hadn't been discovered, she went down the steps and hurried toward the street. She didn't slow down until she was out of sight of the house.

It was too far to the docks to walk. Though she hated to spend the money, she headed toward the block where a carriage or a buggy usually could be hired. She was lucky. A buggy was waiting for someone to arrive wanting a ride.

She wasn't sure where people actually sold the clothes at the dock, so when they arrived in the area, she had the driver let her out at a building which looked like it might be a restaurant or an office. The name on the outside said "Tilley's" and she figured it was the owner's last name. Many of the buildings had names, but this one had curtains on the upstairs windows. She paid the driver and got out of the buggy.

She wondered if she should knock on the door and see if someone inside could help her find the right place to go. As she moved toward the door, her heart pounded.

"Hey pretty lady, you don't look like you belong here. What are you doing in this part of town?"

Valissa whirled around. A man dressed as a seaman, and obviously drinking because he waved a bottle, staggered toward her.

"I…came…

"It don't matter, honey. You're here and getting ready to go into Tilley's. You don't have to give me no more information." He gave her a smile and lurched toward her. "Let's go inside and I'll buy you a drink to go along with mine."

"Thank you, but I don't want a drink."

"Oh come on, sweetheart. Tilley likes his women to sell drinks before they go upstairs."

"I'm sure I don't know what you're talking about."

"Likely story," he said in a slurred voice and waved the bottle again.

The door to the building opened and a man dressed in a black suit and red brocade vest stepped outside. His dark eyes swept over Valissa and he turned to the man. In a firm voice, he barked, "Move along, Harvey."

"Ah, Mr. Tilley, I was only trying to get know your new girl here."

"I said, move along. She don't want to get acquainted with you at this moment."

Harvey shook his head and walked away, muttering, "Why do you always hide the pretty ones?"

"Shut up and get along."

The man turned to Valissa. "I'm sorry you were subjected to him, Miss. My name's Glenn Tilley and I must say, you do seem out of place here. Is there something I can do for you?"

"Oh, yes, Mr. Tilley. I brought some gowns to the dock to sell. Could you tell me where I might be able to do that?"

"This might be your lucky day…Miss….?"

"Prescott. Valissa Prescott."

"Your name sounds familiar, but I'm not sure where I've heard it." When she said nothing, he went on, "Miss Prescott, I'm sure some of the women who work for me would be more than happy to look at your dresses and probably buy them. They're always interested in pretty things to wear and I'm sure a lady like yourself would only have the finest."

Valissa felt he was looking her over too closely, but she didn't say anything. She didn't want to make him change his mind about his employees looking at her gowns. "That would be wonderful," she muttered.

"Follow me." He led her through the heavy wooden doors to a room that was filled with tables and chairs. On the left side of the room a bar stretched from one end to the other. Behind it were racks of liquor bottles, a large mirror and above it hung a picture of a nude woman lounging on a red velvet couch.

Valissa shivered. This was no office business. It had to be a one of those saloons she'd heard about. Nothing else would be decorated in such garish colors with a picture like that one. Though Valissa wanted to run, she knew it was too late. She was already inside and the door was closed. There was nothing she could do but sit at the table he indicated.

"Would you like something to drink, Miss Prescott?"

"No, thank you." She hoped her voice didn't show the fright she was beginning to feel. What had she gotten herself into?

"I'll get the girls and be right back."

He grinned at her and she noticed his dark eyes twinkled, though she thought they were a little too close together. And the twinkle made her a little more uncomfortable. She wondered if she could run out the door and get away before he came back. She then remembered she'd paid the carriage driver and sent him on his way. She didn't have anywhere to go except the street. What if she met someone else like Harvey? Could she get far enough away that he couldn't catch her?

She didn't have to make the decision because Tilley returned.

"The girls will be right down." He pulled out a chair beside her. "So, Miss Prescott, why are you selling your clothes?"

Before she could stop herself, she blurted, "I need the money,"

He grinned and said, "I thought it was some reason like that. A lot of women come to me when they need money."

"Really?"

"Oh, yes. Many of them are in circumstances beyond their control and have to have someone to help them out. Are you in trouble, Miss Prescott?"

She nodded. "I have to move out of my house and I'm collecting all the money I can to help me get away."

"I understand. I assume you're alone in the world."

The way he still sized her up with his eyes made her shiver, but she went on as if she had no control over her tongue. "Unfortunately, yes. They tell me that my only relative, my brother, is in California."

"I assume you're raising the money to join him." Tilley cocked his eyebrow.

"Oh, no. He's the reason I'm in this terrible financial mess." Why couldn't she control her mouth? This man was a stranger. A stranger she didn't think she could trust. She had no business telling him her problems.

"Then, Valissa…May I call you Valissa?" She didn't really want him to, but for some reason she nodded and he went on, "If my ladies don't want to buy your clothes, I'll buy them because I want to help you. I could never have a gentlewoman like you wanting money. It wouldn't be gentlemanly of me, would it?"

"That's very kind of you, Mr. Tilley."

"Glenn, please."

There was a rustling in the room and a large blond wearing a red silk wrapper, which she'd failed to fasten over her revealing nightgown, walked up. In a slurred voice, she said, "Glenn said you were selling dresses."

"Yes, ma'am," Valissa looked at her and knew the woman would never fit into the gowns she had with her. Valissa was slender and this woman was stout, to say the least.

"Well, let me see them."

"Don't be rude, Maude." Glenn snapped and eyed the big blond.

The woman's mood changed. "I'm sorry, but I'm a bit grumpy when I first get up."

Valissa wondered if she'd interrupted Maude's nap. She only nodded and opened the carpet bag. She pulled out the dresses and handed them to Maude, one by one.

"Hey, I like that blue one," another woman entered the room. She walked directly to Maude and snatched the blue dress from her. "How much do you want for it?"

Valissa wasn't prepared for that question. She hadn't given any thought to the price she should ask. She was grateful when Glenn said, "She wants at least twenty dollars for each gown, girls. If there is a haggle over one, whoever is willing to pay the top price gets it."

Valissa looked at him with grateful eyes. If she could get a hundred dollars for the five gowns, it would go a long way in helping her, though any of these dresses cost her many times more than that to have made in the first place.

"Hey, I like the blue one, too." Another woman entered the room.

"I saw it first." The big blond held it up. "I can add some lace in the sides and make it fit me."

"Don't matter. I'll give her twenty-two dollars for it."

Soon the room was filled with eight women and they began to argue over who was to get what dress. All Valissa could do was sit back and let them decide.

When it was all over, five happy women took their dresses and headed up the stairs and Valissa had a hundred and eight dollars to put in her fund. But the best part was that she promised to bring three more dresses for the girls who lost out. Glenn assured her they would pay a minimum of twenty dollars each for them.

After they were alone again, Glenn turned to Valissa. "I'm glad that went well for you."

"Thank you so much for letting me bring the dresses in here to sell."

"I was happy to do it." He stood. "Now I think you deserve a drink on the house. What would you like?"

"I thank you, but I'm not a drinker, Glenn. Besides I must get back before someone misses me."

"Maybe just a little white wine or a glass of sherry?"

"Well, maybe a small glass of wine."

He returned from the bar with a wide grin on his face. Or was it a leer? Instead of bringing her a glass of wine, he brought an empty glass and the bottle. For himself he brought brandy.

Valissa was hesitant about drinking the wine, but he acted the perfect gentleman and he kept telling her he wanted to help her. He even suggested she consider him her new friend.

"I hardly know you, Glenn."

"That can be overcome in a short time, my sweet lady."

She had another glass of wine and began to relax. "I'm probably going to have to look for a job in the near future," she blurted and wondered why she did.

Glenn patted her hand. "Things will work out, I'm sure."

"You're very kind, sir."

It was after her third glass that Valissa began telling him the whole story of how she had been reduced to the fate of having to sell her clothes.

"You poor dear," Glenn said as he refilled her glass. "You do need money, don't you?"

She sighed. "I sure do and selling a few dresses will not bring in nearly enough for my needs."

"I understand that, but there is always another way. You could get a job."

"I know I have to work, but who will hire me? I have no skills."

"Oh, I don't know." He reached for her hand again. When she didn't pull away, his voice seemed to turn to velvet. "I'd hire you in a minute."

Valissa laughed. "What in the world would I be able to do for you?"

"You could do a lot, pretty lady. You have a radiant smile that lights up those beautiful aqua eyes. Any man could get lost in them in no time."

Valissa giggled. "So you're going to hire me to smile?"

"In a way, that's exactly what I'll do. I think you'd make a wonderful hostess and believe me, you'll bring in so much business, I may have to take you on as a partner."

"That doesn't sound too hard."

"Oh, it's not. There are other ways you could add to your income, too."

"Oh?" Valissa began to feel a little dizzy, but she had to listen. A job where she could make lots of money sounded wonderful. "How could I do that, Glenn?"

"I'm sure there are many businessmen who'd want to sit and have a conversation with you."

She giggled and sipped her wine. "So how much money are we talking about?"

"Oh, honey, we're talking about lots and lots. Since you've never been in this business, I won't explain fully how it works right now. You'll just have to trust me, Valissa." He poured her another glass of wine, then leaned back and grinned as she began sipping again. "Do you trust me enough to come with me to my office to discuss it?"

"Yes, I think I do." She giggled again, then frowned. For some reason she couldn't remember where she was or what she was doing here. She started to ask, but the words wouldn't come, so she shrugged and took his hand to stand.

He picked up the glasses and the wine bottle and headed up the stairs with her.

~ * ~

It was late afternoon when Nathan got out of the carriage and headed into the house through the kitchen door. "Hello, Flo," he greeted the woman at the stove.

"Good afternoon, sir. I hope you had a good day."

"It went well, thank you." He paused and looked at her. "Is Miss Prescott around?"

"She went to her room to take a nap right after she ate lunch. I promised to wake her before supper. Shall I do it now?"

"Please. Have her come to the study. There's something I need to check out with her before my guest arrives tonight."

Flo put down her spoon and headed upstairs and Nathan went into the study.

In a minute Flo came running down the stairs. "Mr. Stone!" she cried out.

He came to the study door. "Yes, Flo."

"She's gone. Her bed wasn't mussed and the valise she packed the dresses in to sell is gone."

He frowned. "You don't think she'd…?"

"Yes, sir. I do think so. When Valissa makes up her mind to do something, she does it. I'm sure she's gone to the docks to sell the gowns herself. Oh, the poor dear."

"Damn little fool." Nathan turned back to the peg where he'd hung his gun and holster. He strapped it around his waist and headed out the door. "If Mr. Colbert gets here before I return, serve him a drink. I'll be back as soon as I find that unpredictable hardhead."

"I'll do that, Mr. Stone."

Without another word, Nathan ran out the back door toward the barn. "Hitch up the horses, Phillips. We have to go to the docks right away."

"Yes, sir." Phillips jumped up from the stool where he was polishing a silver-studded harness.

When the team was hitched, Nathan rode on the front seat with Phillips instead of inside the carriage. "Take the shortest route. I know the roads aren't as good as those through town, but it's important to get there as quickly as we can. It's no telling what kind of trouble Miss Prescott has gotten herself into."

"Yes, sir." Phillips turned the horses down a side street.

When they reached the docks, Phillips turned toward his boss. "Where do you want to start."

"Hell, I don't know." Nathan looked around. "Now, where would a lady who has never been to this side of town go to sell her clothes?"

"May I suggest one of the houses or a saloon where a lot of women work?"

"That's not a bad idea, but which one? There are several around here." Phillips didn't answer and Nathan went on, "We might as well start on Dock Street. Let's go to the end and work backward."

"Yes, sir."

After checking three saloons, they had no luck. "I'm afraid we may have missed her, Phillips."

"I don't know, sir. There are a lot of saloons around here."

A seaman came stumbling down the street. "How about a drink, mates?"

"Not now," Nathan said.

"Oh come on. I need one now and it would give me more courage."

"Courage?"

"Yes, sir. I'm trying to get up my nerve to visit Tilley's new girl tonight. She looked top notch. Not like his usual whores."

A shiver went down Nathan's spine. Could he be talking about Valissa? Surely the stubborn little woman hadn't gone into a whorehouse.

"Where is this place called Tilley's?" Nathan looked at the seaman.

The seaman smirked. "So you intend to try her out first."

"No. I'm looking for someone who doesn't belong in this area. Maybe you saw her and mistook her for one of the house women."

"Don't think so. Tilley came out and ran me off. Then he took the woman by the arm and led her into his place. She had her carpetbag with her, so I knew she was moving in."

"Where is this Tilley's?" Nathan's temper rose. "Tell me now."

The man shrugged. "Why should I?"

Nathan had had enough of the man not answering him. It didn't matter that the seaman was drunk. Nathan whipped out his pistol and pointed it at the man's head. "You should tell me because if you don't, I'm going to put a bullet between your eyes."

"No!" The man screamed as his body began to shake.

"Where's Tilley's?"

The man stuttered, but he managed to say, "It's on Pelican Row. Over where the big boats dock."

Nathan holstered his gun and almost laughed when he saw the seaman drop to his knees. He was sure the man was crying, but he didn't bother to find out.

Pelican Row was only two streets over and they arrived in a matter of minutes. Nathan jumped from the carriage almost before it stopped.

He pushed open the door to the saloon and stepped inside. Phillips tethered the horses and followed. A redhead wearing a green satin dress, unlike any a saloon whore would wear, took his arm. "Well, hello big fellow. My name's Angela and you look like you're in need of some heavenly company."

Determined not to lose his temper, Nathan asked in as calm a voice as he could muster. "Where did you get that dress?"

"Oh, do you like it?"

"I want to know where you got it, Angela," he persisted.

"If you must know, honey, I bought it today from a woman who was selling dresses. Now let's go have a drink. I'll call one of the girls to take care of your friend." She nodded toward Phillips, then cuddled against Nathan. "We can take our drinks to my room if you like."

"Where's the woman you bought the dress from?"

"Why do you care? I'm prettier in this dress than she ever was."

Nathan took her arm and whirled her around. "Listen, Angela. I'm not interested in going to your room. Now where is Miss Prescott?"

Though Angela was a little intimidated, she stammered, "I don't know any Miss Prescott."

"If you don't want me to start shooting up this place, you better start knowing."

"He'll do it, too," Phillips said.

Angela must have believed him because she said, "She's in the office with Mr. Tilley."

"Where's the office?"

"Upstairs. The first door on the right, but I wouldn't disturb them if I were you."

Nathan didn't bother to answer. He went up the stairs two at a time. Without knocking, he shoved the door to the office open.

When he saw Glenn Tilley sitting beside Valissa with his arm around her shoulders, he roared, "What the hell is going on in here?"

Tilley jumped off the davenport. "Who do you think you are barging into my office without knocking?"

Nathan ignored him. He stomped to the sofa and took Valissa's arm. "Let's get out of here."

"Wait just a minute. Miss Prescott and I were…"

"I know exactly what you had in mind for Miss Prescott," Nathan snapped.

"And what business is it of yours?" Glenn began, straightening his loose tie.

Valissa gave Nathan a silly grin and said in a slurred voice, "Mr. Stone, I'll be on my way…I mean, I'll move out of your house soon. Mr. Tilley has a job for me."

Nathan looked into her glazed eyes and shook his head when he realized she was near passing out. "You're not working for Tilley, Miss Prescott."

"Of course I am. I'll greet people and seat them and …" she turned to Tilley. "What else did you say I'd do?"

"I don't give a damn what he told you. Let's go." None too gently, Nathan pulled her to her feet.

"But I have more wine…"

"You've had plenty of wine." Nathan turned to Glenn Tilley. There was a look of hate in his eyes. "Miss Prescott will not be coming to work here and you can forget you ever saw her."

"Look, Mr. Whoever-you-are, Miss Prescott is capable of making up her own mind about working here. I suggest you leave before I have you thrown out."

Nathan moved toward him and took hold of his shirt collar with his free hand. "I'm going to say this one time, Tilley, and one time only. If you ever again try to contact Miss Prescott in any way, I'll see that this place is closed down and you won't be welcome in any saloon in Galveston."

"You can't do that," Tilley gasped.

"Try me." Nathan let go of the collar and Glenn stumbled backward.

Without another word, Nathan turned to see Valissa had slumped to the davenport again. He pulled her to her feet. She tried to protest, but her complaints fell on deaf ears. He ushered her out the door and practically carried her down the steps toward the front door where Phillips waited.

"Don't forget to bring those other dresses," a woman's voice called as they reached the bottom of the steps.

Valissa nodded and waved at the woman.

Nathan looked toward the auburn-haired woman who spoke. "She'll not be bringing any more dresses," he snapped.

"But she promised."

"I don't give a damn what she promised. There'll be no more dresses." He didn't wait for an answer as he rushed Valissa through the door Phillips held open.

In a matter of minutes, Phillips was driving the carriage down the street with Nathan and Valissa inside.

~ * ~

Glenn Tilley walked to the mirror and straightened his shirt collar and tie. "How dare that oaf treat me that way? When a woman comes in here needing my help, I intend to help her. Especially when she's as pretty as this woman."

He snarled at himself for talking out loud and continued to think. *Valissa Prescott might have been some society dame before her fall, but I know how things work in Galveston. There's no way any of her so-called friends will accept her as one of them now. She knows it and I know it.*

Stepping back from the looking glass, he set his mouth in a firm line and his eyes glared with hate. "If I have to kill that man, Miss Valissa Prescott will be my hostess within a month. In three, I'll have her taking the finer gentlemen of Galveston upstairs to enjoy her pleasures."

He headed out the door to check on things in his saloon. His snarl turned to a wry smile as he descended the steps. *It'll sure be interesting to watch how she handles it when some of her customers turn out to be husbands and fathers of some of her former friends. I can't wait to talk with my business partner. I bet he knows her. I bet he'll want to be one of her first customers.*

Five

Flo gasped as the back door opened and Nathan came in with Valissa over his shoulder. "What in the world happened, Mr. Nathan?"

"She passed out and I figured I'd better bring her in the back door and go up the kitchen stairs with her. Since my guest has probably arrived, I didn't want him to see her in this condition."

"Is she sick? Shall I call the doctor?"

"No, Flo. She's only drunk."

Flo looked stricken. "She can't be. Miss Valissa doesn't drink. She don't believe in it."

"She must have changed her belief, because she's sure way past tipsy."

Flo shook her head and started after him up the steps.

He paused. "Is Mr. Colbert here?"

"He arrived a few minutes ago."

"Go see if he'd like a drink. I'll put Miss Prescott in her room and you can check or her after serving us supper."

"But…"

"Don't worry, Flo. She's out cold. I doubt she'll be awake before morning."

Flo nodded and turned back into the kitchen.

Nathan hurried up the steps and headed to Valissa's room. He took time to throw back the covers before he laid her on the bed. Shaking his head, he removed her button-up shoes.

"You're going to have one hell of a headache in the morning, Miss Prescott," He muttered. "I'm looking forward to breakfast."

Valissa didn't move.

Nathan chuckled and headed down the front stairs. He wasn't going to be able to use his planned strategy with Lyman Colbert tonight. Miss Prescott had changed the focus of this meeting with her trek to the docks. He plastered on a friendly face as he entered the parlor. "Mr. Colbert, I'm sorry I kept you waiting. There was something I had to take care of."

"That's no problem at all, Mr. Stone." Colbert stood. "I know how busy you must be."

"Yes." Nathan moved to the liquor cabinet and poured himself a drink. "Supper should be ready soon."

"Good. I'm looking forward to it."

Nathan glanced at his guest. "Did you bring the bank ledgers like I asked?"

"I did. I asked Flo to put them on your desk."

"Thank you. I'm sure I can have them back to you in a week or so."

"That'll be fine."

Flo appeared at the door. "Supper is served, Mr. Stone."

Nathan nodded and motioned Colbert out the door. He carried the drink Flo had served him. Nathan followed with his drink in his hand.

Nathan took his seat at the head of the table and Lyman sat in the chair to his left where Flo had placed a plate.

"I see you've retained the Prescotts' servants. That was a wise decision."

"I thought it wise to offer them work since they seemed efficient."

"I'm sure they are. They've been here for years and the Prescotts seemed to like them. I've heard other families have tried to hire them away, but were unable to do it. Some of the townspeople will be upset that they didn't get a chance to hire them before you did."

"I had the advantage, since they already worked here."

Flo entered the dining room with a silver platter of ham surrounded by fried sweet potatoes. Alvin followed with a tray laden with four bowls of different vegetables.

When they were again alone, Lyman turned to Nathan. "My wife chatted so much while you were at dinner at our house last night that I didn't get a chance to ask you how you like your new home, Mr. Stone."

"It needs some work, but I'm sure it'll suffice when I'm in Galveston and need a place to stay."

Lyman cocked an eye. "Do you mean you'll not be living here all the time?"

"I'll be here when it's necessary." Nathan cut into his ham.

"Though you didn't mention it last night, I understand from my nephew that Miss Prescott is still in residence. I expected to see her at supper."

"Miss Prescott isn't feeling well. She sends her regrets." Nathan put a piece of sweet potato in his mouth.

"I'm sorry she isn't well."

"She'll be fine in a day or so, I'm sure."

Lyman cocked an eye. "How long will she stay here?"

"Her solicitor gave her three weeks to move and I'll honor that."

"I understand. It's too bad she can't be with us tonight. I wanted to express my sympathy for what has happened to her. It's a shame she's had to face something so tragic at her young age. Valissa and my daughter, Rowena, have been friends for years and it has been hard to see someone fall so low." When Nathan didn't reply, he went on, "Has she said what she'll do now that she's destitute?"

"I haven't asked."

"It's too bad she didn't marry before all of this happened."

"Maybe she will yet."

"I doubt there's any man in Galveston who'll want to marry her without Heartsong. Word has already gotten around about her plight."

"That's too bad, because I find her to be a quality woman." Nathan eyed him. He wasn't about to further express his opinion of how the people he'd met in Galveston were treating Miss Prescott. "Now if you're through discussing Valissa Prescott, I'd like to turn to business matters."

Lyman reddened a little. "Of course."

"I know I can go over the books, but as president, I want you to tell me about the bank, Mr. Colbert, since this isn't the only one I own and I have to rely on the employees to keep it stable. How safe would my money be if I decided to put the bulk of it in your care?"

"Why, I assure you, Mr. Stone, it would be perfectly safe. Some of the richest men in Galveston bank with us." Lyman Colbert looked at Nathan with interest.

"I'm thinking of buying another business or two while in Galveston and I'm talking about a lot of money. Probably around two hundred thousand. Maybe more. Of course, I'd be depositing it in increments."

Lyman Colbert's eyes grew large. "I assure you, Mr. Stone, we'll do everything we can to be of service to you."

"Then, Mr. Colbert, would you object if I had my accountant go over your books?"

"Well…I…" He swallowed. "I thought you'd be the one to be looking at the books."

"Oh, I am, but sometimes I miss things. I'd feel better about my money if I had someone else look over your records. Please don't be offended. I'm not questioning you. I just want to be sure nothing has slipped by you or anyone else in the bank."

Colbert finally said, "I guess it'd be all right."

"Thank you. I'm sure my bookkeeper will find things in order."

"I'm sure he will, too, Mr. Stone."

Again cutting his ham, Nathan said, "There's a saloon down on the docks called Tilley's. Is there anything you could tell me about it?"

Lyman blushed. "What makes you think I'd know about a place like that?"

Nathan knew that by accident, he'd hit a nerve with this man. Swallowing a smile, he said, "Oh, I don't mean you'd know personally, Mr. Colbert. I meant could you tell me who owns it and if a bank holds a mortgage."

"I see. We do hold mortgages on several of those houses at the dock. Of course, some are paid off. I'll certainly find out about Tilley's for you."

"Thank you. I know some of those places make a lot of money and I happened to drop into Tilley's. It looked successful and I wondered if it could be bought." Nathan knew this statement had cleared up in Colbert's mind why he was asking about the saloon.

"As I said, I'll certainly find out for you, Mr. Stone."

"Thank you."

Flo came in with apple pie for dessert. When the men finished the meal, they retired to the study where Nathan served brandy.

Lyman Colbert left soon afterward. Nathan watched him go down the walk to his waiting buggy. He was sure the man was seeing his bank growing with a substantial deposit. He decided he'd send a wire transfer to his home bank in Fort Worth and deposit some money here to show Colbert he was serious.

Turning back inside, Nathan climbed the stairs and paused to look in on Valissa. Easing her door open, he had to smile. Someone, probably Flo, had removed her clothes and tucked her under the sheets. She looked so small and vulnerable lying there. He wanted to go into the room and cuddle her in his arms. Of course, that could never happen and why did he think of it in the first place? He had all the women he wanted or needed back in Fort Worth. Hadn't he almost decided that as soon as he was back at the ranch, he'd ask Maurine to marry him? After all, it was time to settle down. But for some reason, thinking of marrying Maurine only made him more aware of how pretty and desirable Valissa Prescott was.

He shook his head and headed for his own room.

~ * ~

Valissa rose up in bed and fell immediately back to her pillow. She felt as if her head were going to explode. "Lord," she muttered, "what's the matter with me?"

Squeezing her eyes together, she tried to remember what was going on. She knew she was in her bed or thought she was. To make sure, she opened an eye and looked around. Yes, it was her room, but how did she get here and what time was it, and was she going to die?

She remembered going to the dock to sell her gowns. She met Glenn Tilley and the women in his establishment bought her dresses. Then he offered her a job as a hostess and they discussed the details.

Then what?

She racked her brain. Somehow she thought Nathan Stone was involved, but how could he have been?

It was too much. She closed her eyes and moaned. Never in her life had she been in so much pain.

There was a tap on her door.

"Go away," she whispered.

The door opened and Flo looked inside. "Miss Valissa, are you awake?"

"No."

Flo moved to the bed. "I brought you some coffee."

"I don't want it, Flo. I'm sick."

"You'll be all right, but you need to get up."

"Why? I want to sleep."

"I'm afraid you can't, Miss Valissa. Mr. Stone wants you to come down. He has some things he wants to discuss with you."

"He can talk to me later."

"I'm afraid he won't take no for an answer. You know how demanding he is."

"I don't care about him. I think I'm dying. Flo? What happened to me?"

Flo smiled. "You're not dying, Miss Valissa. You have a hangover."

"A hangover?"

"Yes, ma'am."

"I couldn't have a hangover. I don't drink."

"You did last night. Mr. Stone brought you home and…"

"Mr. Stone? Did he get me drunk?"

"No, Miss Valissa. He went to the docks and found you. You were drinking so much you passed out. Mr. Stone brought you home on his shoulder."

"His shoulder?" Valissa frowned. "What do you mean?"

"He had you flung over his shoulder just like a sack of feed. He carried you upstairs and put you to bed."

"Oh, no. Why did he…"

"You'll have to ask him, Miss Valissa. I've told you all I know." She set the coffee on the table beside the bed. "Now let me help you get dressed. If you don't come downstairs, he might come up here."

Valissa knew Flo was telling the truth. He'd never think a headache was any reason to stay in bed. She somehow managed to sit up. Flo handed her the coffee and turned to the wardrobe to select a dress.

~ * ~

After making it downstairs, Valissa took a deep breath and knocked on the study door. When she heard Nathan call 'come in,' she hoped she could get to one of the chairs in the room without stumbling, or worse still, falling flat on her face.

She opened the door and was lucky enough to reach one of the high-backed chairs in front of the desk without letting him know how wobbly she felt. "You wanted to see me?" she managed to say as she sat.

"I did. I not only wanted to see how you were coping with your hangover, I wanted to discuss something I had in mind to talk over with you last night. Of course, we both know why that didn't happen."

"Who said I had a hangover?"

"My dear, Miss Prescott, it goes without saying anyone as drunk as you were last night would definitely have a hangover this morning."

"I wasn't drunk."

He laughed. "Honey, you were so drunk you passed out as soon as I got you into my carriage."

"I might have had a little too much wine. I'm not used to drinking," She tossed her head, then grabbed it as a pain shot across her temple.

Nathan continued to grin. "I would suggest that next time you limit your drinking to a glass or so of wine. It looked as if you'd consumed a whole bottle."

"I did not. Mr…uh…anyway, we were discussing a job."

His eyebrow shot up. "So you're considering going to work for Mr. Tilley?"

"I have to work for somebody, Mr. Stone, and Mr. Tilley said I could be his hostess. All I would have to do is wear a pretty gown and greet his customers at the door."

"And you believed him?"

"Of course. Why shouldn't I?"

"You are naïve, aren't you?"

"What do you mean by that?" she snapped.

"Valissa, you were on the verge of climbing into bed with Glenn Tilley last night. If I hadn't burst into the room when I did, I'd probably have found you there."

Valissa jumped up. "How dare you say such a thing?"

"Sit down before you fall." He eyed her and she dropped back to the chair, clutching her head. "I say such a thing because I know how men like Tilley operate. He was kind and charming. He offered you only a sip of wine, but when you weren't looking he kept filling your glass. Of course I'm sure you told him the story of how you'd lost your home and how you had no place to go."

"He was trying to help me."

Nathan shook his head. "No, Valissa. He was trying to help himself."

"How?"

"I'm sure he talked about you working as a hostess, but that wasn't his goal for you. He saw you as a beautiful young woman who would bring in lots of customers. Not just to greet them at the door, but to pleasure them in a bedroom upstairs."

Valissa gasped and he went on. "He intended to get you so drunk you would let him take you to bed. Afterward he'd be nice for a few days, then he'd demand you earn your pay and to do that you'd have to do whatever he demanded to entertain any man he sent to your room."

Tears began to run down Valissa's cheeks. "I don't believe it."

"I can't help what you believe, but that is definitely what would have happened. I've met men like Tilley before and as I said, I know how they operate."

Valissa dropped her head. "I guess I'm just stupid where men are concerned. I believed my brother and looked what happened. Now I believe a man who wanted to turn me into a… a…"

Nathan felt a rush of pity for her and interrupted. "Well, it's not going to happen." He stood and walked around his desk. He put his hand on her shoulder. "Why don't you go back to bed for a while? The best thing for a hangover is to sleep it off."

Valissa didn't resist when he took her arm and helped her to the door. "Flo!" he called when they reached the bottom of the steps.

Flo came into the entry. "Yes, Mr. Stone?"

"Please see Miss Prescott to her room. If she needs anything, please get it for her."

"I will, sir."

As they started up the steps, Valissa turned and looked at him through her still-bloodshot eyes. "Thank you, Mr. Stone."

He only nodded.

~ * ~

At noon Valissa slipped down the stairs, hoping to get a cup of coffee before she had to face Nathan Stone again. Luck was with her and she made it to the kitchen. Flo turned from the stove and grinned. "Feeling better?"

"If I could get a cup of coffee, I think I might live."

Flo laughed out loud and poured a cup for her. "Shall I serve you in the dining room?"

"I'll have it here." Valissa sat at the round wooden table. "I'm not up to facing Mr. Stone yet."

"Mr. Stone isn't here, Miss Valissa. Phillips took him into town because he had some business to take care of and he said for me not to worry about the mid-day meal. He was going to meet somebody for dinner in town, but I was to cook supper."

"Good." Valissa breathed easier. "By the way, Flo, where is Phillips staying? I never see him."

"Alvin told him there was a room in the servants' quarters he could have, but he said he preferred to stay in the room over the stable. He does come in for his meals with Alvin and me. In fact, I think he and Alvin are becoming friends."

"I see." She sipped her coffee. "Did Mr. Stone say when he'd be back?"

"He said he'd be home by early afternoon because there was something he needed you to do."

"I wonder what."

"I'm not sure, but I heard him talking to Alvin about designing the fall garden. Maybe he wants your opinion."

Valissa nodded. "Maybe so."

Without asking, Flo sat a saucer containing a piece of bread and a slice of ham before Valissa. "Eat this, miss. You need something on your stomach."

"I suppose you're right." She picked up the bread and nibbled it.

"Now, Miss Valissa, you know I'm not one to interfere, but what in the world were you thinking when you went to the docks by yourself?"

"Since Nathan Stone refused to let you go sell my gowns, I saw no other alternative." She gave a little smile. "I did well with them, too."

"Even so, how did selling your dresses manage to get you home drunk and hanging on Mr. Stone's shoulder?"

"You know I'm not much of a drinker and I had a little too much wine." She slung her hair back. "Even if he doesn't think so, I would have managed to get home without his help."

Though she didn't say anything else, by the look on Flo's face Valissa knew the woman didn't believe her.

"It's true, Flo. I was discussing a job with a man and I guess I picked up my wine glass several times without thinking. I'm sure it was because I was nervous. I would never drink so much if I were paying attention."

"You must have picked it up more than several times. Remember I saw you when you were passed out on your bed."

Valissa slammed her coffee cup down. "I can't believe you're talking to me like this, Flo."

"I'm sorry, Miss Valissa, but I guess since I helped raise you, I have a right."

Valissa dropped her head. "Of course you do, Flo. I shouldn't have snapped at you."

Flo shook her head and turned back to the stove. "I'm making some lemon pies for supper. Do you think Mr. Stone will like them?"

"I don't know if he will or not, but you know they're my favorite dessert." Valissa grinned at Flo's back, knowing the pies were for her, not the new owner of Heartsong.

"Thanks," she whispered, then stood, patted Flo's shoulder and left the kitchen.

Six

At three o'clock, Nathan helped Valissa out of the carriage in front of Mrs. Dupree-Fontaine's dressmaking shop. As soon as her feet touched the sidewalk, she jerked her arm from his hand. "I can get inside by myself."

"Of course."

She knew Nathan smothered a smile, but it didn't stop her from glaring at him with nothing except anger in her eyes. Valissa had been furious when he insisted she come for a fitting of the gown being designed, but of course with his ill manners, he didn't let it deter him from forcing her to obey him. He even threatened to bodily carry her inside if she didn't come along quietly. She knew he'd do it, too.

When they entered the door, the dressmaker came on the run. "Ah, Mr. Stone. I see you've brought the woman you said was the same size as your friend to be fitted. I think the dress will be perfect for her."

"I'm sure it will be."

Mrs. Dupree-Fontaine took Valissa's arm, but still looking at Nathan she said, "I'll get her into the dress, so you can see the results so far."

"Thank you. I look forward to seeing your work."

"Come on, young lady. Let's get you into the dress."

"I think you know my name's Valissa Prescott, Mrs. Dupree-Fontaine. You've made dresses for me."

Mrs. Dupree-Fontaine mumbled something nobody understood and ushered Valissa toward the dressing room. Once inside, she said, "Now listen here, young lady. I know your name, but this is not your gown. Mr. Stone said it was for a special friend of his and he wanted it to be perfect. I'm only trying to please a customer. After all, he's paying a good price for the dresses."

"Dresses?"

"Yes. He said he wanted the gown first, then he wanted me to make three day dresses for his friend. I hope this will be the only one you have to have fitted for him, but in case it's not, please don't irritate him so much that he takes his business somewhere else."

Valissa took a deep breath. "I'll watch my tongue."

"Thank you, Valissa. I don't care what anyone says, you have class."

Valissa didn't say anything, but she wondered who of her former friends were saying she had no class to the dressmaker.

Mrs. Dupree-Fontaine slipped the gown over Valissa's head. "Oh, my, my, my. It looks beautiful on you. The color is perfect. Too bad it's for another woman."

Valissa fingered the lace-covered bodice. "It is lovely. You always do beautiful work, Mrs. Dupree-Fontaine. I'm sure Mr. Stone as well as his friend are going to be pleased with it."

"Thank you, dear. Now, shall we go out there and show him how beautiful it is?"

~ * ~

When Valissa walked out, Nathan's mouth almost fell open. He knew the dress would enhance her natural beauty, but he never dreamed how much. She looked like a princess. A princess he wanted to get his hands on and one he knew he shouldn't have such thoughts about. After all, he had Maurine waiting in the background. A woman he knew well and one who would fit into his lifestyle and on his ranch. He knew a woman like Valissa Prescott would never do that.

Glancing away, he said, "It looks very pretty, Mrs. Dupree-Fontaine."

"Is there nothing you want to change?" Mrs. Dupree-Fontaine looked pleased.

He turned back to Valissa. She looked uncomfortable and he wondered how far he could push her. "Maybe the neckline should dip a little more."

Valissa frowned at him. "I think it's low enough, Mr. Stone."

"Now, dear, let's not argue with the customer. He knows what he wants." The dressmaker pulled the bodice down an inch or so. "How's this?"

Nathan grinned. "That's more like it."

"Then I'll make the change. Is there anything else?"

He shook his head and gave her a big grin. "I think it'll be fine."

Valissa seethed as they left the shop, but she didn't say a word on the ride home.

Nathan decided to go to the stable with Philips when they returned to the house. He wanted to let her stew for a bit. She had to learn he was in charge of what went on at Heartsong, including her comings and goings. For the next three weeks anyway. Besides, she'd get over her mad. Women, in his experience, always did. In his opinion, Valissa Prescott was as much a woman as any he'd seen in this world, and that included his lover, Maurine.

~ * ~

Inside the house, Valissa went directly to the kitchen. "I can't believe that man, Flo."

Flo grinned. "I assume you're talking about Mr. Stone."

"Of course I am. He's the most infuriating person I've ever met."

"What did he do to rile you this time?"

"You won't believe it. He actually had Mrs. Dupree-Fontaine lower the neckline of the gown she's making. I know he did it to humiliate me."

"Maybe not. He could have thought it needed lowering."

"No, Flo. He watched as the dressmaker took her hands and pulled the dress down, exposing a lot more of my breasts. I looked at his eyes and he was ogling me. He wanted me to be uncomfortable and I know it."

"Maybe he thinks you're a pretty woman, Miss Valissa."

"I don't believe it."

"Men have strange ways of doing things and women can't always tell what they're up to."

Valissa picked up a cookie from the plate sitting on the table. "I know what he's up to. He wants me out of here before my three weeks are up, and because I know this, I'm staying until the last minute. I want to aggravate him as much as he does me."

"You know that could turn on you, don't you, Miss Valissa?"

"What do you mean?"

Before Flo could answer, Nathan came through the back door. "Good…you're in here, Miss Prescott."

"Did you want me for some other errand, Mr. Stone?" Her voice was snide.

"I want to talk with you about something else besides errands." He turned to Flo. "Would you please bring some coffee to my study for me and if Miss Prescott prefers, bring her tea?"

"Yes sir."

He looked back at Valissa. "Come with me."

She stood and followed him down the hall without speaking.

"Have a seat," he said and moved behind the desk.

"If this isn't going to take long, I prefer to stand."

"You'll get tired, Miss Prescott. It may take the rest of the afternoon."

Furious, Valissa plopped into one of the chairs in front of the desk without saying a word, though she wanted to slap the smirk off Nathan Stone's face. How could he be such a brute? He thought nothing of ordering her around as if she were one of his servants. The problem was, she couldn't do anything about it. This really was his home, though it still felt as if it were hers, and technically she was going to consider it as hers until her three weeks were up. Why couldn't he accept that and leave her alone?

Flo entered with a tray in her hands. It held both coffee and tea. She'd also added the plate of cookies Valissa had sampled. She served the two of them, then slipped out the door, closing it behind her.

Valissa sipped her tea and glared at Nathan. He was busy looking through a stack of papers on the desk and paid no attention to her. She wanted to demand that he get this meeting over with, but decided she'd wait him out. He wanted her in there and she wasn't about to make it easier for him to get on with his business.

Finally he broke the silence. "I've noticed some of the records you've been keeping on your household expenses."

Valissa bristled. "You were going through my personal papers?"

"They were here in plain sight."

Oh, how she wanted to wipe that innocent look off his face! Instead she snapped, "You had no right. They were personal."

"I have no interest in your personal things, Miss Prescott, but I couldn't help noticing how meticulously you kept the records. I have to commend you for that. Few women are so careful."

Surprised by the compliment, she muttered, "When you don't have a lot of money to spend, you have to keep careful track of it."

He smiled. "That's what I want to talk to you about."

She lifted an eyebrow. For what possible reason did her recordkeeping hold an interest for him? This man could throw her off balance and make her mad quicker than anything or anyone ever had before. But before her anger could build, curiosity settled in. She wanted to know what he was going to say next. "So you want to discuss the way I kept my records?"

His next statement confused her more. "Not really. What I want are those sharp eyes of yours. You seem to be able to keep up with every penny in your account, and for that reason, I want to hire you to look over some accounts for me, Valissa."

She was surprised he'd used her first name. Any other time, she'd have confronted him about it, but today she let it go. She was more interested in why he wanted to hire her. Surely he had many people at his disposal that could look over important papers like accounts for him. Why would he settle for a woman who only kept track of her meager income?

"Why me?" she blurted.

"It's simple. I'm not sure who I can trust in this town."

"How do you know you can trust me, Mr. Stone?"

His grin grew wide. "Though I know you don't like me, Miss Prescott, I'm pretty sure you're completely honest."

She didn't intend to admit, even to herself, that she might like him. She simply asked, "Again, how do you know?"

"It's simple. I figure if you intended to try to cheat me, you would have taken some of the valuable items in this house to sell. A piece of the silver, perhaps. Or one of the paintings from a room I seldom go in. But you didn't. You took your dresses, though they couldn't possibly bring you as much money as one of the more expensive items."

"I'm not a thief, Mr. Stone. I was told I owned nothing in this house except my personal things. My clothes and my grandmother's earrings are the only things of worth that I could sell."

He eyed her. "Have you sold the earrings?"

"Not yet. I planned to sell them today, but I just couldn't do it. I decided to hold them until the last minute. I'm sure I'll have to let them go when I'm forced to move."

"Before you sell them, let me know. I have a jeweler friend here in town. I can probably get you a better price than you could get on the open market."

Since he was a big businessman in town, he was probably right when he said he could get a better price. "I'll do that," she muttered. She didn't really want his help in raising money, but if he could get her a better deal, she'd swallow her pride and accept his offer.

Holding up a ledger, he changed the subject. "This is one of the records of accounts at the bank. I asked Colbert to let me look them over. I've perused it quickly, but there's nothing I can put my finger on. Still, I think something is out of kilter because there should be more profit than what I'm seeing. I want you to go through it and see if anything strikes you as wrong."

"I'm sure Mr. Colbert could explain anything you don't understand."

"I don't trust Colbert."

Valissa frowned. "But he owns the bank."

"No, Valissa. He doesn't own the bank. I do."

"You?" She was surprised.

"Yes, but I don't want Colbert, or anyone else there to know that I'm questioning their recordkeeping."

"Why?"

"As I said, I'm not sure who to trust. At this point, I only trust you."

"But Mr. Colbert has always been at the bank."

"When I bought it, it was on the condition that he stay there as the manager. I didn't see a problem with such an arrangement at the time."

Valissa didn't answer, but took the ledger he held toward her and glanced at the others he pointed to.

He gave her one of his rare smiles. "I could be mistaken about this, but if something is wrong, I want to find who is not to be trusted before I make any changes."

She didn't like the way the smile made her feel, so she dropped her eyes, though she couldn't stop her heart from thumping. She hoped he couldn't see how it affected her. "What makes you think I could see something you haven't already discovered?" she muttered.

"I have a feeling you'll see anything that's not supposed to be there."

"Do you want me to take them to my room?"

"I have an appointment, so the study is available if you want to work here."

"I think I will work here. I always liked working in Daddy's study."

He shrugged and stood. "Then, I shall see you later."

She nodded and moved behind the desk without looking at him as he moved out. She still had his engaging smile on her mind and she was afraid he'd guess it had set her heart to racing. She couldn't understand why it was happening, anyway. Though she knew it might be a lie, she kept telling herself she couldn't stand the man.

~ * ~

Valissa was amazed at how quickly she began to find mistakes in the figures in the ledger. They weren't big mistakes, mainly a few transposed numbers here and there. One was a requisition to purchase some supplies that cost fifty-three dollars and eighty-nine cents and was deducted as fifty-eight dollars and thirty-nine cents.

She looked for the five dollars and fifty cents, but didn't find it posted. She jotted the number down on a sheet of paper.

At the end of January's record, she found that the small mistakes added up to one hundred and eighteen dollars and sixty-eight cents.

When she finished February, there were another ninety-two dollars and twenty cents to add to the list.

In March there wasn't as much wrong. She only found forty-one dollars and no change.

She intended to start April when the study door opened. She glanced up as Nathan entered.

"Still hard at work, I see," he nodded at her.

"I am, and you're not going to believe what I've found."

"Oh?"

"Look at this." She handed him the sheet of figures she'd written on the paper. "It looks like somebody is doing some fancy bookkeeping."

He looked at the numbers. "What are these?"

"It's money that was deducted from the accounts, but it doesn't show up on a record anywhere. It comes from many different subtractions and it isn't accounted for."

He frowned. "Do you mean somebody is taking money from the bank?"

"I'm not sure yet, but it does look like it."

"How can they get away with it?"

"It seems when money must be deducted from the vault or wherever, more is taken than is requested."

"So somebody is putting that extra in their pocket." Nathan frowned. "Can you tell who?"

Valissa shook her head. "I hope something will give them away if I keep looking."

"Show me how you found this." He leaned over her shoulder and looked at the ledger.

She moved a little to the side to get away from the spicy, manly smell of him. It made her heart start up again. She bit her lip and said, "See how it's noted here that the lumber company charged thirty-four dollars and eight cents for building a new railing in the bank." He nodded and she flipped the page. "Now look here. Forty-three dollars and ninety-eight cents were deducted, leaving nine dollars and ninety cents unaccounted for."

"I'll be damned. I knew somebody in that bank was crooked. It looks like it must be the bookkeeper."

"Not necessarily."

He frowned. "What do you mean?"

"There's another record that states the bookkeeper wasn't privy to the bills. He was only given sheets of paper where the bankers had written the deductions."

"So it could be anyone?"

She nodded. "I would need to see the papers the bankers wrote out to know who the thief is."

"I'll see if I can get them for you."

Flo knocked on the door and announced supper.

"Let's go eat. We can get into all of this later." He stood back and held his arm toward her.

For once, Valissa didn't argue. She'd worked all afternoon and she was hungry. Besides he did smell good.

She couldn't help noticing the surprised look on his face when she stood and took his arm without saying a word.

~ * ~

Valissa came down the stairs the next morning humming one of her favorite tunes. She knew it would be a wonderful day. How could it not? Nathan told her at supper last night that he had to leave town early this morning and he didn't say when he'd be back. He also told her to continue studying the bank ledgers and he would discuss them with her when he returned. He even asked if she needed any of her pay in advance, which she refused.

She smiled to herself as she entered the kitchen. Maybe she could even finish the work and be gone by the time he came back. It would be a blessing if she never had to see him again, since she was afraid she might begin to like him.

Then she remembered she didn't take any money he owed her for the work she was doing for him and her smile turned to a frown. Though she had no doubt he would pay her, he might take his time if she were gone. There was no way she was going to leave without her money.

Again her facial expression changed. She felt a surge of pride when she realized that as long as he was gone, she would have free access to Heartsong and everything there.

Yes, it was going to be a good day. A very good day indeed.

"Good morning, Flo," she chirped when she entered the kitchen.

"Good morning, Miss Valissa. You sure seem chipper this morning."

"I feel chipper." Valissa took a seat at the wooden kitchen table. "I'm also hungry. I hope you have made a big breakfast."

"Indeed, I have. Mr. Nathan wanted ham, eggs, potatoes and biscuits before he left. Of course, I made enough for you." Flo turned and smiled at her. "If you'll go into the dining room, I'll serve you there."

"I'll eat right here with you, it that's all right."

"I don't mind, but Mr. Nathan told me to treat you as if you were still the lady of the house."

"He did, did he?" Valissa frowned. "Well, what Mr. Nathan doesn't know won't hurt him. Since I'm no longer owner of this place, I'll eat where I please."

"Suit yourself." Flo handed her a cup of coffee.

"Did Nathan tell you where he was going?"

"No. He only said he would be back, but he didn't say when."

"I guess that means you're stuck with only me until he returns."

Flo laughed. "I don't mind that at all, Miss Valissa."

~ ❋ ~

In the middle of the afternoon, Flo tapped on the study door. "Miss Valissa, there's a woman here who won't believe me when I told her that I didn't know where Mr. Nathan was or when he'd be back."

"Where is she, Flo?"

"I put her in the parlor."

Valissa started to stand, then changed her mind. "Please show her in here."

"Yes, ma'am."

Flo showed a shapely woman, beautifully dressed in a dark blue velvet traveling suit and white silk blouse, into the study. She had big blue eyes and mounds of red curled hair under a hat with a bunch of brightly colored feathers that reminded Valissa of a turkey's behind. Yet even with the comparison, Valissa thought it one of the most handsome outfits she'd seen in a long time.

The woman ruined the pretty picture as her high-pitched voice demanded, "Tell me right now where Nathan is."

Valissa's eyebrow went up as did her temper, though she was able to hide that she was getting angry. She said in a calm voice, "May I asked who wants to know where Mr. Stone is?"

"Not that it's any of your business," the woman snapped, "but I'm Colleen O'Malley, Mr. Stone's fiancée."

Valissa couldn't help the feeling of disappointment that flittered through her mind, but she pushed it aside. "As his fiancée, you probably know more about his whereabouts than I do." She wanted to add, I thought all pretty Irish women had red hair and green eyes, but you have blue eyes, but she didn't.

"If I knew where he was, do you think I'd be asking you? I expected him to be here in his new home."

"He left this morning."

"Where did he go?" She began to look exasperated.

"He didn't tell me where he was going."

Valissa wondered if the woman were going to break out in angry tears when she stuttered, "Then…then, when will he be back?"

"He didn't tell me when he'd return either."

The woman threw herself into one of the chairs in front of the desk. "What kind of servant are you if you don't know where your boss is or when he'll be back?"

"My dear Miss O'Malley, I'm not Mr. Stone's servant. I'm merely doing some work on his accounts for him."

Colleen fanned herself with her lace handkerchief. "Employee or servant. What's the difference?"

"Let me assure you, there is a huge difference."

The woman shook her head and sighed. "I feel like fainting."

"Don't you dare."

Colleen's eyes opened wide and she stared at Valissa. "Sometimes a lady can't help it."

"If she tries hard enough, a real lady can help most anything she wants to."

Colleen continued to stare. "What kind of woman are you?" When Valissa didn't answer, she went on. "You must be one of those who think they're as smart as a man and just as strong."

When Valissa spoke, she didn't take up Colleen's question. She asked, "Is there something else you wanted?"

"I don't know what to do. I came to see Nathan and to look over this house." She glanced around the room. "I must say it's nice. I guess I can live here if this is where he decides to settle."

Valissa wanted to lash out at her and tell her there was no way she'd ever fit into this house, but she held her tongue. What could she do about it if Nathan did move the woman in here?

Colleen jumped up, startling Valissa.

"Show me to a guest room. I want to take a nap. Maybe Nathan will come back by the time I get up."

"I'll have Flo ready a room for you." Valissa stood and moved to the door. "You can wait in the parlor until she sends for you."

"But...I... "

Valissa went out the door, ignoring her protests.

Seven

At suppertime, Colleen came into the dining room. She'd changed from her fancy traveling suit to a yellow silk gown with low neck and heavy lace around the neckline. The sleeves were short and the same lace trimmed them. Valissa thought she'd either redone her hair or she'd slept holding her head off the pillow because there wasn't a hair out of place.

"Has Nathan returned?" she demanded as she took a chair across the table from Valissa.

"I haven't seen him."

Colleen picked up her linen napkin, snapped it and placed it across her lap. "I'm surprised you're eating in the dining room."

"Why are you surprised?" Valissa frowned at the woman.

"I figured the hired help would eat in the kitchen with the servants."

Valissa bit her lip. "Since you're into asking inappropriate questions, I want to ask you something."

"What?"

"Why are your eyes blue instead of green?"

"I've never heard such a stupid question in my life. My eyes are blue because I was born with that color."

"It is a stupid question, but so is yours about why I eat in the dining room."

Colleen frowned and looked puzzled, but didn't have time to answer.

Flo opened the door and came into the room with a platter of baked ham and placed it in front of Valissa.

"I think you should give that to me. I'll be acting as hostess."

"No, ma'am," Flo said. "Mr. Nathan told me until he returned that Miss Valissa was the mistress of this house."

"But I'm here now."

"I'm sorry, ma'am. I don't know you and I only take orders from Mr. Nathan." Flo went out the door and immediately returned with bowls of potatoes, beans, carrots and a basket of freshly baked bread.

Colleen didn't say anything until she was gone. Then she looked at Valissa. "Is she telling the truth?"

"I've never known Flo to lie. Pass me your plate, please."

Colleen handed her the china plate. "Well, when I marry Nathan, things will change. I don't intend to let a servant tell me what to do."

"Flo is only following orders. She'd never disobey anything Nathan told her to do."

"Why do you call him by his first name? I think an employee should call him Mr. Stone."

"Nathan and I are on a first name basis."

"Then what should I call you?"

"Miss Prescott will do fine."

"But…I don't…I mean, if Nathan and you…"

"I'll also be courteous and call you Miss O'Malley." Valissa handed her back her filled plate. "Tell me, Miss O'Malley, how long have you and Nathan been engaged?"

"It's been forever. I think my parents decided I was going to marry him as soon as I was old enough. His stepmother seems to think it's a good idea that we marry soon. She wants grandchildren. Preferably a suitable grandson she can leave the ranch to."

"I see." Valissa busied herself dishing out her food. Why, she wondered, how this woman managed to attract the stern and willful Nathan Stone was beyond her. Of course, she'd always heard that opposites attract and this case proved it to be true. "Have you set a date?"

"Oh, no. That's one reason I came to Galveston. I wanted to see if I could help Nathan make up his mind."

"Make up his mind?"

"Yes. You see, he hasn't formally proposed to me, but that doesn't matter. It's inevitable that we marry. Everyone says so."

"I see," Valissa said again because she couldn't think of anything else to say, since the woman wasn't really Nathan's fiancée.

"Nathan told Daddy he expected there would parties to go to while he was here, so I thought if I could get him to propose, it would be a good time to announce our engagement."

Valissa's lip curled a little as a thought crossed her mind. The dress she'd tried on at Mrs. Dupree-Fontaine's dress shop would never fit this woman, no matter how much Nathan said his friend was the same size as Valissa. Colleen was at least an inch or two shorter and her waistline much thicker. She shook her head. Men were clueless sometimes when it came to women.

"Why do you think we shouldn't announce it here?"

"I didn't say you shouldn't."

"But you shook your head."

"That didn't mean anything. I was thinking of something else."

"Good. I thought announcing our engagement at one of the parties was a chance for me to meet the right people in society here. I want to get started right away with the right families."

"I was under the impression Nathan liked to stay on his ranch."

"Lord, I hope he doesn't want to stay there much. It's miles from neighbors and even more miles from town. After living all my life in Fort Worth, I'd be bored sick living way out there."

Valissa finished her meal and looked at Colleen's empty plate. "Would you like more?"

"Maybe a little." She handed her plate over.

As she spooned up the food, Valissa casually asked, "If you were in town and Nathan was on the ranch, how did you two meet?"

"Daddy is Nathan's lawyer. We were always invited to the functions at the ranch and when there was something exciting going on in town, the Stones were always guests. I've known Nathan all my life."

Valissa handed her back the plate, and said nothing else. She mulled over what Colleen had told her while the woman finished eating.

As soon as Colleen put her silverware down, Flo appeared with cherry pie and coffee, then retreated to the kitchen.

"It's going to get dark soon," Colleen said. "I guess we should hurry. You don't want to be going home in the dark."

"Oh, I thought you knew." Valissa paused with a fork of pie heading toward her mouth. "I live here."

Colleen dropped her fork and stared at her. "You mean here in the house with Nathan?"

"Not exactly with Nathan. I have my own room." She put the pie in her mouth.

There was a long silence. Colleen finally asked, "Is your room downstairs in the servants' quarters?"

"No. It's upstairs."

Colleen frowned. "Flo put me in the room at the end of the hall upstairs. Is your room near mine?"

"Does it really matter where my room is?" Valissa picked up her coffee. Why she was enjoying making this woman feel uncomfortable, she didn't know, but she wondered if it was because if there was ever anyone unsuited to be Nathan Stone's wife, Colleen was it.

Colleen didn't answer, but she kept looking at Valissa as if she wanted to throw the pie at her instead of eating it.

~ * ~

After a late breakfast, Colleen decided to take another nap. "Not much use in sitting around with you glaring at me," she said to Valissa. "I wish I'd never come here."

"Then why did you come?"

"If I'd known Nathan wasn't here…"Her voice trailed off at the top of the stairs.

Valissa shook her head. She wished Colleen had never come to Galveston either. With a shrug, she turned to the study. At least, she could get some work done on the books while the woman was asleep.

She had only finished a couple of pages of the ledger she was working on when Flo announced she had a visitor in the parlor. Valissa put the pen back in the inkwell and stood.

Entering the parlor, she gasped. "Rowena, I can't believe you're here!"

"I had to come, Valissa. Please don't tell anyone. Mother would be furious, and maybe Daddy, too, but I had to come."

"Of course I won't tell." Valissa took a seat in a chair facing the settee where Rowena sat. "Now, tell me why you felt you had to come."

In a rushed voice, she said, "I accept that you've lost everything, Valissa, but I won't accept the fact that people say we can't still be friends because of it. We've known each other too long for that."

"But I thought…I mean, Wilbur said…" Valissa's voice trailed off.

"My cousin doesn't have the best of manners sometimes. And he definitely has no backbone." She let out a nervous laugh. "Not that I have much, but I couldn't completely turn my back on you."

"I will understand if you think it's better for our friendship to end."

"I'm sure it will change, but end… No. I don't want that."

Valissa looked at Rowena for a several seconds. "What do you want, Rowena?"

"I'm not sure. I just know that if I were in your circumstances, you wouldn't turn your back on me."

"You're right. I wouldn't."

"See, I knew you'd be a faithful friend. That's want I'm trying to be, though Mother told me I had to discontinue our friendship. Of course, I guess I'll have to I let her think I agree, but I don't agree at all."

"What if she finds out you've been here?"

"I thought about that before I came. I decided to tell her that I was passing by and decided to visit Mr. Stone. After all, she kept pushing me toward him when he was at the house for dinner the other night."

"Mr. Stone is out of town."

For a minute Rowena looked flustered. "Well, I didn't know that. If she or my father finds out about this visit, I can tell them the truth then."

"Then you must not stay long. I'm sure your father knows he's gone."

"You're probably right. I'll tell them I didn't stay because he wasn't here."

"I do appreciate your visit, Rowena. It means a lot to me to know you are a true friend."

"After all we've shared through the years I couldn't let our friendship end." Rowena began looking in her draw-string purse. She came out with a folded envelope. "I didn't have much money in cash, but there's about eighty dollars here. I want you to take it because I know you can use it."

Valissa was embarrassed and felt herself flush. "I couldn't do that. I don't want my friends to think I'm begging for handouts."

"You didn't ask me for anything. I'm offering it to you of my own free will. I wish I could do more, but I want to help what little I can."

"I appreciate it, but no. I can't accept it."

"Don't be that way, Valissa. Mr. Bower said you had nothing. Not even the furnishings left in Heartsong."

"That's true, but I'll be fine. I'll find a job soon."

"What can you do to make enough money to live on?"

The idea of being Glenn Tilley's hostess floated across her mind, but she didn't mention it to Rowena because she knew Nathan would put a stop to it if she went to work there. Instead she said, "Actually, Mr. Stone is paying me to do some paperwork for him. If I do a good job, maybe he'll put me to work in one of his offices."

"That would be wonderful. I know he's a little scary, but he seems to be a nice man."

Valissa frowned. "What do you mean, scary?"

Rowena laughed. "Don't you find his size a little intimidating?"

"Maybe, a little." She hurried to add, "Though he's been nothing but a perfect gentleman since he's been here."

"He was a gentleman at the house, too, though Mother embarrassed me by the way she kept pushing him to ask me to Mrs. Maxmillion's party."

Valissa remembered Colleen, but didn't mention her. "Did he ask you?"

"No. He finally told Mother that if he came to the party at all, he was bringing a friend of his." Rowena stood. "I think I should go. I'll come again, Valissa. I don't know when, but I'll find some way that we can visit each other without my parents knowing."

"You better keep it away from Wilbur, too."

"Oh, Valissa, Wilbur was devastated because of your loss."

Valissa shook her head. "I think it was more because he thought of it as his loss of Heartsong. I'm sure he had dreams of owning it through me someday."

"You may be right." Rowena turned her back and gathered her purse from the settee.

"Thank you again for coming. As I said, it means a lot to me."

"You're welcome." Rowena gave Valissa a quick hug and headed out the front door.

After closing the door, Valissa turned back to the parlor. She started to close that door then she noticed something on the settee. She picked it up and bit her lip. Rowena had tucked the envelope of money in the back of the sofa.

Grabbing it, Valissa ran to the front door. She had every intention of giving it back to her friend, but she was too late. She watched Rowena head down the street in her small buggy.

"I'll give it back to her somehow," Valissa muttered. She tucked the envelope in her pocket and returned to the study. She wasn't sure the tears forming in her eyes were because of the unexpected visit from her friend or because Rowena had been kind enough to leave the money behind in a way she wouldn't hurt her friend's feelings.

Eight

Nathan didn't come home the next day, or the next. Valissa began to wonder if he'd ever come back. The three days she'd spent with Colleen had been three of the longest days of her life. She knew Flo felt the same way, because the longer the O'Malley woman stayed, the more demanding she became.

Finally, on the third day Coleen got a wire from her father. He said Nathan was in Fort Worth and she should come home. Alvin gladly drove her to the train station that afternoon and stayed to make sure she was really gone.

That evening, Flo served Valissa roast chicken, vegetables and chocolate cake for dessert. After finishing, she left the dining room as Flo cleaned up the dishes. In a few minutes she returned and joined Alvin and Flo in the kitchen.

"I think we should have a little celebration." She held up the bottle. "I went to the wine cellar and got a bottle of my father's favorite wine. I want you two to join me in a glass to toast our good fortune that our guest has finally gone away."

"I don't think we should do that, Miss Valissa." Alvin stared at her. "Mr. Nathan might not like us drinking his wine."

"It really belonged to my daddy." She held the bottle high. "I don't see why Nathan Stone would object."

It took some coaxing, but they finally agreed to have a glass with her. As they were hoisted their glasses into the air to make the toast, the back door opened and Nathan Stone walked in.

Without a word, Nathan stomped to the table and picked up the wine bottle. "Well, well. It looks like my staff tends to play while I'm away. And with some of my best wine."

"I'm sorry, sir…"

Nathan interrupted. "Never mind, Alvin. I'm sure Miss Prescott can come up with a reasonable explanation."

Valissa giggled, then covered her mouth with her hand. She managed to nod, but she seemed unable to say anything without laughing out loud. Why this situation he'd stumbled in on was funny to her, she didn't know. Maybe it was his unexpected arrival or maybe it was because he would be surprised that his girlfriend was the reason for the frivolity.

~ * ~

Nathan eyed her. "I'm waiting on a verbal answer, Valissa."

She giggled again.

"Mr. Nathan, she…"

"I need for her to tell me, Flo." He reached down and took hold of Valissa's arm. "Please bring me something to eat and some black coffee for both of us to the dining room."

"Do you want, tea, Miss Valissa?"

She nodded, but Nathan said, "Not this time. She's going to drink black coffee and sober up."

Before Flo could say anything else, he ushered Valissa from the room.

In the dining room, he led her to her usual chair on his right. She looked up at him and muttered, "I forgot my wine."

"You've had enough wine. You're on the verge of drunkenness again."

She leaned back and looked at him with distain. "I am not!"

He only shook his head as Flo entered the dining room with a plate for him. Alvin followed with the coffee. "The coffee was still hot, sir."

"Good. Pour Miss Prescott a cup first."

She turned up her nose. "I don't drink coffee except with my dessert at night."

"Well, you're going to tonight."

She tilted her head and looked at him. "Why?"

"The food is hot, too, Mr. Nathan." Flo sat a brimming plate before him.

"Thank you, Flo. Now leave us, please." He looked at both of them.

Flo bit her lip, but only said, "If you need anything…"

"I know." He waved her away. Though she and Alvin both left the room, he was sure they were plastered against the door so they could hear what he said to Valissa. He didn't care. They needed to hear it. Besides, he wanted Flo's help if Valissa didn't take the news he heard in Fort Worth well.

He turned to Valissa. "You're not drinking your coffee."

"It's too hot."

He cut into the chicken on his plate. He decided to make small talk first. "Then, while it cools, tell me what was going on in the kitchen when I unexpectedly arrived."

She twiddled a piece of ebony hair that had come loose from the blue bow at the back of her neck. "It was a nice little celebration until you came in and spoiled it."

He chewed the chicken and stifled a grin. "And what were you celebrating?"

She picked up her coffee cup, frowned at it and set it down. "We were celebrating the fact that we were finally rid of your fiancée."

"My *what?*" He coughed because he almost choked on his food.

Valissa giggled. "She was sure a lot of trouble. Kept poor Flo running around all the time and tried to make me be her servant, too."

He knew she was enjoying making him uncomfortable. "What are you talking about?"

She lifted an eyebrow at him. "I told you. Your fiancée. She came to visit you, but when she got a wire telling her to come home and she obeyed it, we felt we had cause to celebrate. None of us particularly took to her." She shook her head at him. "In fact, we all think you could do better in finding a wife, but it's your life."

"I told Maurine Taylor not to come here."

She shook her head and picked up her coffee again, but her hand wobbled and some spilled out of the cup on to her fingers. She plopped the cup down, spilling more. "That burns."

"I told you to let it cool."

"You're always telling me what to do. What gives you that right?"

"Somebody needs to tell you. You're sure not doing very well making decisions on your own." He knew when he shared his news with her, she was going to need a lot of help making decisions to cope with it and he regretted being so sharp.

Like a child, she stuck her tongue out at him.

He dropped his eyes to keep her from seeing the laughter in them. Taking a drink of his coffee, he said, "As I asked, was your visitor Maurine Taylor?"

"Who is Maurine Taylor?" She eyed him.

"I guess it wasn't her."

"Is she your fiancée, too?"

"I told you, I don't have a fiancée?"

"Well, Colleen O'Malley sure thinks you do."

He frowned at her. "How do you know Colleen O'Malley?" He couldn't imagine the young impetuous girl coming to Galveston. Yet, how would Valissa know her name if she didn't?

"I told you. She came to see you. We had to put up with her because she wouldn't leave until you got back, but her father sent for her to come home. I guess she was afraid not to go, so she did. We celebrated when she left." She cocked her head to the side. "Why do you want to marry her, anyway? She's not your type."

"I'm not marrying her, Valissa."

"She said you were."

"She's wrong." He motioned toward her cup. "Your coffee should be cooler now. Start drinking it."

"Honestly, Mr. Stone. I'm not drunk. I didn't have a chance to even take a sip of the wine before you came in and interrupted us. Ask Flo."

He eyed her. Maybe she was telling the truth, but he wanted to be sure. "Doesn't matter. Drink it any way."

She frowned, but picked up the cup.

He finished his supper and watched as she sipped her coffee. Was this the time to share his news? Maybe he should wait until tomorrow. She might have a hard time sleeping if she knew tonight.

When she finally pushed back her empty cup, she started to stand. "I think I'll go to bed now."

"Oh no, you don't."

She glared at him. "And why not?"

"We're not through talking."

"Maybe you're not through, but I am."

"Are you sure you didn't have a couple of glasses of wine, Miss Prescott?"

"I told you, you came in before I could drink any."

"Then why are you giggling?"

She couldn't hold the smile back, though she didn't giggle. "I was thinking of something funny."

"Tell me about it and I'll laugh, too."

She looked up at him and said, "I'm afraid I have bad news for you."

"Oh?"

"I was picturing you and Colleen O'Malley at Mrs. Maxmillion's party. It'll never work."

He frowned. "What'll never work?"

She shook her head at him. "I know you said your friend was the same size as me, but you're wrong. Very wrong. If Miss O'Malley tries to wear that beautiful dress Mrs. Dupree-Fontaine made for her, it'll drag the floor and she'll split the seams. Her waist and her posterior are much bigger than mine."

Before he could answer, Valissa jumped up from her chair and ran out of the room.

Nathan couldn't help chuckling. *So, the little minx is jealous. That's a good sign. Now I'll hold the news for a few days. After all, there's no hurry to tell her that her brother has surfaced.*

He stood, but instead of heading to his study to see if she'd accomplished the job he left her to do, he went toward the kitchen. He knew the Shermans had been near the door by the way they scurried across the room. He went to the table where the wine bottle still sat. He realized Valissa was telling the truth because all that was missing from the bottle was in the three glasses sitting there. Picking up her glass, he glanced toward them.

"Since you missed the toast with Miss Prescott, please join me now."

They looked confused, but picked up their glasses and waited for him to say what they were toasting this time.

"Valissa had everything wrong. I have no intention of marrying Colleen O'Malley, though I think her folks and maybe the woman my father married when I was away at school in the East expect me to. I have my own idea of whom I plan to marry. I decided on it while I was away."

When neither of them said anything, he went on. "Please drink to my future bride." He turned up the glass and drained it.

Alvin and Flo drank, too.

Putting the glasses down, Flo finally asked, "Do we know who the future bride is, Mr. Nathan?"

"It won't be long until you know her very well."

Without waiting for a reply, Nathan turned and left the kitchen. The Shermans looked too stunned to say anything. They simply stared at the door as it closed behind him.

~ * ~

It was mid-morning the next day when Flo knocked on the study door where Valissa and Nathan were had been shut up working since breakfast. "Come in," Nathan said.

"I'm sorry to interrupt, Mr. Nathan, but there's a Mrs. Maxmillion and her daughter here to see you. I put them in the parlor."

"Thank you, Flo." He glanced up from the ledgers spread before them and asked Valissa, "Is that the woman having the party I've been hearing about?"

"I'm sure it is."

His brow wrinkled. "Why is she coming to see me?"

"I don't know, Mr. Stone. Maybe she wants to issue you a special invitation."

"I figured she'd send one by post."

"Then maybe she wants you to get to know her daughter before the party. I hear she's been trying to find Candice a suitable husband for some time now."

"Don't start talking about fiancées to me again."

She grinned. "The Maxmillions are upstanding members of Galveston society. You could do worse than to marry her. Of course she could never fit in the dress you had made any better than Colleen could."

"And why wouldn't she?"

"You'll see when you meet her."

He frowned and shook his head at her. "Why don't you go see what they want, then get rid of them?"

"I can't do that. It would be rude. She came to see you."

He stood. "Then you're going with me to greet them."

"I'd rather not."

"Please, Valissa."

"All right, I'll go, but don't be surprised if Mrs. Maxmillion asks me to leave the room."

"Why would she do that?"

"You know I've fallen from grace with the elite of Galveston's society. And when it comes to society, Eugenia Maxmillion is the queen."

"Sometimes even queens get their comeuppance." He took hold of her elbow and steered her from the study.

When they entered the parlor, it surprised Nathan to see the impeccably dressed tiny older woman with the snow white hair piled on top of her head seated by a woman whose long legs told him she was almost as tall as he. Though that wasn't a problem. Nathan liked tall women. But this woman was about as unattractive as any woman he'd ever seen. Her eyes were too small and too close together, her mouth too large and her face was covered in red blotches which she'd tried to disguise with white face powder. Besides that, Valissa was right. She'd never fit into the dress being made, though the dress fitted the woman it was being made for, perfectly.

He took a breath and moved to the settee. Taking Eugenia's hand, he kissed it lightly and said, "My dear, lady, it's a pleasure to meet you."

Eugenia smiled. "Likewise, I'm sure, Mr. Stone. I've been hearing what a gentleman you are. Now I believe it."

"And you must be Miss Maxmillian." He nodded to Candice, but didn't kiss her hand.

"Yes, sir, I am." She smiled, showing her best asset—even white teeth.

He turned toward Valissa. "I think you know Miss Prescott."

"Of course." Eugenia glanced at Valissa and added, "I thought she'd moved away since you bought Heartsong."

"I convinced her to stay on as one of my bookkeepers. She's very good with finances."

"Good afternoon, Mrs. Maxmillion."

Again the woman glanced at her, but said nothing.

"Why don't I go ask Flo to bring tea for your guests, Mr. Stone?"

"Thank you, Miss Prescott."

~ * ~

Valissa was glad he agreed because she wanted to get out of the room. She knew Mrs. Maxmillion didn't want her there. And to be honest with herself, she knew she didn't belong. She was no longer accepted by these society people.

In the kitchen, she asked Flo to serve tea to Mr. Stone and the Maxmillions. She then went out on the back veranda instead of returning to the parlor. There was a slight chill in the air. She shivered and wrapped her arms around herself for warmth as she watched the fall leaves trickle down from the maple trees scattered in the back yard. She didn't want to admit, even to herself, that she wished she were in a position to chat with the Maxmillions about the upcoming party, then be able to attend it. This would be the first time she'd missed the annual gala since she was fifteen years old. But from the cool reception Mrs. Maxmillion had given her, she knew she'd never be welcomed to one of their festive events again.

"Hello, Miss Valissa," Alvin's voice broke into her thoughts.

"What are you doing, Alvin?"

"Mr. Stone wanted me to dig some beds along the side of the terrace to plant oleander. What do you think?"

"I think it will be lovely. You know how hard I tried to root some from the bushes on the front so I could have it planted here."

"Mr. Stone told me to buy all the shrubs I needed to make it look right." He grinned. "I asked him what color and he turned around and asked me what color you like."

"Did you tell him?"

"Of course I did. I told him you liked the deep pink."

"What did he do, tell you to buy yellow?"

Alvin chuckled. "No, ma'am. He told me to get the pink. He also told me to buy all the other flowers and shrubs needed to make this lawn come alive this spring."

"Sounds like he might be going to make things look like they once did." She sighed. "Of course, I won't be here next spring to enjoy it."

Alvin didn't answer that, but changed the subject. "I thought if you had time one day, you could come out here and make me a list of what we need."

"I think you should ask Mr. Stone to do that. It would make me sad to plan a beautiful garden, then have to leave before seeing it come alive."

"I understand."

Valissa shivered. "I'm beginning to get cold. I think I'll go inside." She smiled at Alvin. "Don't work too hard. I'm sure Mr. Stone is in no hurry."

"What is Mr. Stone in no hurry for?" Nathan's voice sounded behind her.

"We were discussing your plans for the garden." She glanced at him. "I'm glad you're taking an interest. I know the place is beginning to have that rundown look, but there just wasn't enough money to keep it in the pristine condition it was when my father was alive."

"It'll be in that condition again whenever I get through with it." He glanced at her. "You look cold, Miss Prescott."

"I am a little. That's why I was heading inside."

"Good. I got rid of the Maxmillions." He shook his head. "I think you were right. Eugenia had the idea to match me up with her daughter for her ball."

"I suppose you quashed that idea?"

"Immediately." He held the door open for Valissa. "I told her I was bringing a friend."

"Did you tell her who?"

He grinned and shook his head. "No. I thought I'd let my friend's beauty shock everyone there when I introduced her to Galveston's most prominent families."

Valissa couldn't help the shudder that ran through her as she pictured Nathan with a beautiful woman wearing that lovely gown and on his arm at the Maxmillian gala. Everyone in the room would be staring at them. Oh, Lord, she had to get away from here. And the sooner the better. She didn't care any longer that she could stay a few more days to irritate him. She needed to leave now. He was beginning to mean too much to her.

Glenn Tilley crossed her mind. Was Nathan right? Did the man want to make a whore of her or was he offering a legitimate job? If it were the latter, regardless of what Nathan said, she needed to check into it again. Besides, she did still owe the women there their three dresses.

Tossing back her hair, she decided she'd make her way back to the docks the first chance she got. After all, what could happen if she didn't drink any wine?

~ * ~

They were half way through their mid-day meal when Nathan looked at her and said, "I need to tell you something, Valissa."

She cocked an eye at him. He never used her given name unless he was going to reprimand her about something or he was going to say something she didn't want to hear. "Yes?"

"When I was on the way back here, I heard that your brother was in trouble in California."

"What do you mean, 'trouble'?"

"They said he killed a man in a saloon fight there and ran before the law could stop him."

She laid her fork down and stared at him. "I don't believe it."

"It came from a reliable source."

"I don't care. Kyle may be a gambler and a womanizer, but he'd never kill anyone. He's not like that."

Nathan ignored her protest. "It was over some woman."

"Who told you these lies?"

Nathan took a deep breath and looked directly at her. "A friend of mine."

"Well, your friend has it wrong. I know Kyle better than you or he does. My brother might be a lot of things, but he's not a killer."

"My friend is a Texas Ranger and he had a poster of your brother that was sent to him from California. He said the wire the law sent with it said they thought Kyle Prescott was headed for Texas."

"Why would he tell you this?"

"He knew I'd bought the Prescott house in Galveston and he put two and two together. He wanted me to know so I'd be on the lookout for Kyle in case your brother decides to come here."

Valissa pushed her plate back. There was a knot in her stomach and she knew if she ate another bite, she'd be sick. She didn't want to believe Nathan, but she did have doubts about Kyle. After all, he'd left her in a terrible shape, but still she couldn't let it sink into her mind about his taking someone's life. It was too unthinkable even to consider.

"Are you all right?" Nathan looked at her.

She nodded. "I will be whenever your friend is proven wrong. I can believe almost anything about Kyle, except that he's…" her voice trailed off.

"I'm sorry, Valissa, but I felt I had to tell you. I want you to be prepared in case he shows up here when I'm out. I'm thinking of your safety."

"Kyle would never hurt me."

Nathan shook his head. "It looks to me like he's hurt you already."

"He's never touched me."

"I didn't say he had, but he sure touched your inheritance. He ran out and left you penniless and with no home to call your own."

Tears formed in Valissa's eyes. "But a *killer...?*

"I'm sorry, Valissa."

"If you'll please excuse me, I think I'll go to my room." She stood.

"Are you sure you want to be alone?"

"Yes. For a little while, anyway."

"If you need anything, please let someone know."

"I will." She hurried out of the dining room.

~ * ~

In a matter of minutes, Flo came in with coconut cake for dessert. "Where did Miss Valissa go? She only ate half her meal."

"She was upset and went to her room."

Flo raised an eyebrow. "I don't mean to be disrespectful, Mr. Nathan, but what did you do to her this time?"

He chuckled. "I don't blame you for wondering what I'd done, Flo, but this time I had to give her some bad news. She didn't take it as well as I thought she would. If you would, please go check on her in a little while."

"I will." She sat a plate with a big piece of cake in front of him. "I'll save one for Miss Valissa."

"Flo, is Alvin in the kitchen?"

"Yes."

"Have him come in here. I want to explain something to the both of you."

She looked at him strangely, but only said, "Yes, sir."

After he told them about Kyle, they both looked dumfounded. Finally Alvin asked, "How did Miss Valissa take it?"

"Not well, I'm afraid. I expected her to take it differently. I figured she'd get mad, maybe throw a tantrum and want to get even with her brother for what he'd done to her, but she defended the man. A man, who in my opinion, ought to be hung for what he's done."

"Miss Valissa has always looked up to her big brother. When she was small, he took good care of her." Flo bit her lip. "I couldn't believe it when he gambled everything away, but I guess I'm not as forgiving as Miss Valissa.

"How can Valissa be so forgiving?"

"It's just the way she is, Mr. Nathan. She has a heart as big as the moon."

Nathan shook his head. It wasn't the first time it had occurred to him that he'd never met a woman like Valissa.

~ * ~

Valissa didn't want to take to her bed. She didn't want to sit in the pink overstuffed chair by the window. She didn't even want to stand and look out onto the lawn and the street below as she often did when she was upset. All she wanted to do was get her hands on Kyle and give him a good shaking. Since that wasn't possible, she paced from one side of the room to the other.

She didn't want to believe a word Nathan Stone said, but she knew in her heart he was telling the truth. Since her brother had left her destitute, she wouldn't put anything past him. He probably did kill someone in California. He had a hot temper and he lost it often. Ever since she'd been old enough to understand what was going on, she remembered hearing Kyle and her father having terrible fights. Most of these fights were about the women Kyle socialized with in saloons and houses of pleasure. She remembered once he told their father he would marry a whore someday just to put a smear on the Prescott name.

She almost laughed when she thought how being a killer would smear the name worse than any woman of any social class would ever do. If he came back to Galveston, she would have to convince him to leave as quickly as he could. Not to save the Prescott name. That was already ruined in this town. But he'd have to go somewhere he could be safe. The first place the law would look for him would be here. She only hoped he had enough money to get away.

There was a tap on her door and she paused in her pacing. "Yes."

The door opened and Flo came in. "I wanted to check on you, Miss Valissa."

"I'm fine, Flo, but thank-you."

"Mr. Nathan told us what was going on."

"I see." For the first time since coming to her room, Valissa sat. She chose the small chair at her dressing table instead of the bigger pink chair. "What do you think, Flo? Will Kyle come back to Heartsong?"

"I don't know, but Mr. Nathan is right. We need to protect you."

Valissa whirled toward her. "Why is everyone hell-bent on protecting me? Kyle is not going to hurt me."

"I don't think he will either, Miss Valissa, but I know how you've always felt about him. He's your big brother. The man you looked up to ever since you were a little girl. In your eyes, he could do no wrong." She took a deep breath. "If he was to show up here, no telling what he'd talk you into."

Valissa burst into tears. "Oh, Flo. You're probably right. I don't know what I'd do either."

Flo crossed the room and put her arms around Valissa's shoulders. "Hush now, child. Things will work out. You know Alvin and me will always be here for you. Mr. Kyle won't be able to take advantage of you as long as we're here. I think Mr. Nathan feels the same way."

"I doubt that, Flo. He probably figures Kyle will try to reclaim Heartsong or something."

Flo laughed. "Now, don't go thinking like that. Mr. Nathan's not going to let anybody have this house. He's beginning to love it as much as we all do."

Valissa didn't believe her, but it was nice to hear. She only sighed and let her faithful servant rock her back and forth in her arms. It felt almost like she was a little girl again and Flo was making all the hurt and worry go away as she had always been able to do.

~ * ~

Glenn Tilley shook the handsome dark-haired gambler by the shoulder. "All right, man. It's time you woke up and got out of here. This place is closed this time of day. I don't know why they let you stay all night. We don't usually do that."

Kyle looked up at the sharp features of the saloon owner. "I bribed the barkeep."

"With what? I saw you lose all your cash last night."

"I had a couple of dollars stuck back."

"Well, whatever. Get a move on. I don't want you here all day."

"Come on, man. Let me stay here. I'll leave as soon as it gets dark."

"It's only a little past noon. I …"

"I'll go see my sister as soon as I can slip in on her. I hear she's still in the mansion."

Glenn frowned. "What mansion?"

"Heartsong. Ever heard of it?"

He had, but he wasn't sure where or when. "Tell me about it."

"It's the house where my sister, Valissa, and I grew up."

It dawned on Tilley who this man probably was and he grinned from ear to ear. "You're Valissa Prescott's brother? The one who ran out and left her destitute?"

"I'm sure she's been able to find a way to make it without me."

Not as much as you'd hoped, fellow. "I'm not so sure about that."

"How do you know anything about my sister? She's a lady. Not the kind of woman you're used to having around."

"Your sister, the lady, was in here a few days ago selling her dresses. It seems the ogre who got your house is throwing her out and she's in need of money."

Kyle frowned. "You mean she's really broke?"

"According to what she told me. As a matter of fact, I offered her a job as hostess so she wouldn't have to sell her grandmother's earrings. She wanted the job, but before we could seal the deal, that big old cowboy who now resides in your house came and carried her off."

"I didn't lose the house to a cowboy. It was a gambler in Dallas."

Glenn shrugged. "I don't know about that. All I know is the man is a bully. I'm not sure but that he's been using your sister for his own pleasure and now that he's tired of her, he's putting her out."

"That snake. I'll kill him." Kyle started to get up.

"Hold on a minute. There might be a better way to get her away from him."

"What do you mean?"

"Let me think it over. I know I can come up with a plan that will benefit both of us." When Kyle said nothing, Glenn went on. "Why don't you go upstairs and get yourself cleaned up and then come down here for something to eat? We can discuss my plan over a meal."

Kyle grinned. "Sounds good to me. I could use a square meal."

"Use the room with the number seven over the door. We keep it vacant for just such an occasion."

Kyle nodded and headed up the stairs.

Glenn chuckled, sat back and pulled a cigar out of his vest pocket. He knew beyond any doubt that he was going to get Valissa Prescott in his saloon and in his bed and it wasn't going to be as much trouble as he thought it would be. Her big brother was going to serve up the woman to him on a silver platter. Or should he say on the bed in the room connected to his office? Then, after he trained her in what she needed to do to make men happy, he'd make sure she serviced only the wealthiest of his patrons.

Yes, sir. He was glad Kyle Prescott had decided to lose his money here. Now he knew why everyone said Glenn Tilley was the luckiest man alive. The way this was all working out, he was beginning to believe it himself.

Nine

The next morning Valissa hoped Nathan had left the house. She wanted to slip out and take the three dresses she'd tucked into a valise and hid under her bed last night, to the women who worked for Mr. Tilley.

But her hope was dashed when she went into the dining room and found him seated at the table.

"Good morning, Miss Prescott."

She took her chair to his right. "And good morning to you, Mr. Stone."

"Are you feeling better today?"

"I'm fine."

"Good. I have a surprise for you."

"Oh?"

"Yes. Mrs. Dupree-Fontaine sent word that the gown I ordered is complete and she wants you to try it on one more time."

"Trying on a dress that belongs to someone else isn't what I'd call a nice surprise," she muttered.

Nathan chuckled. "Well, that's not the surprise I was talking about."

"Then what is?"

"You'll see at ten this morning." She frowned and he went on, "I want you to be dressed and ready to go into town at ten. You'll get the surprise then."

Flo came in with the usual big breakfast Nathan always wanted. Valissa couldn't help wondering what surprise he had for her, but she wouldn't ask. She knew he'd made up his mind not to tell her until ten. She simply took the full plate Flo handed her and began to eat.

The morning passed quickly. By the time she bathed and dressed, it was almost time for the promised surprise. At ten, Valissa came down the stairs wearing her deep green velvet traveling suit. She was aware that the sleeves of the coat were beginning to look worn as were the edges of the collar and the hem of the skirt. It couldn't be helped. It was the nicest thing she had to wear now that the weather was turning cooler.

Nathan was waiting at the bottom of the stairs. "I'm glad to see that you're on time. Some women are always late."

"When I'm supposed to be at a certain place at a certain time, I make it a point to be there." She turned up her nose a little. "And you made it quite clear that I was to come down at ten."

He nodded but didn't answer her as he opened the front door. "The surprise is waiting outside."

Valissa was puzzled, but stepped outside.

Philips stood at the bottom of the steps holding the bridle of one of Nathan's black horses. Hitched behind him was a shiny black buggy.

At first Valissa didn't understand what the surprise was—then she realized the buggy was the one her father always drove. "Oh, my," she exclaimed. "How in the world did you ever get it looking so nice?"

Philips grinned. "I like to work on old carriages, ma'am. Mr. Stone gave me permission to fix this one up and then clean and polish it and all the horses' gear for you."

Valissa turned to Nathan. There were tears in her eyes. "Thank you."

"I'm glad you like it."

"I love it. I never thought I'd ever ride in Daddy's carriage again."

"So you're pleased?"

"More than I can say." She took a lace handkerchief from her reticule and wiped her eyes. "You surprise me by your unexpected kindnesses sometimes, Nathan Stone. I never know what to expect from you, but this is wonderful."

"I'm glad you approve." He took her arm. "Shall we drive it to town?"

"Oh, yes." She let him help her climb inside then she turned. "Thank you, Mr. Philips. You did a wonderful job."

"You're welcome, ma'am."

Nathan moved to the other side and climbed in. Before they drove off, she smiled and said, "This makes trying on your girlfriend's dress much easier for me."

~ * ~

Valissa paced the floor in her bedroom when she finally went upstairs for the evening. She thought about the afternoon and how it made her feel to ride in her father's buggy once again. Maybe her last ride. She was sure Nathan had Phillips fix it up so he could use it in town. It wasn't as bulky as his big carriage and it only required one horse to pull it. She remembered well sitting beside her father, then beside Kyle, and going to town in the buggy with the beautiful red gelding with the black mane and tail pulling it. She wondered what went with that horse. The last time she saw it, Kyle had ridden it to

Huston, then he came back on the train. Did it mean so little to him that he thought of it as just another possession? Another possession he'd lost at the gambling table?

She shook her head and her thoughts turned to that beautiful gown she had tried on. It looked and felt like it was made for her. It fit every bend and curve of her body and she had to admit that with the neckline lowered as it had been, it was a fetching garment. The way the imported cream-colored silk lent itself to the sunlight almost looked like there was some green hiding in the folds of the skirt. Green that would be reflected perfectly if one were wearing her grandmother's beautiful emerald earrings.

Taking a deep breath, she knew she was putting off thinking about the inevitable by dwelling on the buggy which was in the barn, and the ball gown which was packed in a box and lying somewhere in Nathan Stone's bedroom. Now it was time to face facts.

Tomorrow two weeks of her three were up. She still hadn't been able to get the three dresses to Glenn Tilley's saloon, but she did have the money the first five she'd sold there had brought. And if she wanted to use it, there was the money Rowena had left her. But sadly, it wasn't enough. There was nothing else left to do.

She crossed to her dresser, took out the jewel box containing the emerald earrings and looked at them. Gently she removed them from the satin lining of the box and put them on her ears one last time. Though it felt as if her heart were breaking, tomorrow she would give them to Nathan Stone and ask him to sell them for her.

It dawned on her that Nathan was still up and working in his study. She'd give him the earrings tonight. That way she wouldn't be able to change her mind. She removed them from her ears, put them in their original little box and headed out the door.

~ * ~

The next week was a busy one. Nathan kept bringing papers and books for Valissa to study for him. "I'd take you to the bank with me to look things over," he'd said at one time, "but I don't want anyone there to know who is pointing out their mistakes."

She understood, but wished it could be different. She'd mentioned him hiring her to work in the bank or one of his other businesses and he'd said he'd think about it. He hadn't said anything about it again and she didn't want to pressure him. He was the type who would tell her 'no' if she managed to irritate him enough.

She did work up the courage to ask him if he'd sold her earrings and he told her that two different people wanted them. He said he wasn't going to rush because he wanted to get her as much money as he could. She agreed it was the smart thing to do.

Though Valissa knew she was beginning to dread leaving Nathan almost as much as she was leaving Heartsong and everything connected to it, the time was drawing nearer.

When the last day of her legal stay at Heartsong arrived, Valissa got out of bed with a lump in her throat so big she wondered if it was permanent. This was hard. Harder than she ever dreamed it would be. She dressed in her green velvet skirt and a white blouse. She laid the jacket on the valise and looked at the meager amount of her worldly goods lying on her bed. "Don't you dare cry!" she commanded herself.

Squaring her shoulders and with determination, she opened the door and headed downstairs.

In the kitchen, she spoke to Flo, then asked, "Is Mr. Stone out?"

"Yes. He had an early meeting and asked Alvin to take him to town."

"Good. I'm glad he's gone, but I would have liked to have seen Alvin."

"Why, child?"

"I guess you've forgotten what today is."

"No, Miss Valissa. I remember." She turned and looked at Valissa. She was biting her lip. "Would you like your breakfast in the dining room?"

"No. I want to eat my last breakfast here with you." Valissa sat at the kitchen table. "I know you've eaten, but please get a cup of coffee and join me, Flo."

"I will, but I have to watch the pies I'm baking for dinner."

"I smell lemon."

"I knew that's what you'd want for dessert."

"Oh, Flo. You know I have to leave early. I won't be here for dinner. I even had a breakthrough on the books I've been going over for him so I left Mr. Stone a note to check it out. I didn't want to face him to tell him about it before I left."

Flo looked confused. "But Mr. Stone said he'd be back by noon because he wanted to talk to you about something important."

"What in the world does he want now? Last night he paid me for the work I've done for him."

Flo put Valissa's breakfast in front of her, then poured two cups of coffee. As she slid into the chair across from Valissa, she said, "I don't have any idea what he wants, but please wait until he returns to leave."

"I'd rather be gone when he gets back."

"I know you would, but he told me to keep you here." Flo took a deep breath. "Please don't put me in a bad light with him, Miss Valissa."

Valissa reached across the table and touched Flo's arm. "I would never do that. I know what a bear he can be when he doesn't get his way."

"Thank you, child."

Valissa ate every bite of her breakfast and had an extra biscuit with peach jelly. "I will miss your cooking something fierce, my dear friend."

"I'll see that you get some of it."

"I don't see how you can do that."

"Me and Alvin talked about it last night. He said no matter where you are, we're going to keep an eye on you. We don't have much, but we'll also see you don't go hungry."

Tears welled up in Valissa's eyes. "You're two of the most wonderful people in the world."

"Oh, Miss Valissa. If we could afford it, we'd quit these jobs and go with you wherever you go." A big tear ran down her withered face.

"Please, Flo. If you cry, I'll cry even harder."

"There are times when tears are called for, child." She stood abruptly.

"Are you all right?"

"I need to check the pies. I don't want them to burn." Flo turned to the stove.

Valissa drank the rest of her coffee and stood. "I guess I'll go see if I missed anything in my room that I can take with me."

Flo nodded, but didn't speak.

Valissa didn't say anything else either. She knew she would dissolve into tears if she tried to talk.

~ * ~

At twelve-thirty, Valissa went into the dining room. Nathan stood and held the back of her chair when she moved to her place on his right. Flipping her napkin into her lap, she said, "I hear you have something to talk over with me."

"I do." He sat and unfolded his napkin. "We'll discuss it whenever Flo brings the food."

As if on cue, Flo entered with sizzling steaks. Valissa was surprised. Steak wasn't her favorite meat and she had expected Flo to serve the baked chicken and rice she loved. Alvin followed with potatoes, peas and corn. They went back into the kitchen. Flo returned with bread and butter. Alvin had a bottle of the wine Valissa had told him her father loved.

"I'm permitting you to drink two glasses, Miss Prescott. We don't want a situation like we've had before."

"Permit me, huh?" She glared at him.

"That's right. I don't want you so drunk you can't concentrate on the options I'm going to explain to you."

Again he'd thrown her off track and her anger dissipated. "What options?"

"As I'm sure you're aware, today ends the three weeks you were promised to live here in my house." He motioned for her to hand him her plate.

She reached it to him. "Yes, I'm fully aware. I have my bags packed and I would have been gone if I hadn't had to attend this command performance with you."

"I figured if I didn't demand you be here, you'd slip out before I got home." He handed her back her plate with a huge steak on it.

"I planned to do just that." She stared down at her plate. "Do you expect me to eat all that?"

"Of course. You're going to need your strength."

She nodded. "You're probably right."

As they passed vegetables back and forth, he went on. "Have you decided where you're going when you leave here?"

"I have the money from selling my clothes and what you paid me, so I thought I'd go to Miss Dobb's Rooming House for a few days. It's nice and clean and doesn't cost as much as some of the others. You can find me there when you get the money for the earrings."

He nodded. "Do you still intend to work?"

"I have no choice, Mr. Stone. I have to work."

"You're not still thinking of working at Tilley's, are you?"

"I would have considered it until you put doubts in my mind about the man. Now I'll look somewhere else. I'm still hoping that, since you own the bank, maybe you would tell Mr. Colbert to give me a job."

"I could."

She looked at him and her eyes grew big. "Would you do that for me?"

In a flat voice, he said, "No."

She dropped her fork. "Well, for heaven's sake, why not?"

"You and I both know there's a crook at that bank. Maybe more than one. I don't want you caught up in the mess when I discover who it is."

"Oh."

"I have a much better idea." He cut a piece of steak and put it in his mouth without explaining.

Valissa waited for what seemed a long time before she blurted, "Well, what is your better idea?"

"I'll explain it all to you after we finish eating."

"Please, Nathan. Don't keep me in suspense."

"It won't be for long." He continued to eat.

Though frustrated, Valissa knew she wouldn't get any more out of him until he was ready to talk. Automatically she began to eat and watch him. Every so often, he'd throw her a smile, but still said nothing.

Finally he finished eating and called for Flo. "Would you mind serving dessert and coffee in my study?"

"I'll be happy to," she muttered, though she looked disappointed.

Valissa could tell it wasn't what Flo wanted to do. She and Alvin had probably been listening to the conversation at the door. She almost grinned because she knew it was their concern for her that would make them eavesdrop.

"Then shall we retire to the study, Miss Prescott?"

"Whatever you say, Mr. Stone." She threw her napkin down and couldn't help noticing that she'd eaten most of her steak. She knew she must have done it without thinking because she couldn't remember taking a bite.

When they reached the study, she was surprised when Nathan took one of the pull-up chairs and indicated for her to sit in the other one facing him. She'd expected him to sit behind the desk as he usually did. She began to suspect he had something important to talk about with her or he wouldn't put them in such friendly proximity.

After Flo brought a tray with the coffee and pie and put it on the table then left, he turned to Valissa. "When I first came to Heartsong, the last thing I expected to find was a family member still living in the house."

When she didn't reply, he went on, "I have a lot of business in Galveston and decided to buy this place because I was spending a fortune on hotels when I came here. I also thought it would be a good place to have if I decided to marry and settle down."

"Are you getting married?" For a strange reason, Valissa didn't like the idea of him marrying. Maybe she was jealous because another woman would make Heartsong her home.

"I hope to, eventually. In fact, there's a woman on the ranch next to mine whom I think would make a good wife. She'd probably enjoy coming here with me when I needed to be in Galveston, but I think she would be happy to live most of the time on the ranch. I love ranching and plan to raise my children there."

"I see." Valissa bit her lip. She wondered what the woman rancher looked like.

He abruptly changed the subject. "How much do you like Heartsong, Valissa?"

"I don't just like Heartsong, Nathan. I love it. I was born here, as was my mother before me. Grandfather built this house for his wife and he always intended for a Prescott to reside here. I'll always consider it my home."

"Then what would you do to keep it in your family?"

She frowned, not knowing what he was getting at, she decided to be honest. "I'd do anything as long as it wasn't illegal. I'd give up anything I have to live here the rest of my life."

"I thought as much." He picked up the small plate his piece of pie was on and took a bite. "I can see why you like Flo's lemon pie so much. It really is good."

She took her pie. "Yes. It's my favorite dessert." She wondered if he wasn't a bit nervous about what he wanted to say to her since he kept changing the subject. She decided to wait him out.

He took a drink of coffee and turned back to her. "I thought about offering you a job as my housekeeper here since I knew how much the place meant to you."

She felt hopeful. "Oh, Nathan that would be wonderful. I'd be able…"

He interrupted. "But I decided it wouldn't work."

Her heart plummeted and she cried. "Why not?"

He stood and walked to the liquor cabinet and poured a drink in a heavy crystal glass and returned to his chair. Valissa knew he was nervous because it was the first time she'd ever seen him drink this early in the day.

"Because I've lived here for three weeks with you, Valissa Prescott."

"What does that mean?"

"It means that, though I had planned to ask Maurine to marry me, I can't keep my mind on her when I'm around you."

"Why not?"

"Damn it, woman, don't you realize how beautiful you are?"

She shrugged.

"Or how many times I've wanted to take you in my arms and kiss those tempting lips of yours and run my hands through that silky black hair and feel your body pressed against mine?" He downed his whisky in one swallow.

Though she felt uncomfortable with his saying these things, Valissa could only stare at him.

"Or how I've wanted to rip your clothes off and make love to you right here in this study?"

She finally found her voice. "Mr. Stone! That's enough."

"You're right, Valissa. It is enough. It's also why it would never work out for you to be my housekeeper. My name may be Stone, but I'm not made of rocks. I have feelings and urges like any other man."

She dropped her head. "I guess you're right. Being your housekeeper wouldn't work out."

"But there is a solution that will give us both what we want."

She looked up at him and whispered, "What is the solution?"

Before he could answer, Flo knocked on the door. "I'm sorry to interrupt, sir, but Mrs. Colbert and her daughter are here to see you."

Ten

"Damn," Nathan muttered. "Of all times for a visitor."

"Should I tell them to go away, sir?"

"No, Flo. I guess I have to see them." He looked at Valissa. "We'll go greet our guests, then we'll continue our discussion when they're gone."

Though she wanted to know what solution Nathan had come up with, there was nothing Valissa could do except nod.

Flo moved from the door and Nathan took hold of Valissa's arm. "Would you do me a favor?"

"If I can."

"Go greet the guests and tell them I'll be there shortly. I want to look over something Lyman gave me this morning before I see his wife."

She knew there was no use to ask what Lyman had given him. "I guess I can do that for you."

"Thanks, Valissa."

She headed to the parlor. Taking a deep breath, she opened the door, plastered on a smile and said, "Good afternoon, Mrs. Colbert and Rowena."

"Hello, Valissa," Rowena said.

Beverly Colbert stiffened her back. "Since the situation has changed at Heartsong, Valissa, I think it would be befitting if you called my daughter Miss Colbert."

"Mother, I can't believe you'd say that. Valissa and I have been friends all our lives."

"Things change, my dear." Beverly looked at Valissa. "I thought you'd be moved out of Mr. Stone's house by now."

Valissa bit her lip to keep from saying something she shouldn't to the woman. Finally she muttered, "I'll be moving soon."

"That's good. You know your reputation is going to be soiled since you're single and you chose to stay here with an unmarried man for this length of time."

"I assure you, Mrs. Colbert, Nathan Stone has been a gentleman. Nothing improper has happened in the short time I've been here."

"Of course, I never doubted he'd treat you properly."

Valissa looked the woman in the eye when she said, "And you think I haven't acted properly?"

"Don't be difficult, Valissa. Of course, as I said, no lady would reside in the home of an unmarried man without a proper chaperone."

"Mother, you're not being fair to Valissa."

"Be quiet, Rowena. I know what I'm saying is true. Everyone is talking about the situation." She looked back at Valissa. "I've even heard that you tried to …." Her voice trailed off when the parlor door opened.

"Good afternoon, ladies."

Beverly giggled. "Hello, Mr. Stone. I hope you don't mind that we stopped in."

"Of course not." He took Beverly's hand and nodded to Rowena. "It's always a pleasure to greet two lovely women."

"I'm glad you feel that way." Beverly smiled at him. "I must admit that I had an ulterior motive for coming."

"And what might that be, dear lady?"

"Someone told me that your friend wasn't going to be able to attend Mrs. Maxmillion's party with you. I know you don't want to have to come to the event alone and I wanted to let you know that Rowena would be more than happy to have you escort her to the party."

Rowena turned almost scarlet. "Mother, I promised Henry…"

"Hush, Rowena." She patted her daughter's arm. "I think it's more important that Mr. Stone have a proper date for the party. You can see Henry anytime."

"Mrs. Colbert, your daughter is a lovely young woman and any man would be pleased to escort her to a party…"

"Wonderful. Then you'll pick her up…"

He interrupted her. "As I was trying to say, whoever told you my friend wouldn't be able to attend the party is wrong. She will most definitely be my date for the night if she and I decide to come."

Beverly Colbert looked confused and defeated. "But I thought…"

"Mother, the man has a date. I can't believe you brought me here and humiliated me like this. If I had known this was your plan, I'd have never come." Rowena jumped up. "I apologize for my mother, Mr. Stone."

"You don't have to apologize, Miss Colbert." Nathan smiled at her. "If I didn't have a date already…"

"No, Mr. Stone. You don't have to explain anything. I don't know why she's been so set on pushing us together, but I want you to know that I didn't know what she was up to when we came. She told me that Daddy wanted her to come by."

Beverly began to regain her composure. "He did, Rowena. He wanted to make sure Mr. Stone had a date for the party."

"That's enough about dates, Mother. Let's go home." Rowena turned to Valissa. "I also want to apologize to you. Mother had no right to say the things to you that she did."

"I understand, Rowena. Don't think a thing about it."

"You don't have to apologize for me, Rowena. I was only trying to give Valissa some good advice."

Rowena shook her head and took her mother's arm. "Good-bye," she said in a soft voice and hurried her mother out the front door.

Nathan looked down at Valissa. "I don't think young Miss Colbert had any idea what her mother was up to."

"I know she didn't."

"Oh?"

"Rowena and I have been friends since we were babies. I could tell she was embarrassed by the situation."

"It baffles me as to why all these women think I'm a good catch for their daughters." He frowned.

Valissa chuckled. "It baffles me, too, Mr. Stone."

~ * ~

Though it had been several hours since Nathan astounded her by his solution to their problem, she still couldn't believe he'd suggested they get married. Of course, he'd gone on to say he didn't expect her to tell him how she felt about the idea right away. He sent her to her room to think the situation over. He even said that he would be away for supper and she was to stay at Heartsong until she made up her mind what she wanted to do. She realized that was a smart move on his part, because if she'd had to answer right away, she'd have given him an unequivocal no.

Now she wasn't so sure. As she thought about the situation, little questions crept into her mind. Would marriage to him be so bad? She knew there were people who had been married for years who had only met once before the nuptials. Or people whose family arranged the marriage for them. She'd even heard about men in the West ordering a bride through an ad in a newspaper. At least she'd lived in the same house with Nathan Stone for three weeks. Being in such close proximity with him, she had to admit to herself that there were occasions she'd enjoyed many of the times they'd been together. He had a way about him that made her feel good about herself, even if she'd become a penniless heiress. At least he'd respected her knowledge of figures, something Wilbur Colbert or any other man she knew wouldn't do. They'd expect her to be a demure little woman only interested in parties and dresses and having teas with their friends and catering to her husband's every need. Nathan, on the other hand, seemed to want her to use her mind. But was this reason enough to marry him?

She'd always dreamed that she'd be fiercely in love with the man she married, and he would feel the same way about her. Not that she didn't have some strange twinges and feelings when she was near Nathan Stone. Feelings she'd never felt when she was with any other man. And he certainly had expressed his want of her. But that wasn't love, was it? Of course, he never mentioned the word love. He only said he wanted her in a physical way. Love would be more than physical, wouldn't it?

Of course, she had always planned to raise her children at Heartsong, and if she accepted his offer, she would be able to do that, only part time. She knew he wanted his children raised at his ranch. But was keeping Heartsong important enough to tie herself to a man she hardly knew and agreeing to live on a ranch? She knew nothing about ranches, but maybe it wouldn't be so bad. Still, was she being crass to even consider his stipulations and marrying him to save her home?

Valissa batted the thoughts back and forth throughout the afternoon. Then, when she went down to eat supper, she only told Flo that she'd be in the house at least one more day.

"Yes. Mr. Nathan said you would be, but he didn't say why."

And I'm not going to say why. But she didn't express this thought to Flo. She ate her supper quickly and returned to her room.

According to the small clock which sat on the table beside her bed, it was half past nine o'clock when she noise in the hall floated to her. She held her breath until she heard the door to his bedroom open, then close again. He was home.

The word 'home' stuck in her mind for a moment. Then it hit her. This was his home. Not hers. No matter who she married, she would never own Heartsong again. If she married Nathan Stone, he would share his home with her, but it would always be his. She would only be his wife. Was that enough?

In a split second, she made up her mind about what she was going to do. There was no need to wait until morning to tell him her decision. She'd do it before she went to bed and maybe they could both get a good night's sleep.

Pulling her robe tightly around her, she opened her door and stepped down the hall. Taking a deep breath, she knocked on his door.

~ * ~

Kyle Prescott wished he'd worn a heavier coat. He'd been there since it became dark, and it had grown chilly in the wooded area across the street from the Prescott estate. But he hadn't planned to stay this long. It was only after he realized the man who lived in his old house was out, that he continued to wait. It might be the perfect time to pay a call on his sister. A lamp burned in her room and he knew she was still up. He only had to wait until the lights went out in the servants' quarters so he wouldn't run into Flo or her husband. They'd probably keep him from getting to Valissa. Those two had always been protective of her and he was sure they were irate at him for losing her home.

Finally the lamps went out and the servants' quarters were dark. He waited another thirty minutes to give them time to drift off to sleep. Pulling his jacket tighter, he was about to make his move when a carriage pulled into the gate of the estate.

"Damn," he muttered. "If that's the owner, I'm out of luck again tonight."

In a short time, a light came on in the rooms above the stable.

"Maybe it was only the stable man. He could have been doing something in town with the horses. Or he could have simply had a night off and the boss permitted him to use the carriage.

He stepped back into the shadows and waited again for several minutes. He was about to believe it had only been the man in the stable, then a lamp lit up the window in the room upstairs that had belonged to his father until his death.

Hell and damnation. Now I'm going to have to tell Tilley I failed to get to my sister again. He's not going to like it. I only hope he won't refuse to let me stay at his place again tonight.

Hurrying down the street, Kyle kept rehearsing the words he would say to Glenn Tilley when he got back to the saloon.

~ * ~

Nathan Stone threw his coat on a chair and pulled his shirt from his pants. He had it unbuttoned when there was a knock on his door.

He frowned. *Who could that be? I know Flo and Alvin have gone to bed.* He headed to the door. *If it's Valissa, I'll wager she's decided she's going to leave in the morning and wants to tell me tonight. Oh, God, I hope it's not her.*

Nathan swung the door open and swallowed as he saw Valissa standing there in her night clothes. He didn't think he'd ever seen her look so fetching.

For a minute they stared at each other. She finally broke the silence.

"Mr. Stone, I've decided I'd be honored to become your wife, but not for the reason you think."

"Oh, Valissa, you don't know…"

She interrupted. "Don't say anything tonight. I'll explain my reasons at breakfast and if you agree it's the right thing to do, we'll discuss the details of our wedding then."

He started to speak again, but she shook her head. "Not tonight. We'll talk in the morning."

With that, she turned and hurried back to her room, leaving a stunned Nathan standing in his doorway with his mouth open.

~ * ~

"So you didn't get her tonight?"

"I'm sorry, Tilley. Every time I think I have a chance to talk with her, he shows up."

"I'm getting tired of your bumbling around, Prescott. I want your sister to come to work here for me as my hostess and I want her soon."

"What's the big rush?"

"I told you. The other owner had thought of her for a job here and he was ecstatic when I told him I'd met and offered Valissa Prescott work. He thinks it's the perfect solution for us as well as for her."

"I can't believe she's as broke as everyone says."

"Well, she is. You left her in desperate need of money. What did you think she was going to live on when you depleted her bank account? And where did you think she was going to live when you gambled away her home?"

"I thought I had won the hand. I had three kings. My mentor told me you always bet all you have because you most always win when you have three kings."

"Well, you didn't win. You not only became a loser, but so did your sister. Now we have to make sure she gets a job so she can live without having to beg on the streets." Glenn turned from the table and motioned for the barkeep to bring him another drink.

"But I'm not sure it's fitting for a lady like my sister to work in a place like this."

Glenn chuckled. "You think it's all right for her to come down here and sell her dresses, but not work. Right?"

"I'm trying to make enough money to help her out." Kyle looked as if he were near tears.

"You're a fool, Prescott. You're never going to win enough money to help your sister or anyone else. Already you're in debt to me for almost a thousand dollars. You only get to eat your meals and sleep here because I'm a generous man. And out of the goodness of my heart, I lct you live here because you promised to bring your sister to me."

"I know. I'll get her here sooner or later."

"It better be sooner. I'm about ready to throw you out and go get the lady myself."

"She'll never come with you."

"She'll come if I have to…"

"To what, Tilley?"

"It doesn't matter. When you get her here, if you manage to do it, our deal will still be valid."

"You'll forgive the debt I owe you if I bring Valissa to you?"

"I said I would and I will."

"And you said you'd only work her as a hostess. My sister is a lady. You wouldn't try to get her to work upstairs, would you?"

"I said I wouldn't. That is, unless she wants to go upstairs. When she sees all the money the girls are raking in, she may ask for that job."

"Not Valissa. She'd never stoop to that." Kyle's voice was becoming slurred.

Glenn noticed. "Why don't you go on up to bed? It's almost morning and you need to sleep so you can go back to watching her house tonight."

"I guess you're right." Without further conversation, Kyle stumbled toward the stairs.

"What a fool," Glenn muttered as he watched him climb the stairs and disappear into room seven.

"I hope he's worth all the trouble he's been to you, boss," Sid, the bartender, said as he wiped the bar to a sparkle.

"If he gets his sister here, it'll all be worth it, Sid. That woman will bring in the business by the droves."

"She is a right pretty thing. I noticed that when she was here with her dresses."

"You've got a good eye. She's class all the way. Until she fades, like Angela has, she'll be well worth all the trouble." Glenn finished his whiskey and moved to the bar.

"Want another one, Boss?"

"I don't think so, Sid. My partner is coming in later and I want to be sober as a judge when he gets here."

"He is a stickler for business, isn't he?"

"Almost too much so, but it's paid off."

"What does he think about Miss Prescott coming?"

"As I told her brother, he's delighted. As I figured he would, he says he intends to be one of the first customers to take her upstairs, since he'd been hoping things would work out this way since she lost everything."

"I bet you have something to say about him being first."

"You're damn right. That woman has been a hard sell. I intend to get all I want from her before I turn her loose for others. After all, it's been a while since I've had a relationship that lasted more than a few nights."

"You know she's going to fall in love with you, don't you, Boss?"

"Of course I do. That's what makes them all do whatever I want them to do, Sid. They think if they please me, I'll come back to them someday."

"Like Angela does?"

"Yeah, like Angela. Of course that one will always be special. She was the first lady I had to break into the business. It wasn't easy, but it was fun."

"And you're expecting the same experience with Miss Prescott?"

"Damn right, I am." Glenn turned. "Looks like you have everything taken care of in here, Sid. Why don't you turn out the lights and get some rest, too? You never know. Tomorrow may be our lucky day."

"I'll do that, sir." Sid put his rag under the counter and watched his boss stride confidently across the saloon floor and head up the stairs.

~ * ~

When Valissa went down the next morning, she was surprised to see the dining room vacant. She went on into the kitchen. "Flo, has Mr. Stone gone somewhere?"

Flo shook her head, but said, "Oh, Miss Valissa, am I glad to see you."

"I'm pleased you're happy to see me, but why? You knew I was here."

"I know, but it's Mr. Stone. He's about to drive me crazy wondering where you are. He's been in here at least four times since he got up asking about you. He actually told me I should go up and wake you if you didn't come down soon." Flo wiped her forehead with the back of her sleeve. "He also asked me to cook all kinds of things for breakfast. I want to know what's going on with him."

"He'll be fine. Now, where is he?"

"I told him to go to his study and count his money or something until I came for him. He promised he would, but as nervous as he is, I don't expect him to keep that promise."

"I'll go tell him I'm up."

"Wait a minute. He demanded that I make pancakes. I've already fried bacon and ham and make a mountain of potatoes. I have biscuits baking and I cut up some fresh fruit. I have the eggs whipped and ready to scramble. Now he wants pancakes. How much can one man eat in the morning?"

"Forget about the pancakes, Flo."

"I can't do that. He was adamant."

Valissa touched the upset servant's arm. "I promise you, Flo. He'll never remember he asked you to make them. Now, relax. You've cooked more than enough."

"Are you sure he won't mind?"

"Trust me, Flo."

"Thank you, Miss Valissa. I was getting a little upset by his actions this morning."

"Put a pot of coffee and two cups on a tray. Nathan and I are going to have a little talk. I'll let you know when we're ready for breakfast."

Flo looked confused, but did as Valissa asked. "Do you want anything to eat on the tray?"

"No. Coffee is fine. Now I want you to sit down and have a cup of coffee yourself. You'll have more than ample time to relax a bit."

"If you're sure."

"I'm positive. Now do it." Valissa smiled at her and headed out of the room.

Holding the tray in one hand, she eased the study door open without knocking, and had to smile when she saw Nathan. He was seated behind the desk with his elbows on it and his head between his hands. She wanted to go put her arms around him, but instead in a cherry voice, she said, "Good morning."

His head jerked up. "You're finally up."

She smiled. "It's about the regular time I get up. You must have gotten up awfully early."

"I didn't sleep much."

"I'm sorry."

"You seem bright and chipper. Did you sleep well?"

"Oh, yes. Just like a baby." She placed the tray on the desk and poured a cup of coffee for each of them.

"I'm glad somebody could sleep." He came around the desk. "Let's sit down and have that talk you promised."

"But you have Flo cooking everything imaginable in the kitchen. Don't you think we should go in to breakfast?"

He took the coffee she handed him and, with his other hand, he led her to one of the pull-up chairs. He took the other one. "I've waited all night for this. Now, talk."

"Let me get a sip of coffee and I will." She smiled at him, then sat the cup on the desk. "When you told me yesterday I could save Heartsong if we were to marry, I thought you'd lost your mind."

He gave her a sheepish grin. "Maybe I had."

"I still think it's a preposterous idea, but after thinking about it long and hard, I've decided I can't marry you just to save my home."

"But you said last night…"

"Please, let me finish." He nodded and she went on. "Heartsong is no longer the Prescott family home. It now belongs to you and it will begin to bear your name. Unless you decide to sell the place, it will be handed down to the Stone heirs for generations. Unless something unforeseen happens to one of your descendants as it did to me, it will become your family legacy."

"But as my wife, you'll be a part of that."

"That's true, and if anyone checks back, they'll see I was a descendent of the original owner of Heartsong." She gave him a smile. "You will continue to let it be called Heartsong, won't you?"

"If that's what you want."

"Thank you. I do." Valissa took another sip of coffee. "I guess you want to know why I decided to marry you, though it wasn't for Heartsong."

"I most certainly do."

"It's because you need a woman like me, Nathan Stone."

His brow wrinkled. "What do you mean?"

"I've only met one of your fiancées, but from the looks of Colleen O'Malley, she'd drive you to a mistress within a year."

"Colleen O'Malley is not my fiancée."

"I know that and you know that, but Colleen doesn't know it. She's sure she'll be Mrs. Stone in the near future."

"Well, she won't."

"There's another name you keep mentioning. Maurine, Marissa, something like that."

He blurted. "How could you know I'd thought about marrying her?"

She eyed him. "You told me, but you didn't tell me how seriously you had thought about it."

"Not very seriously. Maurine is a widow who lives on a neighboring ranch. Her husband and I were friends. They'd been married a couple of years when he was killed and since she was a city woman, I helped her out on the ranch. We became good friends and she was convenient when I needed…a …never mind." He shook his head. "What has this got to do with our getting married?"

Valissa looked at him for a long minute. Was she doing the right thing? Did she really think it through enough? She was sure of her decision last night, but now…No. she wouldn't think that. She knew deep in her heart this was the right thing to do. Besides, it was all she could do not to throw her arms around him and tell him to please love her because she was sure she'd fallen in love with him.

"If you're sure you're not in love with this woman, I guess it has nothing to do with us."

"I assure you, I'm not in love with Maurine Taylor. I had only toyed with the idea of marrying her because everyone kept saying that I should settle down and start a family."

"Good. Then we'll proceed with our plans." She threw him a smile. "As I said, I think you need a woman like me. I can't see you with someone who only wants to sit around and drink tea and gossip about their so-called friends. Or one who only wants to talk about the upcoming parties and what ball gown she's going to have made this time."

"You don't like those things?"

"Of course I like pretty things, but they're not the most important thing in the world to me. I only want to wear them to make my husband proud, not to make other women jealous." She chuckled. "Well, maybe a little jealous."

"Good. I don't want to think I had that ball gown made for you for nothing."

"What do you mean?" She frowned at him. Did he actually have that beautiful gown made for her?

He ignored her question. "Go on with your story."

She shook thoughts of the ball gown from her mind. "I realized when I worked on your bank ledgers that I enjoyed it. I was glad I could find some mistakes and I was also pleased that you had the faith in me to let me do it. Though I know now I should have been more inquisitive about my brother's activities, I still think I'm fairly good with facts and figures. Of course, I could never replace your lawyers or managers, but I think I could be a help in the running of your affairs."

She stopped talking and he asked, "Is that it?"

"What more do you want me to say?"

He finished his coffee and put his cup down. He reached for her cup and put it on the desk beside his. He then stood and pulled her to her feet. "I want you to say why you really decided to marry me."

"I just told you."

He wrapped his arms around her. "No, you didn't, Valissa. You said some things that made good sense, but you didn't say what feeling made you decide."

She looked into his brown eyes for several seconds then she whispered, "Because you excite me as no other man ever has."

He grinned and his eyes twinkled. "That's all I wanted to hear."

Without another word, his lips found hers.

Valissa was surprised, but didn't resist. If she were going to marry the man, she should at least be kissed by him.

What she thought would be a gentle peck flourished into something she wasn't expecting. At first she was amazed at how soft his lips were and how the kiss began awakening parts of her body that she didn't know had feeling. The kiss grew deeper and she felt as if she were going to float away to a different world. Maybe paradise. For some unexplained reason, she wanted to go there with Nathan Stone. She felt her heart pound against his chest and his against hers.

When she thought she could stand the pleasure no longer, he gently pushed her from him. "If we don't stop now, there'll be no way I can resist carrying you up those stairs to my room and starting the honeymoon before the wedding."

Valissa didn't tell him that she wished he would. Instead she said, "You're right. We're not married yet."

He turned her toward the door. "But we will be before the day is out."

"You mean….?"

"Yep, but we'll finalize the details while we eat. I'm suddenly awfully hungry."

She grabbed his arm and stopped him. "I'm glad you're hungry. Flo has cooked a lot of food. By the way, what do you mean finalize the details?"

He slid his arm around her shoulders. "I simply mean that as soon as we go have breakfast, we're going to get dressed up and find a preacher."

Eleven

Valissa automatically walked to what had become her regular seat at the dining room table, the chair to the right of Nathan's place at the head of the table. She watched as Flo brought in the mounds of food she had cooked per Nathan's request.

Nathan frowned. "Did you plan on feeding an army this morning, Flo?"

"No, sir, I didn't, but you kept telling me what I needed to cook for breakfast and the menu grew." She shook her head. "You told me to make pancakes, too, but Miss Valissa said not to do it. If you want them, you'll have to discuss it with her."

"I don't remember telling you to cook all this."

"Well, Mr. Nathan, you did."

He raised an eyebrow. "If I ever tell you to do something like this again, I hope you'll tell me to hush and go away."

"I couldn't do that, sir. You might fire me."

"There's no way in the world, I'd fire you, Flo. You're too good of a cook. Besides, Valissa would probably bash my head in if I let you go."

Flo looked confused. "No disrespect to you, Miss Valissa, but sir, what does she have to do with it? I know her three weeks are up."

"That they are, Flo. That they are." He put eggs on his plate and passed them to Valissa. "Now, Flo, before you do anything else I want you to go find Alvin and bring him in here. I have something important that I want the both of you to do."

Flo looked at Valissa, but Valissa only shrugged. Still looking confused, Flo muttered, "Yes, sir," and left the dining room."

"What are you up to, Nathan?" Valissa cocked her head to the side and looked at him.

"You'll see." He began eating with gusto.

Valissa also began to eat. She knew there was no need to ask him anything further. He'd tell her when he was ready.

~ * ~

Nathan was happy with the way things were going. He never dreamed Valissa was coming to him as a wife because she wanted him. He thought it would only be because she wanted her Heartsong back. But after that kiss, he didn't doubt that she was excited to be with him.

Now he was rethinking his reasons for marrying her. Sure, he knew he was almost thirty-one years old and it was time he married and started a family. But when he decided they should get married, a family was a long way from his mind. He was only thinking of how it would be to hold the tempting woman in his arms and introduce her to the sensual side of life.

He'd even thought of trying it without marriage because in the back of his mind he was still thinking that Maurine Taylor would be the woman to have his children and live on the ranch with him. Though it didn't matter to him, his stepmother liked Maurine. At least he thought she liked her. No, he knew she did. If Ada Stone didn't like someone, it wasn't long until everyone around her knew it. And she had told him more than one time she had to approve of his wife and she'd refuse to let any woman come on the ranch she didn't like.

Of course, Nathan ignored her threats. She was always threatening about something. He knew he'd end up marrying whomever he wanted, regardless of her feelings. After all, his father had left a third of the ranch to him and he had no intention of giving it up to Ada or anyone else.

Then there was the problem of Colleen. Yes, Ada had mentioned that she would make a good wife on more than one occasion. Maybe because she didn't see the relationship between him and Maurine progressing fast enough. But Colleen was young and spoiled. He could never see her as wife material.

And when he brought Valissa home as his wife, what would his stepmother think? He almost laughed out loud because he knew the two women would probably clash. They were both strong and independent and each one would think they knew what the right way to do a thing was.

Hell. They're a lot alike. Neither will give an inch to the other. I'm surprised I feel the way I do about Valissa because I can't often stand Ada and her fancy ways. But there is the big difference. Along with being hard to handle, Valissa has her sweet side. She's loving and kind and she'll make a wonderful wife and mother. She's also very smart. She'll work beside me in most of my endeavors. She won't be the kind of wife who is only interested in making a name for herself and stepping on others to do it the way Ada does.

He smiled again when he remembered how often he'd said to Ada in a sarcastic voice, "My dearest step-mama. When I find a woman as hard-headed and smart-mouthed as you, I'll get married and settle down and have you all the grandbabies you want. You'll have the rest of your life to complain and tell me how much you dislike her and how the children are driving you crazy." *Trouble is, I think Valissa can hold her own with you or anyone else, though if she's miserable around you, I'll buy a different ranch to live on with her. You've about run Stone ranch into massive debt anyway. I may just give it to you completely. If Valissa is willing to start over, so am I.*

The door to the dining room opened and Flo appeared with her husband. "We're here, Mr. Stone."

"Thank you for coming. Would you and Alvin like a cup of coffee?"

Alvin looked at his boss as if he'd lost his mind. "I had some earlier, sir."

Nathan wiped his mouth with his napkin. "While Flo puts these dishes away, I want you to draw a nice bath for Valissa and me. In our separate rooms, of course," he added when he saw the look on Flo's face.

"Yes, sir."

"Then I want you and Flo to go to your rooms, clean up a bit and put on your best Sunday-go-to meeting clothes."

"Sir?" Flo stared at him.

"You heard me. When you're dressed, Flo, you come to Valissa's room and help her into her prettiest dress. Alvin, you go make sure Philips has my carriage sparkling and the horses ready to harness up."

"We can do all this, sir, but do you mind telling us why?" Alvin looked at him.

"I thought you'd never ask." He stood and moved behind Valissa. "You see. This beautiful lady and I are going to find a preacher or a priest, whatever she wants, and we're going to get married. You are the two closest people in this town to us and you will be our witnesses."

After a moment of shocked stillness, Flo finally burst into smiles. "Miss Valissa, is this true?"

Valissa laughed. "Yes, Flo. It's true. I hope you'll agree to see us married."

"Oh, child, you know we will. It's almost like my own baby is getting married. I've got to hug your neck."

Nathan stepped back and took the withered hand Alvin offered. "I hope you don't mind me saying you'd better be good to her, Mr. Nathan. Miss Valissa is a special lady to us."

"Don't worry, Alvin. I know I can make her happy."

~ * ~

Valissa finished her bath, put on her dressing gown and opened her door. Nobody was in the hall so she hurried down to the end and opened the door that led to the seldom used attic. She slipped up the stairs and closed the door behind her.

While she was bathing, she'd had an idea and she hoped it would pan out. She knew there was a trunk of things her father had kept for sentimental reasons and she hoped the object of her search was one of those keepsakes.

The sun beamed through the windows in the attic and she didn't have to light a lamp. She edged her way beside some discarded furniture and old picture frames. The trunk was under one of the eaves. She moved it out from the wall and hoped it wasn't locked. It wasn't.

First she pulled out some pictures and her eyes became misty as she studied her parents in a long ago joyful time. Her mother, Agatha, had beautiful raven hair and her father, Edward, looked handsome with his high-buttoned collar. They both looked happy and in love. Oh, how she missed them.

Putting the pictures aside, she fumbled through different items, then spied what she was looking for. She gently pulled it out from between two folded sheets of tissue paper and shook it out. Standing up, she held it to her. It looked as if it would fit. She was pleased. Maybe she wasn't as much in love as her mother was when she wore it, but she did love Nathan and she hoped in time that he would love her back. At the moment it didn't matter whether he loved her or not, this was going to be her special day. She was going to get married in her mother's wedding dress. She knew it would bring her luck.

An hour later, Flo came into Valissa's room with the wedding dress over her arm. "I have it all pressed and ready. I was even able to get the stored smell off it."

"How did you do that?"

"I put it on the clothes line and shook it until most of the wrinkles and smell came out. Then I put a little of your perfume in the water I used to sprinkle it with to press. Now it smells like you."

"Oh, Flo. You're a genius."

Flo laughed. "No, I'm not, child. I just happen to know how to do some practical things. I've learned most of them over the years taking care of you."

Valissa let Flo slip the dress over her head. The skirt fell to the floor in a puddle of satin beauty and the high-necked lace bodice fitted under her chin and framed her jawline with touches of more gathered lace. The sleeves were long and the back had a row of a multitude of buttons.

Flo was busy closing them. "It fits you beautifully, Miss Valissa. You look so much like Miz Agatha in this dress."

"Mother was a beautiful woman, Flo. Much prettier than I am, but I am thankful that I inherited her lovely hair."

"Yes, she was beautiful and she had a beautiful daughter." Flo straightened up. "There, that does it."

"Thank you." Valissa whirled around. "How do I look?"

"You look like a happy bride."

Valissa looked in the mirror. "I do like the way you put my hair up on my head. It's too bad Mother's veil wasn't in the trunk."

"I think these will do fine." Flo picked up the fall flowers she'd gathered in the garden. "I'll place them in different places in your hair and you will look stunning."

"Thank you, Flo."

"Now, I'm going downstairs and make sure the men are ready. You give me about three minutes and come on down slowly. I want Mr. Nathan to see you appear at the top of the steps. He'll know then he's about to marry an angel."

Valissa did as she was told. When she was sure it had been about three minutes, she left her room and closed the door. She turned the corner and paused at the top of the winding stairway.

Nathan, in a formal black suit, grinned from ear to ear and his eyes grew big as he looked at her. She knew by his reaction he was pleased with her looks. Smiling back at him, she put her feet on the top step and began her slow walk toward him.

At that moment there was a loud banging on the front door which startled all of them. Alvin was the closest, so he turned and opened the double doors.

A woman in her mid-forties rushed in followed by a younger woman with long blond hair.

"Ada," Nathan roared. "What the hell are you doing here?"

"I'm here to keep my son from marrying that tart and ruining his life. Thank God, it looks like I got here in time."

Twelve

For a minute it was as if time had frozen. Nathan broke the silence. "You're not here in time to stop anything, but you're here in time to attend my wedding if you'd like to see your only stepson get married."

"I will see him get married when he comes home and marries the right woman." She glared at him. "As you can see, Maurine is with me. If you're hell bent on getting married, I'll go with you and her to find a preacher."

"I'm not marrying Maurine and I told her so when I was home. I am marrying Valissa Prescott."

Ada Stone looked up the stairs and her eyes locked with Valissa's. "Young woman, I don't know what kind of game you're trying to pull, but my son is engaged to Maurine here. He's not going to marry you today or tomorrow or not ever. Now get back up those stairs and get that ugly old wedding dress off."

Valissa didn't move. She couldn't. What was happening? A few minutes ago she was a happy woman. Now everything was crumbling around her again. It was the same as when Heartsong was snatched from her. Now this woman was taking Nathan.

"Ada Stone, don't talk to her like that."

"How should I talk to her, Nathan? She wormed her way into your life, and now she's trying to force you into a marriage you don't want."

"You're wrong. I asked Valissa to marry me. It took her a long time to decide she wanted to do it."

"If it was that hard for her, she probably doesn't want to marry you anyway." Ada smiled at Nathan. "Now, Maurine here has wanted to marry you ever since her husband died. Don't you think it's time you made an honest woman out of her?"

"She's right, Nathan." Maurine spoke for the first time. "We've been engaged for a long time. I think we should go ahead and make our relationship legal."

"I told you when I was at the ranch that I wasn't going to marry you because there was someone else, Maurine. You said you accepted that."

"Well, she didn't accept it. As soon as you headed back here, she came to me and told me what you were up to. We decided then and there we had to come to Galveston and stop this foolishness. I'll not have my son marrying a woman I don't know."

"As I said, I'm marrying Valissa, Ada. Now if you and Maurine want to attend my wedding, fine. If not, go to a hotel and I'll deal with you later." He turned and went up the stairs as he held his hand toward Valissa.

She didn't move.

"Please, Valissa. I want us to go on with the wedding just as we planned." His brown eyes pleaded with her.

Valissa reached for his hand. "Are you sure?"

"I'm positive."

"Yeah, he's positive all right," Maurine said in a mocking voice. "Go ahead and marry him. I guarantee that as soon as he tires of you, he'll be coming back to my bed just like he does when he always tires of every new woman he takes a fancy to."

Valissa started to turn, but Nathan held tight to her hand. "Don't listen to her. She's only jealous. I'll never be unfaithful to you."

"Maybe you should go sit down with your mother and discuss this," Valissa whispered to him.

"She's not my mother, Valissa. My mother died when I was a teenager."

"I'm the only mother he has," Ada snapped. "So he sure had better discuss marrying you with me."

"There's nothing to discuss. I'm marrying Valissa and that's that."

"I'd think twice about that, Nathan." Ada's eyes were hard as she glared at them. "On the way here, I made up my mind about something."

He glanced at her. "What was that?"

"I know how stubborn you are. Even if you didn't want to marry this strumpet, you would do it just to spite me. Well, I've had enough of you doing everything you damn well please against my wishes."

Nathan frowned, but said nothing.

Ada went on. "I've made up my mind. If you marry her, things will change at the ranch. Though you've worked hard and built it up and own a third of it, you know I'm the major owner with two thirds of the interest in it. I decided that unless you give up the idea of this marriage, I plan to disinherit you. I can do it, too. I've already checked with the bank. You'll never get a foot of my two thirds of the Stone Ranch if you marry this woman."

Valissa watched disbelief wash over Nathan's face as he let go of her arm, and turned toward his stepmother. "You can't mean to take everything my daddy worked for just because you managed to get him in your bed and married when he was grieving the loss of my mother."

"I mean every word, Nathan Stone. The only way you'll be able to get any of my part of the ranch is to marry Maurine within the next month."

"Surly this is only a threat. Even you can't be that evil. I want my children to have a piece of what my parents gave up most of their life for." His face showed not only anger, but also how hurt he was by her words.

"It isn't a threat; I do mean every word of it. If you don't believe me, just continue with this farce of a wedding."

Turning his back to Valissa, he took Ada's arm. "We need to discuss this before you make the biggest mistake of your life. Let's go to my study."

"Of course, dear." Ada took his arm, then turned back to Valissa and gave her a sneaky smile.

Maurine followed them to the study.

Valissa was still standing on the stairs when the study door slammed shut. She looked at Flo and tears welled up in her eyes.

Flo went to her and put her arm around her. "It'll be all right, honey. Mr. Nathan will make his mother see."

"No, Flo. He will give in to her."

"I don't think so."

"He will. I know how much he loves his ranch. He loves it the way I love Heartsong." She brushed the tears away and forced a smile. "You and Alvin may as well go to your room and get out of your Sunday clothes. There'll be no wedding tonight."

~ * ~

As soon as she was in her room, Valissa refused to let her mind dwell on what had happened. It was too painful, and besides, there was nothing she could do about it. Even the betrayal and humiliation she'd felt when she learned Kyle had lost Heartsong didn't hurt as much as the treachery and degradation she felt now. Not only had Nathan thrown her over for a ranch, he'd broken his promise to always care for her. Besides that, he'd shattered her heart.

Pushing it from her mind, she slipped out of the wedding gown and into the green traveling suit. Throwing the shawl she'd planned to wear that night around her shoulders, she picked up her still-packed valise and the small package with all her other valuables and opened the door. There was nobody in the hall, so she crept to the back stairs. She knew Flo would dress quickly and come to comfort her, so she had to hurry. Going through the kitchen and out the rear door, she managed to work her way toward the back street before Flo or anyone else could suspect she was gone.

She hadn't gone far when seemingly from nowhere an arm went around her and a hand clamped down on her mouth. She struggled, but couldn't scream.

Then the man whispered, "Calm down, little sister. It's me, Kyle. I had to see you."

"Oh, Kyle," she cried when he uncovered her mouth. "I'm so glad you're here. I need my big brother right now." She fell into his arms and began to sob.

~ * ~

"Ada, I want to know why you're so upset about my marrying Valissa Prescott." Nathan turned from the liquor cabinet with a glass of bourbon in his hand.

"Please have your maid fix us some tea and I'll be glad to talk with you about it." Ada put her purse down beside her on the leather chair. "It was a long ride from Fort Worth and I'm tired."

"I'm sure Flo is taking care of Valissa and I will not interrupt her to get tea for you. You can drink some of my liquor or nothing."

"Do you have wine?" Maurine asked.

"It's on that table over there." He indicated the table in the corner. "Help yourself."

"Would you like a glass, Ada?"

"Please, dear."

"Okay, ladies, enough of the stalling. Why are you here and what do you want?"

"I thought I had made myself clear to you, son. I want to stop you from making a mistake. Miss Prescott may have turned your head for the moment, but you know you don't want to marry a woman like her. She'd never fit on our ranch and you know that's where you want to raise your children."

"Valissa will live anywhere I want to live."

"Oh, she says that now, but I know these city women. When they have the ring on their finger, they get stubborn. She'll demand that you live here in Galveston with her."

"I told her we'd live in Galveston part of the time. You know I often have to come here to take care of my businesses."

"That doesn't matter. Maurine told me how you get involved with a woman, then toss the new companion aside and come back to her. The same thing will happen with this one. Only this time you'll be married and it won't be so easy to get rid of her."

"I have no intention of ever getting rid of Valissa. She's going to be the mother of my children and we're going to raise them together."

Ada sipped the wine Maurine handed her. "Then I told you what I'd do. You know when your father married me, I became the only mother you have."

"You've never been a mother to me, Ada. You were only the woman my father married. He did that against my wishes, but there was nothing I could do about it."

"But I've love you as my son, because that's what you are. As your mother, I have to protect you. If refusing to let you get the ranch your father left mostly to me is the only to save you, I'll do it."

"You better listen to her, Nathan." Maurine smiled. "She decided all this while we were on the train ride down. I'm sure she means it."

"Then so be it." He downed the rest of his liquor and slammed his glass down on the desk. "I have enough money to buy a ranch anywhere in Texas or any other state I choose. I don't have to have the Stone ranch to fulfill my dream of working as a cowboy. Besides, without me overseeing what goes on there, you'll end up losing it anyway. I'll be able to buy it for its debt. Then you can get the hell away from the ranch and out of my life."

Ada's eyes grew large. "You wouldn't do that to me."

"Oh, yes I would. You were nothing but a saloon dancer when you got your claws into my dad. I've tried to be half way decent to you because he thought he loved you. But I don't give a damn what happens to you from here on out." He turned to her and glared into her eyes. "I'm in love with Valissa Prescott and I intend to make her my wife tonight. There's nothing you can say or do to stop me."

"What about me, Nathan?" Maurine asked. "What about all those plans and promises we had? I thought we'd be getting married."

"So did Colleen O'Malley when she showed up here while I was in Fort Worth. She told Valissa she was my fiancée." He looked back at Ada. "How many women are you going to try to pick out for me?"

Maurine's eyebrows shot up. "Colleen O'Malley? Had you thought about marrying her?"

"Not really, but Ada had an idea that maybe I should. I guess she saw I wasn't going to and she decided you'd do as a second choice."

"That's not so, Nathan." Ada turned to Maurine. "Don't listen to him. I think you would be a wonderful wife for my son."

"You wouldn't think so if you knew everything about the situation."

"What do you mean?"

"I'm not the only man Maurine is sleeping with."

"Nathan!" Maurine was shocked and showed it.

"What?" His mother almost screamed. "You must be lying."

"You can't tell her that, Nathan. You know you're the only one I care about."

"From what I hear, you told your foreman the same thing. Said if he'd marry you, you'd drop me in a heartbeat."

"Maurine, is this true?" Ada stormed out at her.

"Of course not. I love Nathan."

Before anyone could say anything else, there was a sharp rap on the door.

"Come in," Nathan called.

Flo came through the door. There were tears in her eyes. "Oh, Mr. Nathan, Miss Valissa is gone."

"What do you mean, gone?"

"The valise she packed to move out this morning is not in her room and she threw her wedding dress on the bed. I have Alvin searching the grounds, but I'm worried."

"Try not to worry, Flo. I'll find her." He grabbed his gun belt from the peg where he always kept it. "When Alvin gets through searching the grounds, have him drive these two women to a hotel."

"Surely you're not going to throw me out of your house." Ada glared at him.

"Frankly, I don't care where you go. I have to find Valissa."

"But we're not through talking."

"Oh, yes we are."

"I'll fix guests' rooms for them, Mr. Nathan."

"All right, Flo. Whatever you say, but if they give you any trouble, send them away." As he headed out the door he added, "If I'm not back, as soon as it gets light, see that Alvin drives them to the train."

The door closed behind him before anyone could say anything else.

Thirteen

Kyle and Valissa hurried down the back street. He held her arm tightly. "Now, little sister, can you tell me what's going on?"

"No. We've got to get away from here. Nathan will be looking for me, I know."

"Are you sure?"

"Yes. Flo will see that I'm gone and tell him. He'll come looking for me whether he wants to or not."

"What do you mean?"

"Never mind. I'll explain later. We've got to think of somewhere to go, somewhere safe, somewhere that he won't find me, somewhere he'll never think to look."

"I've been staying with a friend down on the docks. Surely he wouldn't look there."

"Who's your friend?"

"Does it matter?"

"Yes."

"His name is Glenn Tilley. He's been letting me use a room in his place. I'm sure he won't mind if I bring you there."

"No!"

"Why not, Valissa? It's a nice place and…"

"That'll be the first place Nathan looks."

"Why would he do that?"

"I said I'd explain everything later." She glanced at the street corner. "I have an idea. Let's go this way."

"But we're getting deeper into the residential area. I want to head for the outskirts."

"I do too, but right now I think this is our best chance of getting out of town."

Kyle didn't argue. He let her lead the way.

After turning at the next three street corners, he blurted, "That's the Colberts' house."

"I know. I also know that Mr. Colbert has his board meeting tonight and Mrs. Colbert meets with her ladies group. If we're lucky, Wilbur will be out and Rowena will be home. I know she'll help me."

"Why should she? I heard society has turned its back on you."

"Not Rowena. We've been too close for…" She grabbed Kyle's sleeve. "Hurry. Hide in these bushes. I hear a carriage coming down the street."

Valissa held her breath and knelt behind the azaleas and boxwood hedge as she watched a black carriage drawn by two black horses approach. She saw Phillips driving the carriage and she knew without looking close that the man on the seat beside him was Nathan Stone. Her heart pounded as they drew closer.

~ * ~

"Glenn, do you really think Kyle Prescott will deliver his sister to you?"

"Absolutely. I have him so deep in debt to me that he'll grab his sister as soon as he gets a chance."

"Looks like it's taking a while."

"It is, but don't you think it'll be worth it to have her here?"

Glenn's partner gave him a wry grin. "I most certainly do. I've always thought she was something special to look at. Of course, I never dreamed we'd be lucky enough for her to fall so far from society that we could get her to work here. I figured she'd marry one of the young businessmen in town and become a lady of leisure like most of the women I know. Of course I hoped all along that if I managed to see that she lost her home, she'd agree to be my mistress."

"If things hadn't worked out as they did when her brother lost their home, she probably would've been everything you say. But they didn't work out that way and I knew the minute she came in here selling dresses that we had to have her."

"I know the husbands and fathers of her former friends will be lining up as soon as we have her working upstairs. No telling how much they'll pay for the privilege, either. I know for a fact that she's as pure as the dew drops on a warm morning. Being married to a stuffy wife myself, I know how much that means to a man." He laughed. "I've been to enough dances and parties where she was that I've even had fantasies about the girl."

"I guess that's why you helped her brother cause her downfall."

"I did no such thing. I simply didn't tell anyone what was happening until it was too late to save her." He chuckled again and looked up toward the ceiling. "Oh, yes. It will be wonderful to feel that naked little body in bed, all sweet and innocent."

"I figured she was an innocent. That's why I'm sure we'll have to take it slow with her."

"Of course, I know you, Glenn. You intend to break her in and show her how things have to be done upstairs."

"Well, you can't do it. She knows you too well. She'd somehow turn that back on you."

"You're right. She'd go running in the other direction if she saw me too soon." He sighed. "You do understand that I'll be the second man with her, don't you?"

"I wouldn't have it any other way, my friend." Glenn sipped the whisky he had left in his glass. "Got any extra money to spend here tonight?

"I do. I was able to get fifty-three dollars out today."

"Good. I'll set up a faro game so you can round it up a little. Who do you want tonight?"

"Who do you think?" He chuckled. "Angela. Always Angela, that is, until Valissa is available."

Glenn nodded. "I thought you'd feel that way. Have another drink and I'll be right back and tell you which table to go to so you can win extra money to spend."

"Thanks, Glenn. A man couldn't ask for a

Valissa and Kyle hid behind the shrubs near the back veranda of the Colberts' Victorian mansion. "Rowena's room is the one on the left of the upstairs porch," she whispered. "There's a light on."

"Want me to go knock on the door?"

"No. One of the servants might come to the door. I want you to gather some of those small pebbles and toss them at her window."

"What if someone hears?"

"We have to take that chance."

"No, we don't, Valissa. I told you we could go to Glenn's place at the docks."

"I'm not going there, Kyle."

"I think you're mistaken about him. He's really a rather nice man. He's been letting me stay there…"

"I know. You've already told me you were staying there, but I think you're the one who is mistaken about the man. Now, stop arguing and gather some pebbles. I want to get Rowena's attention before one of her parents gets home."

It took several tosses, but finally the curtain stirred on Rowena's window. As planned, Kyle darted back behind the bushes and Valissa moved into the yard enough for her friend to see who was making the noise. With hand signals, she made Rowena understand that she wanted her to come down. Rowena nodded and closed the curtain.

"She's coming."

"What will she do when she sees me?"

"She's always liked you, Kyle. When I explain that you've rescued me from a situation that I couldn't seem to get out of myself, she'll help us both."

The door to the veranda opened and Rowena appeared. "What's going on?" She kept her voice to a whisper.

"I'm sorry I had to come here, but I need your help, Rowena?"

"What can I do?"

"Kyle is with me," Valissa explained as Kyle stepped out of the bushes. "He found me running away from Heartsong and he's trying to help, me."

Surprise covered her face when she spied Valissa's brother. "Hello, Kyle." He nodded and she went on, "It's almost time for Mother to get home. I don't want her to see you two here. She'd probably send for the police."

"I know. I only want you to do one thing for me."

"You know I will if I can."

"We need to get out of town tonight. Please let us borrow your horse and buggy. I promise we will leave it where it will be easy for you to find."

Rowena looked puzzled. "What has happened, Valissa? Why do you have to leave?"

"It's complicated, but I promise to write you a long letter and explain everything."

"All right, but you know if Daddy finds my buggy gone, I'll have to let him think somebody took it."

"I understand. Can we have it?"

"Do you know how to harness the horse…"

"I know how, Rowena," Kyle said.

"Then go to the stable and get it. Just hurry. I need to get back inside in case Mother comes in."

"Thank you, my friend." Valissa tiptoed to the edge of the veranda and hugged Rowena. "I promise to write tomorrow."

"Thank you, Rowena." Kyle smiled at her.

It took almost twenty minutes to get the horse harnessed and hitched to the buggy, but luck was with them. Neither Mrs. Colbert nor her husband arrived before they were on the next street over.

"Now that we're safely away from the Colbert house, where do you want to go, Valissa?"

She bit her lip. "I'm not sure."

He jerked his head toward her. "Then why in hell did we go get this buggy? I thought you had a plan."

"Don't be angry, Kyle. I'm thinking as we go. My first goal was to get this buggy so we could get away. I guess we should head toward Houston."

"Houston?" His voice grew angry. "Why would you want to go to Houston? We would've been perfectly safe at Tilley's place. Now you want to go running off to Houston."

Tears sprang to her eyes. "You don't have to be angry. I told you I couldn't go to Glenn Tilley's place."

"But you didn't tell me why."

"It's complicated."

"Looks like we'll have plenty of time for you to explain if we're going to Houston."

She sighed. "I was desperate for money, Kyle. You left me in a dreadful mess when you gambled away my home."

"I'm sorry about that, Valissa, but I know my luck will change. I'll win your home back."

She shook her head. "It's too late for that. Nathan Stone, a rancher from near Fort Worth, bought the house from the man you lost it to. He's in possession of it and he has no intention of selling it."

When he didn't reply, she continued. "Anyway, as I said, I needed money. I knew that a lot of women sold their gowns down on the docks so I went through mine and picked out what I could sell."

"Surly you weren't so desperate you had to sell your clothes."

"Yes, I was, Kyle. I was down to almost nothing. Mr. Stone was moving in and I needed money to move away and find somewhere else to live. I took my dresses to the dock and happened to sell them at Glenn Tilley's saloon."

"So? That shows he wanted to help you."

"He wanted to help me so much that he plied me with wine and would have taken advantage of me if Mr. Stone hadn't shown up and rescued me from him."

"I can't believe that."

"I didn't want to believe it either, but Nathan said the man planned to set me up in one of the rooms he has women in upstairs."

"That can't be right, Valissa. Glenn is a good-hearted man. He has a good business and he makes lots of money. If he likes someone, I'm sure he only wants to help them."

"But Mr. Stone said…"

"Valissa, if you put so much faith in what this Mr. Stone says, why are you running away from him?"

She didn't answer.

"I see you're thinking about what I said. Maybe Mr. Stone had his own plans for you. He probably didn't want you to turn to anyone else for help."

She still didn't answer.

"I think it's time you told me the rest of the story. The man must have had some sinister plan or you wouldn't have been sneaking away."

"We were going to get married," she whispered so low that Kyle barely understood.

"Then he changed his mind?"

She shook her head. "His stepmother showed up with his fiancée. He took my hand and told them he was going to marry me and asked them to leave, but they didn't."

"Then?"

"His mother said if he married me she wouldn't leave the ranch that he loved to him."

"What'd he do?"

"He dropped my hand and went into the study with his mother and his fiancée."

"Without you?"

"Yes."

"See, Valissa. He was only interested in you for one reason. He would probably have pretended to marry you, then when he decided he was tired of you being around, he'd have thrown you out. I guess he'd marry his real fiancée then."

"I can't believe he'd do that to me."

"But…"

"Oh, Kyle." She burst into tears. "I don't want to talk about it any longer."

"Then we won't." He reached out and put his arm around his sister. "Now rest your head on your big brother's shoulder and cry it out. You don't have to worry about Mr. Stone anymore. I'm here and I'll take care of you."

"Oh, Kyle. I'm so glad you came home." She closed her eyes and rested her head like he told her to. The ordeal had exhausted her more than she realized because in a few minutes she became drowsy.

She was actually asleep when Kyle turned the buggy in a new direction. Valissa had no way of knowing that, instead of heading toward Houston, they were on their way to the docks.

~ * ~

"I tell you, Mr. Stone, Valissa Prescott is not here." Glenn's eyes blazed as he stood face to face with the big cowboy.

"Then you won't have any objections if I look around."

"Of course, I object. My patrons pay a lot for the pleasures they receive here and they have a right to their privacy."

"I don't give a damn about your patrons. All I want to do is find Valissa Prescott." Nathan headed for the stairs. "I'm starting with your office."

Glenn followed him and opened the door. "Then look around good."

The office and the connecting bedroom were empty.

"See, I told you."

"I'm checking these other rooms." Nathan started down the hall. The first door he came to, he reached for the knob.

"At least let me warn them," Glenn said.

"Hell, no. It'd give them a chance to hide." He jerked open the door and a woman with long black hair sat up and screamed when he looked inside. The cowboy with her reached for his gun, but Nathan closed the door before he could fire a shot.

He had the same results in the rest of the rooms. Though he saw a few men he recognized from his business dealings in town, none of them were with Valissa.

Returning to the bar, he met Philips. "Did you find anything?"

"No, Mr. Stone. I checked the kitchen and the cook's quarters. I even checked the outhouses. She's not here."

Nathan nodded then turned to Glenn. "This isn't the end of my searches here. I'll be back in the morning in case you've stashed her somewhere and plan to bring her back here. I may even come back tonight."

"I'm sure you will, but you'll find nothing on each of your visits." Glenn ground his teeth, showing his anger. In his mind he formed a plan of what he'd do with Valissa if Kyle happened to show up with her.

Nathan took hold of his brocade vest and moved his face close. "Have you ever seen a man die from being shot slowly? You start with his feet, then his hands, and you go from legs to arms. It takes a man a long time to die and it's very painful. Do you want that to happen to you?"

"Are you threatening me?"

"You're damn right I am. If I find out you've laid a hand on Valissa Prescott, I'll kill you just like I described. Slowly and painfully." He let Glenn go. "You keep that in mind if Miss Prescott happens to show up here."

~ * ~

Valissa woke and found herself alone in the buggy. "Kyle," she whispered, but there was no answer.

Looking around, she realized the buggy was parked in an alley, not the open road leading to Houston. Why were they here? Did something happen while she was asleep? Had Kyle gone for help?

Valissa wondered if she should climb out of the buggy and go look for her brother when she heard someone talking. They were speaking low, but she knew by the tone the voices belonged to men.

In a moment they came into view in the moonlight. *Oh, no. That's Glenn Tilley with my brother. I told him I couldn't come to Tilley's place, but he brought me anyway. What was he thinking? Nathan told me I wouldn't be safe here.*

Glenn Tilley walked up to the buggy. "Miss Prescott, I'm so sorry you had to run away from your home."

"I'm going to Houston." She sat up straight and glared at him, showing more strength than she had.

"I don't think that's a wise decision. Stone would track you down before you got half way there." Glenn gave her the smile Nathan warned her about.

"I have to go out of town."

"I know. Your brother explained what happened and I want to help you."

"By making me work in your saloon." She couldn't keep the sharpness out of her voice.

"Not now. We can talk about the hostess job later. At this point, it seems hiding you is the most important thing I can do for you."

Kyle broke into the conversation. "I told you Glenn would help us, Valissa. He has a fishing cottage on the coast heading toward

Brownsville. He says we can go there and Stone will never find us. Very few people know about the place."

Surprised, Valissa looked at Glenn. "Is this true?"

"Of course. I'm the type of person who wants to help his friends when they need it."

Valissa felt a little doubtful, but it sounded like a good place to go for the time being. "How far is it to your cabin?"

"Far enough that nobody goes there unless I invite them or they're headed to Brownsville or even Mexico. Now, don't you worry. I'll take care of everything. Cook is gathering some supplies for you to take with you and I'll send someone to check on you in a couple of days."

Valissa swallowed. "I owe you an apology, Mr. Tilley."

"No you don't, Miss Prescott. I know Stone tried to poison your mind about me, but he's wrong. It's my pleasure to help you and your brother any way I can."

Valissa looked around in alarm as she heard a noise headed in their direction. "Who's that?"

"Don't worry, pretty lady. It's only my cook with the supplies you'll need."

"Glenn, I appreciate this more than you can know," Kyle said.

"Don't mention it, Kyle. As we talked, I'll have my buggy hitched up for you. I'll get this one back to the Colberts and nobody will ever know you were anywhere near it." Glenn turned to meet the cook.

"Kyle," Valissa said. "Are you sure we're doing the right thing?"

"I'm positive we are, little sister. I told you that you were wrong about Glenn. He's really a nice man. He cares about his friends."

She bit her lip. "I hope you're right." Inside, she couldn't help remembering the warnings Nathan had given her about Glenn Tilley.

Fourteen

When Nathan came into the kitchen through the back door, it was just before dawn; Flo handed him a steaming cup of coffee. "I didn't have any luck, Flo. It seems Valissa has disappeared into the night."

"She has to be somewhere, Mr. Nathan."

"I know, but where?" He dropped to Flo's kitchen work table. "I checked the saloon twice because I was sure she'd go there. I don't think I've been able to convince her that Glenn Tilley is a disreputable character. She still insisted he was only trying to help her. I figured she'd run right to him."

"And she wasn't there?"

"No sign of her. I searched the place myself. So did Phillips."

Flo sighed. "I'm so worried. I'm not sure what Miss Valissa might do. Did you check the rooming houses?"

"Of course. She wasn't at any of them." He drank his coffee. "Did you get Ada and Maurine settled last night?"

"Finally. I put them in guest rooms on opposite sides of the hall, but they were still arguing when I went to my quarters." She had a plate in her hand. "If you'll go to the dining room, I'll serve you your breakfast."

"Ada would be stunned, but I'm going to eat right here." He shook his head. "I can't believe they showed up like they did. It sure was bad timing."

"It was a little awkward."

"You're damn right it was. I think they're the reason Valissa ran off." He looked down at the egg and bacon Flo set before him. "Where's Alvin this morning?"

"He decided to take a walk around the neighborhood and talk to some of the servants and day workers. He said maybe somebody heard or saw something." She refilled his coffee. "You know how servants talk."

He couldn't help grinning. "They do?"

Flo turned red. "You know Alvin and I would never say a thing, but we do listen sometimes."

"I know, Flo. Valissa has more than convinced me of your loyalty. I also know you're as concerned about her as I am."

"She's like a daughter to me, Mr. Nathan."

"I'll find her if I have to turn this town upside down to do it."

The door opened and Alvin came in. When he saw their expectant looks, he said, "I didn't find her anywhere, but I may have picked up a clue."

Nathan stopped eating and Flo stared at him. "Well, tell us. What did you find?"

"One of the Colberts' day maids was laughing about the fact that when she came to work she saw Miss Rowena's buggy sitting in front of their house all hitched up as if she planned an early morning ride."

"Had she planned such a ride?"

"No, sir. The maid said the girl was still in bed."

Nathan frowned. "You don't suppose…"

"Well, well, well," a sharp voice butted in from the door to the dining room. "I never dreamed you'd sunk so low, Nathan Stone. I thought you knew better than to fraternize with the hired help."

"I see you're still in your gracious mood, Ada."

"I'll have my coffee in the dining room. At least one Stone knows her place." She glared at Nathan. "If you're not too comfortable here, maybe you'll join me."

When nobody answered her, she turned and closed the door.

"I'll get her coffee, Flo," Alvin said. "Maybe you better fix her something to eat."

Nathan stood. "Thanks for the breakfast, Flo. I guess I'll go have coffee with the queen. Then I'll check with the Colberts. Something is wrong about that carriage being in the street."

"I agree, sir."

Nathan nodded at him and headed to the dining room. He was surprised to see Ada seated in his chair. He cleared his throat and put his hand on the back of the chair. "If you'll move to the left, I'll join you. I always sit in this chair."

"But I always sit at the head of the table at the ranch."

"We're not at the ranch and the way things look, I won't be back there for some time, but I am here. And here I'm the head of this household." His voice was firm.

Though she looked like she would argue with him, she didn't. She moved to the chair on his left side as Alvin appeared with a cup and coffee for her. She didn't speak.

"Thank you, Alvin," Nathan said. "I'm sorry that a member of my family has chosen to act as if she's better than anyone else. I guess the fact that she managed to leave her job as a dance hall girl and marry a rich rancher makes her think she has the right to act this way."

"How dare you say that?"

"It's the truth, isn't it?" When she didn't answer, he went on. "Do you have your clothes ready for the return trip to Fort Worth?"

"I decided I'll not go back to Fort Worth until you decide it's time for you to come home."

He glared at her. "I am home."

"Be reasonable, Nathan. I'll send Maurine on her way today since you've made me see the light about her past, or should I say present? But I want to make sure you don't do something foolish like finding that silly girl and marrying her."

"Ada Stone, I'm going to marry Valissa and you might as well get used to the idea. Whenever Flo brings your breakfast, eat and then go get ready to travel. You're leaving here on the morning train."

"But I don't want to go, son."

"For the name of heavens, quit calling me son. I'm not your son and I never have been. I might as well add that I never will be."

"Nathan, please. When you're at the ranch we manage to get along most of the time. Why are you being so difficult now?"

Nathan didn't like hurting anyone, but he decided it was finally time to level with Ada. He took a deep breath and said, "We manage to get along at the ranch because I spend most of my time out on the range with the hands. You and I only see each other at meals and occasionally when we meet in the house." He looked at her. "You know I've resented you, no, I'll change that, I've almost hated you since the day Dad brought you home and introduced you as my new mother."'

"But I thought you'd grown to care for me." She gave him a coy smile. "After all, that was almost fifteen years ago."

"It was exactly fifteen years ago this past spring. I was sixteen at the time."

"So you're saying you always resented me?"

"What I'm saying is that my feelings haven't changed. Even going away to college didn't change them."

"I tried to be a good mother to you, Nathan. You just wouldn't let me."

"I had a mother. A wonderful mother. She was good and kind and she never hurt a soul in her life."

"I haven't hurt anyone."

Nathan sneered. "Oh, no? Do you think I don't know that you and Sanford O'Malley were sleeping together while my dad was dying?"

Ada gasped. "That's not so."

He sighed. "Yes, Ada. It is so and there's no use denying it now."

"So, what? It's not important now. Your father is gone."

"Yes, he is. And thank God, I don't think he ever knew you betrayed him."

"Sanford was a good friend to me when I needed someone, Nathan. You don't understand how it was."

"I understand more than you think, Ada. Why do you think I moved all my business that had nothing to do with Stone ranch to another lawyer? I had to leave the ranch affairs with him because Dad thought he was his friend. But I refused to let him know what was going on in my holdings. I knew he'd tell you anything you wanted to know about what I was involved in."

"I knew you were keeping secrets from me."

"It has nothing to do with the ranch, so it was none of your business."

Flo came in and set a plate before Ada. "Would you like some more coffee, Mr. Nathan?"

"No, thank you, Flo. But would you please go upstairs and wake Miss Taylor? Tell her she has one hour to get dressed and eat and one more hour to get herself packed and out of my house." He stood and looked down at Ada. "That goes for you, too. I'm going out for a little while, but I'll be back in two hours. I want the both of you to be gone or at least leaving when I get back."

"Nathan, please wait. We need to talk…"

"I've said all I want to say and you have nothing to say that I want to hear." He headed through the door to the kitchen without another word.

~ * ~

Valissa struggled awake, raised up on her elbow and shock covered her face when she looked around the dingy room. The cabin Tilley had sent them to turned out to be no more than an unkempt one-room shack. Spider webs dripped from the ceiling and the rough walls had mud missing between several of the logs. A small rusty looking iron stove and a crude table with four chairs sat in the middle of the room. Along the wall behind where she had slept someone had built four rough bunk beds—two lower bunks and two upper. The shelf between the two bunks held a bucket, used soap, the stub of a smoked cigar and a wash rag that should have been thrown away months ago.

She'd somehow been able to sleep on one of the lower bunks and her brother was still asleep on the other. Sitting up straight, she was grateful the bunk above her was high enough that she didn't hit her head.

She eased to a standing position and moved to the shelf with the bucket. Immediately she turned up her nose. The water inside must have been standing in the bucket for several months. It had a film on top and some dead insects she didn't recognize floated in the scum.

Downhearted, she walked to the one door and pushed it open. A sandy beach stretched out in front of her and led directly to the Gulf of Mexico. Though her surroundings in the hut were terrible, the sight of the aqua blue water stretching as far as the eye could see filled her with awe.

Valissa had always loved the sea. She found it huge and scary and knew many unknown creatures made their lives under its pristine waves, but it still inspired her. She felt the vastness of the universe when she looked at it and this made her reflect on her one, small seemingly unimportant life.

"Hey, you're up." Kyle's voice made her turn around and close the door.

"I was just checking out where we are located."

"Glenn said we were about five miles from the heart of the city. He said there weren't any close neighbors."

"I didn't see any other houses."

"Good. You'll be safe here."

Her eyes got big. "You're not going to leave me here alone in this awful place, are you?

"Not today. I'll help you clean it up and get you settled. I'm not sure what supplies the saloon cook gave us, so I might have to go to town and get some things."

She looked at her brother. "Kyle, this place is awful."

"Mr. Tilley said it hadn't been used in a while, but we'll soon get it in livable shape."

Valissa shrugged. She wasn't sure the place could be made livable, but she decided not to argue with Kyle. "Where did you put the supplies?"

"Over there on that shelf under the window."

Valissa moved to the area and looked in the canvas bag. "Looks like there are several things here."

"I hope there's some coffee."

"There is, but there's no water in here. You'll have to go find some."

"What about that bucket?"

"Look in it. I don't think you'll want to do any cooking with that."

Kyle moved to the shelf and peered inside. He wrinkled his nose. "You're right."

"I don't know if there's a well or what here, but you should go look. I'll check around and see if there are pots and pans enough to put a meal together for us."

Outside, Kyle found a small pump and fortunately it worked. Kyle also brought in dry wood and started a fire in the stove. Before she would use any of the utensils, Valissa heated water and washed everything as best she could. She then made coffee and fried some bacon. The saloon cook had sent bread so she said they'd have to make do with bacon and bread. There were no eggs. Neither was there milk or sugar for coffee.

Though she hated the thought of being left here alone, Valissa knew Kyle was going to have to go into town with a list if they were to survive in this place. She decided she'd use that time cleaning, and maybe taking a walk on the beach.

~ * ~

Deciding to leave his carriage in the barn, Nathan saddled one of his horses and headed toward the Colberts' house. The only thing he could figure out was that somehow Valissa got to her friend Rowena and managed to talk her into lending her the buggy to escape. But if that were so, why was the buggy returned home? There were no trains that left the station during the night and that was the best way to leave town other than by horse or buggy. Since she wasn't using Rowena's buggy, Valissa must be somewhere in town. But where?

He'd certainly spent enough time searching Tilley's place and the woman wasn't there. Neither was she in one of the boarding houses. Then a thought hit him. No, she wasn't at Tilley's, but could she be at one of his friends' places? Did he know someone who would hide Valissa for him? Though Nathan doubted Glenn Tilley could have such a friend, he knew he'd have to check out that possibility.

Then another thought hit him. Was Kyle Prescott in town? Could he have kidnapped his sister? Certainly if he did, he didn't snatch her from the house. It would have had to have been after she left Heartsong.

"Damn," Nathan muttered. "Why did she have to run away? She knew I was only going to be with Ada for a few minutes, then the wedding would have still taken place."

He gave the reins a sudden jerk and the horse reared. "Damn." His pulse quickened. "Surely she didn't think because I went into the study with Ada that I was abandoning her."

This realization stunned Nathan. It was then he knew that was exactly what she thought. He probably would have thought the same thing, though it was the furthest thing from the truth. And it could have been easily remedied. He should have had her come into the study with them. She had a right to hear everything that was said there. But fool that he was, he'd left her standing on the stairs, wondering why he'd suddenly gone away from her.

Nathan dug his heels into his horse's flanks and proceeded to the Colbert house in a gallop. He had to find out if anyone there had helped Valissa run away, then he'd return home to make sure Ada and Maurine were out of his house. He'd then return to his search for Valissa. If he didn't find her soon, he had the sinking feeling that something terrible might happen to the woman he wanted in his life forever. He wasn't sure when he'd come to realize he was in love with her.

~ * ~

Beverly Colbert was all a dither when the maid knocked on her door and told her Nathan Stone was there and wanted to speak with Rowena. "Put him in the parlor, Nellie and tell him we'll be down shortly."

"I did that, ma'am." Nellie twisted her hands in front of her. "He seems to be a very impatient man."

"What do you mean?" Beverly frowned.

"He said he was in a hurry, ma'am."

Beverly shook her head. "Don't let his gruff manner bother you, Nellie. All men are in a hurry. I'll get Rowena dressed and her hair done and we will be down. It shouldn't take more than an hour. I'm sure Mr. Stone won't mind waiting that long."

Nellie looked doubtful, but hurried out of the room.

Beverly put on her wrapper and went into Rowena's room. "Get up, dear. You have company waiting to visit you."

"Who?" A sleepy Rowena pulled the covers up under her chin and didn't bother to look at her mother.

Beverly rushed to the bed and pulled back the covers. "Nathan Stone is calling on you and you have to hurry and get yourself presentable. He's finally showing attention to you and your father is going to be very pleased. Now come on, dear, and get out of bed."

Rowena rubbed her eyes and sat up. "Why would he come to see me?"

"I'm sure it's because he's interested in you, Rowena. Now don't dawdle. We need to get downstairs as soon as we can. If we hurry…"

A knock on the door interrupted her. "Who is it?" Rowena called.

The door opened and Nellie stepped in. She had tears in her eyes. "It's me, Miss Rowena. I told Mr. Stone you'd be down within an hour and he yelled at me."

"What did he say?" Beverly frowned.

"He said for me to march right back up here and tell Miss Rowena if she wasn't in the parlor within five minutes, he was coming up here to get her."

Beverly gasped. "He wouldn't dare do that."

"I don't know, Mother." Rowena swung her legs from the bed and stood. Grabbing her robe, she added, "I fear he might do just what he said."

"But you can't go see him without dressing and fixing your hair and…"

Rowena grabbed a brush and smoothed her hair. Laying the brush back down on her dressing table, she said, "That'll have to do."

As she started out the door, Beverly cried, "You can't go down there. You'll be scandalized. It's not proper to receive a man in your night clothes."

"Would you rather he came up here, Mother?"

"Oh, my, no." Beverly put her hand to her breast. "I feel faint."

"Take care of her, Nellie," Rowena said and went out the bedroom door.

Rowena found Nathan pacing back and forth on the brightly colored Oriental rug in the parlor. "Good morning, Mr. Stone."

He whirled around. "Miss Colbert, I'm sorry to barge in on you like this, but I need your help."

"What can I do for you?"

Beverly came rushing through the door with Nellie right behind her. "Mr. Stone, this is so, so…I mean, I can't permit you to call on my daughter in this manner. It isn't…"

"I have to discuss something with your daughter, Mrs. Colbert."

"Well, the least you could do is let her get dressed and make herself presentable. It just isn't seemly for a young lady to meet with a gentleman while she's still in her night clothes. Surely you…"

"I don't give a damn if she's stark naked. Now, please leave us."

"Oh, my goodness…" Beverly again grabbed her breast and looked faint.

"Mother, why don't you go have cook send some coffee in here?"

Before anyone else could say anything, Nellie put her arm around Beverly Colbert. "Come with me, ma'am. I'll see that you have your smelling salts."

"Yes. I do need them." She let Nellie lead her from the room.

"I'm sorry about that, Mr. Stone." Rowena shook her head. "Please have a seat and tell me what it was you wanted me to do for you?"

He dropped to the fancy carved sofa. "First of all, Miss Colbert, I want you to tell me the truth about your relationship with Valissa."

"It's not secret. Valissa and I have been friends since we were babies." Rowena took the chair facing him.

"And you haven't decided you'll turn your back on her as has the rest of Galveston's society set?"

"I could never turn on her."

"Then you'd be willing to help her if she were in trouble?"

"Of course I would."

He paused and looked into Rowena's green eyes. His voice was blunt and demanding when he asked, "Did you loan her your buggy last night?"

"I…uh…I…"

"I see. You did."

Though flustered, Rowena said, "She said it was necessary for her to get away last night. I couldn't refuse her."

"Then how did the buggy get back to your house this morning?"

Rowena looked startled. "I didn't know it was back. Valissa said she'd leave it somewhere it would be easy to find, but I didn't expect them to bring it back here."

It was Nathan's time to be surprised. "Them? Who was with Valissa?"

Rowena hesitated.

"Come on. It's important that I know."

"I feel as if I'm betraying her."

"You may be saving her life, Rowena."

Her eyes widened and she muttered, "It was her brother."

"Damn. I hoped he'd not come back to Galveston."

"Why, Mr. Stone? Valissa and Kyle have always been close."

"I know. That's the problem."

"What do you mean?"

"I'm afraid he'll get her into something that will be hard for her to get out of."

"But…"

"I don't suppose she told you that Kyle killed a man in California and is a wanted man."

"Oh, no. Are you sure?"

"I'm positive."

"Then I did the wrong thing by letting her have my buggy."

"It's too late to think of that now, Miss Colbert. It's now time to see if we can figure out where they would have gone. It would have to be close enough for them to get the buggy back to your house before anyone saw them return it."

"What can I do to help?"

He stood. "I have an idea that might work, but I will need your help. I'm going to make sure my uninvited guests are put on the morning train to Fort Worth, but I'll be back for you. Can you be ready to go with me in an hour?"

"If it's necessary to save Valissa's life, of course I can."

"Very well. I'll be back." He nodded and went out the door without waiting to be escorted.

Beverly came back into the entry as Rowena was going up the stairs. "Where's Mr. Stone? I had Cook make breakfast for him because I thought you and he could eat on the veranda after you were dressed."

"He's gone, Mother."

"Why in the world would he leave? I'm sure he's interested in you if he insisted on coming here to see you like this, which I can overlook this one time. After all, he's an important man."

"I'm sure you can overlook it, Mother." Without giving her mother a chance to say anything else, she hurried to her room to dress.

Fifteen

"Do you think you can get into town and back without anyone seeing you, Kyle?" Valissa handed him the list of what she needed in the way of groceries and bed linens.

"I'm sure I can. I'll avoid the streets where I'd be known. There's a market close to the docks that the saloon cooks use. I'll go there for the food. I'll find a store that carries the other things."

She dug into her purse and handed him ten dollars. "This should buy all we need."

He looked disappointed as he glanced at the money. "Maybe I should go back to Tilley's and see what they have on your list in case this won't pay for it."

"I'm used to budgeting money for food and necessities, Kyle. I assure you that will pay for what I want with some left over."

He looked skeptical. "I still think I'll go to Tilley's first."

"It doesn't matter to me where you get the supplies. I only want them so we can be as comfortable as possible while we're here."

"We shouldn't have to stay here long. Soon your Mr. Stone will give up searching Tilley's for you and we can go back there."

Valissa give her brother a frown. "I have no intention of going to Tilley's, Kyle."

"I think you'll change your mind as soon as you see that's the best answer for both of us. I don't see why you're so hesitant about going there. Glenn is a nice man and he wants to help."

"I hope you're right, but I have my doubts." She eyed him. "What if I agreed to go to Tilley's and he wanted to put me to work?"

"There's no shame in work, Valissa. He said he only wants you to serve as his hostess. Most of the saloons have one."

"Then why doesn't he?"

"I don't know. It's his business." He shook his head and looked at the list she gave. "I'll get this and be back before evening. You will be safe here and there's no need to worry about me. I'll be careful."

"If you're not back before dark, I'll know something went wrong."

He leaned down and kissed her forehead. "You're such a worrier, little sister. Everything is going to be fine. Just you wait and see."

"I hope so." She didn't sound convinced.

Kyle shook his head again and headed for the buggy without saying anything else.

Valissa watched him drive off, and then turned back into the shack. She knew she had to keep herself busy or she would worry. She found a stub of a broom in the corner and tackled the floor. She then heated some water and scrubbed the table and the area around the stove. Putting the mattresses on the rail around the porch to air was her next job.

Finally, she looked through the supplies Tilley's cook had sent with them. She put the dried beans in a pan of water to soak and sliced more bacon. There was meal to make corn bread and a couple of apples. She was getting tired and hungry, so she ate one of them.

She figured by the position of the sun it was somewhere around three o'clock in the afternoon. It was time for Kyle to return, but she knew he'd probably take his time. With nothing else to do, she walked down to the water's edge and began to stroll along the white sandy beach. It had a calming effect on her and she didn't notice that the time was sliding into early evening.

~ * ~

Kyle Prescott was feeling good. His luck had turned. He was sure of it. He knew it was no coincidence that when he came by Tilley's and asked Glenn about linens for the cabin, Glenn sent him into the saloon to wait until he could get his cook or housekeeper to find some.

Not only had he just sat down to have a beer when two drunken sailors came in wanting to play cards. Seemed that they'd just gotten their pay and were spending it as fast as they could gamble and drink it away. "Jest gotta hold back a little for a woman tonight," one of them said with a snigger.

At first Kyle thought he'd better not use the money Valissa had given him for supplies to gamble, then he changed his mind. These fellows were so drunk he felt it would be easy to win more money off them. Valissa would be happy if he returned with all the stuff she wanted plus a handful of extra money.

His instinct had been right. The ten dollars she'd placed in his hand earlier had now turned into seventy-two. If he could keep these men playing until they ran out of their pay he was sure to see that seventy-two double. Maybe even triple or more.

He was right. Within an hour, his money had slid over the hundred dollar mark. He felt if he could keep this up, not only would he be able to give his sister her money back with extra, he'd also have enough to stake himself for a large game where he could win some big money. Money he could use to have him and Valissa living the kind of life they were born to live.

He sipped his sixth beer and continued playing.

Then something went haywire. He lost forty dollars. This didn't bother him too much. He knew the best of gamblers would have a losing hand now and then. But he lost the next four hands. His money had dwindled to thirty dollars.

In the recesses of his foggy mind, he wondered if he should quit and go for the food supplies Valissa wanted. He had enough to buy her some special things. Maybe that tea she liked so much or some candy. She was always fond of sweets.

But he continued to play. The next hand reduced his holdings to fifteen dollars.

Determined to get back to the amount he'd previously won, Kyle bet the fifteen dollars on two nines.

One of the sailors had three twos.

Throwing his cards on the table, he grabbed his beer glass and stumbled to the bar. Glenn was leaning against it. "Bad luck again?"

"I was doing good. I had over a hundred dollars. Then I started to lose a little at a time."

"I know. I've been watching. You should have quit when you were ahead."

"But I thought…" His words were slurred.

"I know what you thought, Kyle. You're like all men with the gambling fever. You began to feel you were going to win every hand. Drinking all that beer didn't help you keep your head clear either."

"I didn't drink much."

"The hell you didn't. Your bar bill is now over thirty dollars and you can hardly stand up. You'll be asleep on your feet soon."

"I can't. I've got to get back to Valissa."

"Are you going back without the food she wanted?"

"I… Maybe… She'll be upset."

"You're right about that. How are you going to explain to her that you lost her money and then some in a card game? How are you going to explain your drunken condition to her?"

Kyle looked at Glenn with glazed eyes. "I'm not that drunk."

"No?' Glenn shook his head and turned to the barkeep. "Give him some black coffee, Sid."

"I want another beer."

"Well, you're not going to get it. You're going to drink black coffee then go out in the crisp evening air and see if you can get yourself in shape to face your sister."

"She'll understand that I was trying to make more money for her."

"Well, you didn't make her a dime. You only lost what she had given you." He passed the mug of coffee the bartender gave him to Kyle and shook his head again. "It looks like we're going to have to put her to work here sooner than I thought. You're sure not going to be able to take care of her, so I guess I'll have to do it."

"You do need a hostess," Kyle muttered and sipped the hot coffee.

"I don't think she'll be able support your gambling habit on what she'll make being my hostess." Glenn had a sneer on his face.

"I won't gamble anymore."

Glenn threw back his head and laughed. "And I'm going to become mayor of Galveston."

Though he could hardly stand up, Kyle leaned on the bar and said, "If she can't work as a hostess, what can she do?"

"My friend, she can do what women have been doing for hundreds of years. She's young and beautiful and she'll soon have customers lining up and down the street to enjoy her favors."

Though Kyle was drunk, he knew exactly what Glenn was talking about. A sudden fury came over him. Valissa had been right. You couldn't trust Glenn Tilley.

Before he could stop himself, Kyle threw the hot coffee toward Glenn's face. He missed and the coffee dribbled down the red brocade vest. "Nobody is going to make a whore out of my sister."

Glenn was livid as he struck Kyle on the head with the whisky bottle at his elbow then wiped the front of his clothes with his silk handkerchief. "You bastard. After all I've done for you. Get out of my saloon."

"I don't think he heard you, Boss," Sid said. "Looks like he passed out when you hit him."

"Good. Throw him out of here. I got what I wanted from him and I don't need him anymore. If he comes back around here, shoot him." With that, Glenn turned and nodded toward the barkeep.

Sid returned the nod and moved from behind the counter.

Glenn didn't look back as he headed up the stairs to change his clothes. He'd go to the kitchen to gather the supplies Valissa wanted. He had a grin on his lips as the evil plan of what he'd do from there formed in his mind.

~ * ~

Sid dragged the unconscious Kyle by the back of his shirt out of the bar area, through the kitchen and toward the back door.

"Trouble?" The cook glanced at him.

"A little, but I can take care of it. Keep an eye on the bar until I return, Cookie."

Cookie nodded and Sid continued out the back door. They had reached the area behind the outhouse when Kyle began to stir. "What's going on," he muttered.

Sid dropped the grip he had on the collar and let Kyle's head hit the ground none too gently. "The boss wants you to stay out of his place."

Kyle started to sit up, but Sid kicked him in the ribs and he went back down. He moaned then said, "I don't understand."

"You don't have to understand. All you have to do is get the hell away from this saloon and never come back."

"But Valissa…"

Sid sneered. "Mr. Tilley has plans for your sister. It's best that you don't interfere with those plans."

"He's not going to make a whore out of my sister," Kyle roared through his pain.

"The hell he's not." Sid laughed and kicked Kyle again. This time in the stomach.

Kyle doubled up. "Why are you doing this?" His voice was breathless.

"This is just fair warning. Don't ever let the boss see you here again. If you come around when your sister starts to work, he'll kill you."

"I won't have Valissa coming…"

He didn't finish his sentence because Sid's big boot hit him in the face. Several kicks to Kyle's upper torso followed. Finally a last kick to the head sent the man into utter blackness.

Sid took a deep breath and looked at his victim. "You better heed what I said, fool. That is if you live to heed anything."

With that, he dragged Kyle to the back of the property that dropped off to a small creek. With his foot, he gave the body a shove and let it roll forward. He didn't wait to see if Kyle's body reached the creek.

~ * ~

The weather turned cooler in the afternoon. Rowena pulled her cape tighter around her as she sat in the buggy beside Nathan.

"Where to now?" Nathan looked at the woman beside him. He'd never dreamed that Rowena Colbert would have been as willing to go from place to place where she thought Valissa might have gone. It was a wise thing he did when he asked her to help him. She knew the city and she knew all the places the two women had visited together, both as grownups and as children.

Rowena took a deep breath. "Valissa's not Catholic, but she has often helped the nuns feed the poorer children in the city. Maybe we should try the church. I think they have vespers in a little while, but we should get there before they start."

"Point the way." Nathan turned the carriage when she indicated they should go down a street to the right.

"I know I've said this a dozen times today, Nathan, but I really don't think Valissa wants to be found."

"I know she doesn't, but that doesn't mean I don't intend to find her."

"You really like her, don't you?"

He chuckled. "I don't think like is a strong enough word. Believe it or not, I love the woman."

She eyed him. "If you love her, why did you take her home away?"

"I didn't take it away. I bought if from a cousin of mine who won it in a card game with her brother. He had no real use for it and I needed a home in Galveston. He wanted the money for it so the deal worked out well for both of us." He smiled a little. "Only thing, I didn't expect to find Valissa still living in the house. That irritated me at first, but it wasn't long until I got used to her presence."

"You understand, don't you, that when it became known Valissa had lost the house, it brought shame upon her name?"

"I know it did. I just didn't understand why. It wasn't her fault her brother gambled it away."

Rowena sighed. "I didn't understand it either. Valissa is the same person she was before Kyle lost the estate or you took over

Heartsong. I can't understand why everyone had decided it was somehow her fault that Kyle did such a thing,"

"I think the man should be shot."

Rowena couldn't help it. She laughed. "Well, maybe not shot, but I wish somebody would shake some sense into him."

"If they did, it would still be too late to help Valissa." He arched an eyebrow. "I guess the fact that she stayed in the house with me there hasn't helped her reputation, has it?"

"I'm afraid you're right. People, mostly women, are saying she should be ashamed of staying there un-chaperoned since she's an unmarried woman. The fact that she didn't have the money to move out didn't matter to them." She touched his arm lightly. "The church is on the next corner."

The nuns tried to help, but none of them had seen or heard from Valissa in several weeks. They promised to send word if they heard anything in the future.

Back in the buggy, Nathan said, "It's way past the noon hour. I'm hungry and I know you must be."

"I could eat a bite, but I don't want to give up until we find my friend."

"Then do you mind if we go back to my house? I'm sure Flo will have something we can eat. Besides, Valissa could have decided to come home."

"I think it's a good idea to check your house."

Nathan turned the buggy in the direction of Heartsong.

~ * ~

Lyman Colbert was looking at the books and wondering how thorough Nathan Stone had been going over the copies he'd given him. It was only during this second scrutiny that Lyman had noticed some of the discrepancies in the figures. He was feeling a little scared about what Nathan would do when there was a knock on his office door.

"Yes." He couldn't keep the irritability out of his voice.

Before she could be announced, Beverly swept through the door. "Lyman, I have to see you."

He frowned and put the book aside. He nodded at the clerk, who promptly stepped back and closed the door.

"What in the world is the matter, Beverly? You never come to the bank to see me."

"It's about Rowena."

"Don't tell me she's gone to see that Prescott girl again and you're upset about it."

"I wish it were that simple." Beverly lowered her ample form into one of the chairs in front of Lyman's desk. "It concerns that businessman, Nathan Stone."

"What in the world does he have to do with Rowena?"

"I don't know."

"Then why are you concerned?"

She sighed. "He came to the house before we were out of bed this morning and demanded to see Rowena. He wouldn't even give her time to dress and make herself presentable to be called upon. He demanded she come down in her nightclothes."

"He must have had something important to see her about."

"I don't know what it was. When I went to have breakfast made for the two of them, he left. Rowena hurried upstairs and got dressed. By the time she ate a small breakfast, he returned and they left together. He wouldn't give me time to get dressed to chaperone them."

"Well, my dear, maybe he didn't want a chaperone."

"I know he didn't. He told me so. He said they had something to do and I would be in the way. Can you believe it? Me, be in the way? How could he be so crass?"

"Mr. Stone is a forthright and demanding man. You must have misunderstood his meaning."

"I did not. He took our daughter off in a buggy and I haven't seen hair nor hide of her since. I want to know where they were going and why they haven't come back."

"I assure you, Beverly, I have no idea, but I wouldn't worry about it. Mr. Stone is an upstanding citizen and it wouldn't upset me one bit if he and Rowena ran off and got married or something."

"Lyman, how could you?"

"It's true, my dear. Nathan Stone owns this bank and it's not the only one he owns. I also found out he has an interest in the shipping industry here and there are real estate properties in the downtown business section that he owns. He rents it out to the merchants. I know he has a big ranch somewhere and from what I'm to understand, he's thinking of buying some more businesses in town. Our Rowena could do a lot worse."

"But, Lyman, I'm afraid since he's been living with that Prescott girl, her shame will somehow reflect on us."

"I doubt that."

"It could. What would Mrs. Maxmillion say if she heard Rowena entertained Mr. Stone in her nightclothes?"

"Probably nothing."

"You don't know that."

He smiled. "I'll tell you something if you promise not to tell another living person, Beverly." He knew when he asked this, she'd probably tell it before he came home for supper.

"What?"

"Do you promise not to tell?"

"Of course."

"Nathan Stone owns the controlling interest in Maxmillion Cooperation."

Beverly dropped the handkerchief she was twiddling into her lap. "You don't mean…"

"Yes, my dear. I do mean what you're thinking. The woman who marries Nathan Stone will certainly replace Mrs. Maxmillion as the queen of society in Galveston. Wouldn't you just love for that to be our Rowena?"

"Oh, Lyman, that would be the most wonderful thing I could imagine."

"I thought so. Now you go along home and don't worry another minute about Rowena and Mr. Stone." He stood and smiled at her. "You might even say a prayer that our Rowena will be that lucky woman. It would be a crowning glory for all our family."

Beverly walked out of the office as if she had wings on her feet. Lyman knew she'd not spend another minute worrying about what people would think of Stone calling on Rowena when she was in her robe. He, on the other hand, was quite worried about what was going to happen if he didn't find out who was playing with the bank books before Nathan Stone did.

Sixteen

The sun had slipped low in the horizon when Valissa heard horses coming up the path to the shack. She gave a sigh of relief. "It's about time you got back, Kyle," she muttered and went to the door.

The buggy pulled to the side of the porch and she was surprised when Glenn Tilley hopped out.

"Where's Kyle?" she demanded.

The man had the audacity to smile at her. "He took sick and I insisted he be put to bed at my place."

"Then I must go to him."

"No, Valissa. He'll be all right." He reached into the back and brought out a box. "I knew you needed these supplies tonight, so I decided to bring them to you before things got busy at my place."

There was nothing she could do but step aside and let him carry the box into the cabin. He then returned and got another one.

After placing the third and last one on the table, he looked about the place. "You've been cleaning."

"Yes. It was a terrible mess."

"I'm sorry. It was never meant for a nice lady like you. Only a few fishing friends of mine use this place."

Valissa didn't tell him that while she was cleaning she'd found evidence that women had been in the cabin. "I didn't mind straightening up. I had to have something to do."

"I understand." He looked at the boxes. "Shall I help you put these supplies away?"

"No. I want you to tell me what happened to my brother. He was fine when he left here."

"He'll be fine again. Just give him a little time."

She eyed him. "You're evading the issue, Glenn Tilley."

He took a deep breath and put a sorrowful look on his face. "I wish you wouldn't press the issue, Valissa."

She put her hands on her hips. "Quit quibbling and tell me. What is wrong with my brother?"

Glenn shook his head. "I didn't want to tell you, but since you insist, Kyle is drunk. Too drunk to handle a horse and buggy. In fact, he's so inebriated he passed out and I had him put to bed."

Valissa felt her heart sink. She was so hoping he'd get the supplies she wanted and come straight back to the cabin, but she feared he wouldn't. "Was he gambling, too?"

"I'm afraid so."

"Then how did you get these supplies?" When he didn't answer, she went on. "I won't take charity, Mr. Tilley. How much do I owe you?"

"You don't owe me a thing, my dear."

"Yes, I do and I insist on paying you."

He shook his head. "If you must know, when Kyle had won a couple of hands, I managed to snatch some money from him. I was sure I'd have to get the supplies for you and I was just as sure that you wouldn't want me paying for them."

"You're right there."

He took her hand in his. "Not that I would have minded. I only want to help you in your plight, my dear."

She almost believed him, but something kept telling her to be careful. "I appreciate that, but as long as I can, I'll pay my own way."

"I understand." He dropped her hand. "I would insist that you come back to my place with me for the night, but I'm still afraid you'd be discovered there. Stone actually sent his man Phillips to search the saloon for you today. I just can't take a chance on you being found."

She nodded. "I'm sure I'll be fine here."

"But I don't want to leave you alone." He shook his head. "I should have brought Kyle with me, drunk or not."

"I'll be fine."

Glenn slipped his arm around her shoulder. "I suppose you will. It's just that a lady shouldn't be left alone on a deserted beach."

Valissa tensed and told Glenn a lie. "I heard some children playing in the water not far from here. I'm sure if I needed someone, I could scream loud enough for those people to hear."

"Good. I was going to offer to stay with you, but you're right. You could probably make them hear if you got in trouble." He smiled down at her. "Of course, I want you to trust me and I guess the only way to do that is to leave."

"I appreciate your concern, Glenn, but I'd really be uncomfortable with you here."

"I understand." He kissed her forehead and let her go. "I'll send your brother back in the morning. You be sure to lock up before you go to bed."

She nodded. "I will. Thank you for everything, Glenn."

"You're welcome, my dear." He bent and kissed her forehead again then strode out the door.

~ * ~

Glenn pulled the buggy into the road leading back to town. He was pleased with himself, though it had taken restraint. When he went into the cabin and saw Valissa there with her trim figure, the dress hugging her ample breast and the beautiful raven hair piled on top of her head, all he'd wanted to do was grab her, throw her on one of the beds and have his way with her. But he'd known right away if he did, he'd never bend the stubborn woman to his will. He had to win her confidence and respect first and the only way to do that was with patience and kindness.

This evening he knew he'd made inroads. Of course she'd lied when she said there were children on the beach, but he let her think he believed her. He knew that was a point in his favor. It was also in his favor that he'd not make one inappropriate move toward her. The gentle kisses on the forehead had shown that he really wanted to be her friend and he knew she'd accepted it in that manner.

As for the lie about Kyle, he had that thought out, too. Tomorrow he'd return sometime after mid-day and tell her he was sorry, but somehow Kyle had slipped out and he'd spent most of the morning looking for him. He'd then tell her that he was missing a couple of bottles of his good whiskey and the money they kept in a box behind the bar at all times.

He expected she'd be upset and begin to cry. He'd comfort her and he'd be a little more aggressive than today, but not much. He'd hold her in his arms and then he'd gently kiss her lips. That would be all for the day. He'd stay with her. Maybe let her fix them some food, then he'd leave her alone again with the promise that he'd search again for Kyle.

Grinning, he continued to work out the scenario in his mind. He'd managed to hook some women in a few days, but he decided he'd spend a week with Valissa. First he'd show his concern and caring, while getting a little more aggressive with his attention each day. At the end of the week, he was sure she'd trust him completely. He'd then make love to her on one of the beds and tell her how he'd grown to love her. He was sure she would feel the same way about him.

He knew he was a handsome man with his flashing dark eyes, always neatly trimmed black hair and his impeccable dress. It didn't take most women he wanted long to fall for his charms.

It was the perfect solution. He'd done it before and right here on the beach in this very cabin. Hell, the world might think it was for fishing, but he knew better. It was where he brought the women to make them fall so in love with him that they'd gladly go to the upstairs rooms in his saloon just to please him.

A little frown crossed his face. For the first time, it bothered him that after getting her in the right frame of mind to be one of his girls, he didn't like the idea of her giving her favors to other men.

Shaking his head, Glenn muttered, "Get a hold on your thinking, man. Valissa Prescott is going to make you a lot of money working in your upstairs."

That thought didn't make him feel much better.

~ * ~

Something wasn't right. Every bone in his body hurt. It was cold and damp and dark and he smelled blood and dirt. He tried to sit up, but it was near impossible. Lying there on his stomach, Kyle wondered if he was dying. Somebody told him once that when he was about to enter hell he'd feel pain, smell bad smells and it would cold and dark. If they were right, he was on the verge of getting his afterlife reward or punishment, which seemed to be the more appropriate description.

Kyle wasn't mad. How could he be? He deserved hell if anyone did. The things he'd done in his past assured him of that. Why, the fact that he'd ruined his own life was bad enough, but he had the knowledge that he'd ruined his sister's as well. Then there was the fact that he'd shot a man in California. It didn't' matter that the man was coming at him with a knife. What had mattered to the authorities was the fact that the man had been married to the mayor's daughter. A woman of questionable character. A woman who had not only seduced Kyle, but had planned to run away with him just because she wanted to make her husband jealous.

Worst of all, he'd come back to Galveston and brought not only shame to his sister, but was responsible for the evil plans Glenn Tilley had made for her. Plans he knew Valissa would be forced to accept, since there was nobody to protect her now.

Kyle frowned into the night. Was the man who was looking for his sister as bad as Tilley? He couldn't be. At least from the gossip he'd heard around the saloon, the man had threatened to kill Tilley if he laid a hand on Valissa. He hoped the gossip was true.

Again Kyle tried to get up. This time he made it to a standing position. Though he thought he was going to die from the pain, he forced himself to take a step up the bank. He then paused and decided he'd better not go back in the direction of Tilley's place. He turned to his left and headed along the stream. After he'd gone several yards, he decided to climb back toward the street. He headed away from the docks, thankful that Tilley hadn't thrown him in the bay instead of the creek behind his saloon.

After stumbling along for several yards, he did turn toward the street. Though he wasn't sure it would be safe to be seen, he managed to get several blocks from the saloon before his legs began to crumple under him.

"No," he said aloud. "You have to keep going. You've caused Valissa enough harm. You have to keep going."

This renewed him and he trudged on, not sure of where he was going. He only knew he had to find somebody to help his sister.

Kyle came to a stop at the edge of town. At least he was away from the docks. He struggled to the side of a sign near the residential area he was entering. "Keep going," he whispered. "You can do it."

But this time it was too much. Kyle's legs buckled and he fell. The last thing he remembered, he was trying to get back on his feet.

~ * ~

Rowena came in the door at supper time. She tried to slip upstairs, but her mother had been watching for her.

"Oh, darling, I'm so glad you're home. I've been waiting breathlessly to hear about your day with Mr. Stone."

"Why, Mother? I thought you were upset because he showed up here this morning."

"That was before I talked with your father. He made me see that it was all right for you to go with the man without me as a chaperone."

"Good." Rowena again tried for the steps.

"You can't go to your room without eating, dear. Come along. You can tell your father and me all about your day as we dine."

"There's really nothing to tell." Rowena wished Nathan hadn't asked her not to let her parents know he was searching for Valissa. She wasn't sure why, but she wouldn't break her word to him.

"I'm sure that's not so. You must be full of news." Beverly turned toward the dining room. "Come along, now."

Rowena sighed, removed her bonnet, placed it on the rack in the entry and followed her mother. She thought fast, trying to invent a good story to tell her family as she went. Maybe she would tell her family that Nathan Stone had asked her to show him the town since he hadn't lived here long.

She might even say they were going to finish the tour later. Surely that would satisfy her mother. She wasn't sure about her father, but she'd make it up to him later. He was the one person Rowena had never been able to lie to.

~ * ~

"Mr. Nathan, you've got to get some rest. You look as if you're about to fall on your face." Flo put a plate of fried pork, stewed turnips, chopped turnip greens and honeyed carrots in front of him.

"I can't rest until I find her, Flo. Anything could happen to her out there."

"I know, sir, but if you drop dead, you're not going to do Miss Valissa or yourself either one any good." She poured him a second cup of steaming coffee.

Nathan gave her a smile. "Thank you for caring, Flo, and I promise you I will rest tonight. I'm going to Tilley's to make one more search. If I don't find her there, I'll come back and sleep a little before I start looking again."

Flo sighed. "You didn't get any good leads today, did you?"

"Not a one."

She shook her head. "I was hoping that little Colbert girl would be able to help you."

"Oh, she did. Now I know where not to look."

There was a moment of silence and Flo started back for the kitchen, but turned. "May I ask you something?"

"Of course."

"Why did you turn your back on Miss Valissa and leave the room with your mother and that woman?"

He looked up at her. "She thought it meant I didn't care, didn't she, Flo?"

203

"Yes she did. She said your ranch was more important than her or anything else. She also thought you wanted to make up with the woman."

He dropped his head. "I know I didn't handle it right, but Valissa is so wrong. I was only stunned when Ada said she was going to disinherit me. I wanted to let her know once and for all that it didn't matter if she did. I intended to marry Valissa anyway."

"I wish Miss Valissa had known."

"How could she, Flo? I may have thought the way she did if the situation were turned around. That's why I've got to find her. She might do something rash."

"What do you mean?"

"I'm afraid she'll go to Tilley's place. She only half believed me when I told her he only wanted to be nice to her because he wanted to trick her into working in his bordello."

Flo gasp. "Surely not."

"I hope not, Flo. I really hope not." He pushed back his plate. "I'll be back soon. Pray that I find Valissa this time."

"I will, Mr. Nathan."

Nathan had been gone only about ten minutes when Flo and Alvin discussed the situation in the kitchen. As she dried the dishes, he waited for her to finish so they could go to their rooms.

"It's a mess, Alvin. I'm like Mr. Nathan. I don't think I can sleep again until Miss Valissa is found."

"I know how you feel. I took another walk after finishing up my work thinking I might get a clue as to where she went. Of course I didn't find any trace of her."

There was a sudden noise on the back porch. Flo looked at her husband with fright in her eyes. "I wonder if that could be…"

"I'll see what it was, Flo. It could have been a dog or something."

She nodded as Alvin went to the door.

As soon as he opened it, he exclaimed, "Oh, my lord. It's Mr. Kyle."

Flo ran to the door. "He looks like he's hurt bad. Bring him in here."

Kyle muttered something, but neither of them could understand what he said.

"Let's put him in his old room, Alvin. I'll see what I can do for him and you can go fetch a doctor."

"How about Mr. Nathan?"

"He'll be back soon."

Alvin nodded and put Kyle's arm around his neck. He practically had to drag the man into the house. "I'll get him to bed. You get some hot water to wash him and we'll do what we can for him. I'll go get the doctor then."

Seventeen

It was almost eight o'clock the next morning when Nathan came into Kyle's room. "He still the same?"

Alvin turned from his vigil beside the bed. "The same. He hasn't said a word except mutter Valissa's name a time or two, just like he did last night."

"Since the doctor said if he was going to wake up at all, he could do it at any time, and I sure wish he'd go ahead."

"Though we'd like to, we can't rush these things, Mr. Nathan."

"I know, Alvin." He glanced at the empty coffee cup on the table beside the bed. "Have you had breakfast?"

"Not yet, but Flo brought me some coffee a little while ago."

"Why don't you go on down and eat? I'll be here for a while."

"Flo will probably have your breakfast done. You can go eat first."

"No. I'll wait. I want to sit here and think about things for a while."

Alvin nodded and left the room.

Nathan took the chair Alvin had vacated. He watched Kyle carefully and wondered what was in the man's head that would lead him to Valissa. He also wondered what had gone wrong that had made him end up in this condition. He knew when Rowena saw him with Valissa, he'd been in a healthy state. If he hadn't been, she would have surely mentioned it.

"Wake up and talk to me, Prescott," Nathan demanded, but Kyle didn't open his eyes or move.

Nathan looked him over. The man was tall. Not as tall as Nathan, but tall by the day's standards. He wore his dark hair neatly trimmed and it was the same color as Valissa's. He wondered if his eyes were the same aqua blue. He shook his head and wondered why a man who seemed to have everything going for him would do the things this one had done.

When he'd returned from Tilley's the night before, Nathan had wanted to beat the man into talking. Of course he realized that would be impossible since Kyle was already clinging to life from a beating from someone. The doctor was here and said he'd never seen anyone so bruised and battered, but he would probably pull out of it. He did tell them to watch for any signs of gasping for breath or unusual moans. It could mean Prescott was injured on the inside so bad that no doctor could do him any good.

Nathan guessed since the man had made it through the night, he would eventually recover. He just wished he'd do it sooner than later.

A knock sounded on the door, then it opened. Flo appeared with a tray. "Alvin said you refused to come down so I brought your breakfast to you."

Nathan grinned. "Thank you, Flo."

"I knew you wouldn't bother coming down for a while." She set the tray on the table and looked at him. "You eat, now, Mr. Nathan. I know you're going to set here until Mr. Kyle wakes up, but you have to keep up your strength."

He nodded. "I guess that's why you made me go to bed last night with the promise that you or Alvin would sit with him."

"Yes it was. You were near dead on your feet, but I must admit you look much better this morning."

"I feel much better, Thank you again for making me get some rest."

"Are you going out again to look for Miss Valissa?"

"Not for a while. I think the best chance of finding her is waiting until I can talk to her brother."

She nodded and started for the door. "I'll check on you in a little while."

He reached for his food and only nodded as she went out the door.

~ * ~

It was almost ten o'clock when Rowena left her house. Her mother had wanted to accompany her, but Rowena said no. She told her she wanted to pick up something at Mrs. Dupree-Fontaine's shop and she planned to call on Candice Maxmillion. She assured her mother it wouldn't be wise for her to be along. After all, Mrs. Maxmillion didn't receive callers without knowing they were coming.

This was another lie Rowena had told her mother. She had no intention of going to either the dress shop or to the Maxmillions. She wanted to talk to her father.

Pulling her buggy up in front of the bank, she climbed down and hurried inside. "Is Daddy here?"

"I think he's in Mr. Bower's office, Miss Colbert, but I'm sure he wouldn't mind your waiting in his office."

"Thank you." Rowena went into the private office. She started to take a chair in front of her father's desk, but noticed the door to the little room adjoining the office was ajar.

She smiled and went into that room. It was small, but her father called it his getaway spot when things got too harried in the bank. Actually it was a small room with a safe, some files and a bench in one end. She knew he not only came here to hide, but he often worked in the area.

Since she'd been a little girl, the room had been a play area to her. He often let her bring toys and stay here while he conducted business. He was especially good about letting her and her girlfriend Valissa have tea parties on the bench when his wife and Valissa's mother needed to shop alone.

Grinning, Rowena moved to the bench and sat down. She was awash in memories of the good times of her childhood when she heard her father enter the office. She knew Milton Bower was with him because the two men seemed to be in some kind of spat.

Rowena stood to greet them, but stopped when she heard her father say, "How could you have done it, Milton? I might have suspected a common thief, but you're our solicitor as well as a board member of the bank."

"It wasn't all that bad, Lyman." Milton's voice sounded strained. "I'll put the money back and nobody ever needs to know."

Rowena sat back on the bench with her eyes wide. She couldn't believe what she was hearing. Was her father saying that Milton Bower was stealing from the bank?

The chair behind her father's desk squeaked as he sat. "I'm afraid it's not that simple. I gave Nathan Stonc a set of the books because he wanted to check on them. He plans to put a lot of money into this bank. If he hasn't already seen the discrepancy, he will find it soon."

"You didn't give him a copy of the Prescott trust fund, did you?"

Rowena could tell her father was agitated because he quickly snapped, "Don't tell me you've pilfered money from the Prescotts."

"Not much."

"What the hell do you mean, not much? Have you taken some of their money or not?"

"You've got to understand, Lyman. I had to do something."

"Why?"

"You know how Thelma is. She keeps all the money in the household and she'd know if I spent a dime more than what she allots me."

"What does that have to do with anything?"

"Well, I'm not sure if I can make you understand because you and Beverly have a good marriage."

"I thought you had a good marriage, too."

"Oh, to the public, we do have, but at home it's hell living with Thelma."

"You're not making any sense, Milton."

"I bet you didn't know that Thelma and I have separate bedrooms. We have had for the past fifteen years."

There was a moment's silence. Finally Lyman said, "So a lot of couples managed to have a good marriage and sleep in separate rooms."

"We're not one of those lucky couples. In all those years, I haven't touched Thelma. The one time I tried, she threatened to divorce me. She'd do it, too."

"Maybe you should get a divorce."

"I can't do that. All that we have comes from Thelma's family money. She said she'd be my wife in public, but as for our life at home, it would remain nonexistent until one of us dies." Milton laughed. "I've actually thought of creating an accident so she would be out of my life forever."

"I can't believe all this. How did it come about?"

"It was such a simple thing. I went to a convention in New Orleans without my wife. It was a festive time and at one of the parties they threw, I drank too much. I ended up with one of the ladies of the night." Rowena heard him sigh, then go on. "I felt so guilty that I came home and confessed to Thelma. She hasn't forgiven me to this date."

"I'm sorry that happened, but it still doesn't give you the right to steal from the bank or the Prescotts."

"I guess not, but a man has to have some things just to get by."

"Like what?"

"Damn it, Lyman. I'm not that much older than you and like you I need a woman now and again. If a man's wife denies him, the women he can get are not cheap."

"You mean you're going to prostitutes?"

"Yes, occasionally I do."

"I still don't understand why you had to steal."

"I already told you. Thelma controls all our money. She'd know if I used a dime in a bordello."

"Then why the hell didn't you take a mistress, Milton?"

"That was my goal."

"What do you mean?"

"Ever since I met Valissa Prescott as a budding teenager, I've wanted her."

"You're kidding." Rowena heard the shock in her father's voice.

"No, I'm not kidding. When I'd go to Heartsong to conduct business with her father, she'd serve us coffee or she'd greet me with a nice smile. I liked the girl. Then when she came back from school, I knew I had to have her someday. Then I saw my chance to make her my mistress."

"How in the world were you going to do that?"

Milton seemed to warm to his subject. "It was easier than you think. I began to take some of Kyle Prescott's money, too. I knew he'd never miss it because he was too busy drinking, gambling and lying up with whores. I'm the one who convinced him to let me have the authority over his sister's estate, then I assured him that he could make back his fortune by gambling. I pushed him to leave Galveston and seek his fortune in the saloons and gambling houses out west so I'd have a better chance of getting Valissa. It was easy to cut down on the allowance he was supposed to validate for her each month. I knew if I could break her, she'd have to do something. It was then I planned to step in and offer to keep her home going for the both of us. Then that damn fool brother of hers lost the estate in a poker game. I still thought I might be able to buy it back because I've hidden the money I took from them. I just didn't count on Nathan Stone buying the place. He messed the whole thing up."

"I don't think so, Milton. It looks to me that you've not only messed up things, but your mind seems to be messed up, too."

"Not really. You see, I've invested some of Valissa's money in a saloon and brothel down on the docks. She happened in there to sell some of her dresses and the owner decided then and there he wanted the beautiful Valissa to work as one of his girls."

"There's no way Valissa Prescott would ever become a whore in a place like that."

"She may not have a choice. Glenn has her brother so deep in debt to him he'll never be able to pay it off. Glenn told him he wanted his sister to come to work there as a hostess and he'd forgive the debt." He chuckled. "Of course Glenn lied to Kyle. He means to send Valissa upstairs soon. Then I'll have my time with the beautiful woman."

Rowena heard her father stand. His voice sounded disgusted as he said, "I've heard enough, Milton."

"Then you see. Things can be worked out."

"Why don't you go back to your office? I have some thinking to do."

"Thank you, Lyman. I knew you'd understand." His chair scraped on the rug when he got up. "Who knows, if Beverly ever fails you, you may want to take a turn with Valissa Prescott, too."

Lyman's voice sounded even more disgusted when he said, "Go on, Milton. I'll talk with you later."

The door closed and Rowena sat frozen in unbelief, not knowing what to. She couldn't let her father know she'd heard the entire conversation. He'd be mortified. On the other hand, she couldn't stay in this room hoping he'd leave his office again. He could come in the little room at any time.

Though it consisted of anther lie to her father, Rowena had an idea. She moved back to the bench stretched out on it and dropped her purse to the floor. She then groaned and muttered something.

The door to the room jerked open. "Rowena, what in the world are you doing here."

She sat up and stretched. "Oh, Daddy, you're back."

He nodded.

"I wanted to speak to you and I must have fallen asleep. What time is it?"

"It's a little after ten." He looked worried, but he didn't elaborate.

"Oh, my goodness. I need to hurry. I was going to Mrs. Dupree-Fontaine's shop for a pair of evening gloves."

"But you wanted to see me first?"

"Yes." She bent and picked up her purse. "Do you have a minute for me?"

"Of course I do, dear. What did you want to talk to me about? Do you need some money?" He looked as if he were relaxing a little.

"No. It's nothing like that. I just wanted to apologize to you." Rowena tried to keep her voice even so he'd never suspect she'd overheard the conversation he'd had with Milton Bower.

He frowned. "For what?"

She dropped her head. "I lied to you and Mother last night. I can't apologize to Mother because she wouldn't understand, but I can't keep lying to you."

"What did you lie about, honey?"

"I told you that Nathan Stone wanted me to show him Galveston, but that's not so. He wanted me to help him look for Valissa. She's disappeared."

"What do you mean, disappeared?"

"She ran out of the house night before last and didn't tell anyone where she was going."

Lyman lifted an eyebrow. "Why would he ask you to help find her?"

"He knows Valissa and I are good friends."

"But he's a big businessman. Why would he care if Miss Prescott left without telling him?"

"Can you keep a secret, Daddy?"

"Yes, I certainly can."

"He doesn't want anyone to know it yet, but Nathan Stone is in love with Valissa."

Layman looked stunned, but he finally asked. "Will you be seeing Mr. Stone again?"

Rowena thought fast. "Yes. He asked me to come by his house this morning and let him know if I'd heard from Valissa."

He didn't ask why his daughter might hear from Valissa Prescott. He only looked into her eyes. "Will you do me a favor, child?"

"Sure, I will."

"Would you go see Mr. Stone before you go to Mrs. Dupree-Fontaine's dress shop?" When she nodded, he went on. "Please tell

Mr. Stone that I need to see him right away. Ask him to please come to the bank."

"I'll do that."

He leaned down and kissed his daughter's forehead. "Thank you, Rowena. Now don't you worry about your mother. We'll be able to handle her together."

Rowena smiled. "I knew you'd understand, Daddy."

Eighteen

Less than an hour later, Rowena sat by Kyle's bed and studied the man's face as her father's conversation filtered through her mind. Would he have really taken his sister to a brothel to clear his gambling debt? She guessed he would. After all, a man who would gamble his sister's home away would do anything.

She shook her head. Why couldn't Kyle Prescott be more like Nathan Stone? Why, the minute she told the man that her father wanted to see him, he said, "You'll have to tell your father I'm sorry I can't come, Rowena. Finding Valissa is my top priority today."

It was only after she told him that the visit with her father would probably give him clues as to where Valissa was that he got up and rushed out. Of course, he was thoughtful enough to ask her if she'd sit with Kyle until he got back.

Now here she was in the room of the man who she'd secretly loved most of her life. Although she'd pretended in her daydreams that he had thought she was special, too, he'd never even shown the slightest interest in her. Looking down at the cuts and bruises on his once handsome face, she wondered if he'd have many scars. Or would he be blind in one eye as Flo had indicated he might. Whoever had beaten him had meant to kill him. That was obvious.

He might deserve the beating, even killing, if what her father and Milton Bower had said was true. Yet she couldn't help herself. She still felt something for him. She didn't want to. He was a scoundrel. A low-down mean man and in her mind, an outlaw. He'd not only ruined Valissa's reputation in Galveston, but he'd ruined her life and he probably didn't care what happened to her anyway. If that man who owned the saloon got his hands on Valissa and turned her into a whore, it would be all Kyle's fault.

Oh, how Rowena wanted to hate him, but for some reason she couldn't. Maybe it was because she remembered the many times she'd visited at Heartsong and Kyle had insisted he accompany them on their excursions because he said he didn't want anything happening to his little sister and her friend. Maybe it was because he was the first man to kiss her and make her shiver inside.

At the time, she'd thought it was the most wonderful kiss in the world. All other kisses she'd received from boys to that date had been on the top of her hand, usually through gloves. But Kyle had kissed on the face and it was the first time anyone other than her father had ever dared to kiss her face. It had been a wonderful sweet kiss, though admittedly it had been planted in a brotherly way on her forehead as he was welcoming her and Valissa home from boarding school when he'd met them at the train station. Still Rowena had spent many nights dreaming about and hoping that one day Kyle would kiss her again. Maybe even on the mouth next time.

"Oh, Kyle," she whispered with tears in her eyes. "How could you have done such a terrible thing to your sister?"

Kyle muttered.

Rowena's eyes got big and she stared at the man. "Are you trying to say something?"

He muttered again.

She didn't understand what he said, so she leaned over him and put her ear to his mouth.

This time she was sure he said, "Save Valissa."

~ * ~

Nathan stared across the banker's desk. "Are you sure about this, Colbert?"

"I'm positive. I had him in my office less than an hour ago and he confessed."

"Then he needs to be arrested today."

"I thought of that, but I was hesitant about calling in the law before I talked with you. I knew you'd know what to do in case there's more to it."

"What do you mean, more to it?"

"I'm not sure Milton Bower acted alone in taking money. He may have had help from right here in the bank. If there was someone else, I don't know how to proceed to find out who it was."

Nathan cocked any eye. "You're probably right. Maybe we should lay low until he leads us to his accomplice, if there is one."

"That's what's bothering me." Layman looked uncomfortable. He took out his handkerchief and wiped his brow. "I hate to admit this, but since I found out what he was doing, I'm not sure who to trust to help me keep an eye on him. I thought he was one of the most upstanding men in the bank. A week ago I would have staked my life on it."

"What about your nephew? Doesn't he work here?"

"He does, but I don't think Wilbur is the one we want. I find him irresponsible in some of his duties and he's lazy as well." Colbert shook his head. "I think ever since he came to live with us, he's only had one goal in mind and that was to marry Valissa Prescott and inherit Heartsong."

"We both know that's not going to happen." Nathan couldn't keep the anger out of his voice.

"Speaking of Miss Prescott, Milton also confessed that he'd pilfered the trust account of both the Prescott heirs."

Nathan sat up straight. "He what?"

"Said he'd been taking from the fund. He said he'd been encouraging Kyle Prescott to gamble and he'd been cutting down on Valissa's monthly allowance to run the estate. I don't understand it, but he had some crazy notion of making her so desperate she'd become his mistress."

Nathan was shocked, but not enough to become livid. "There's no way in hell she'd succumb to that."

"That's what I told him. Then he said he'd still have her because he'd invested in a saloon and the owner is planning to make a whore of her. He even had the gall to suggest I'd like to come there to sample her favors."

Nathan stood so quickly that the heavy chair he sat in rocked and almost toppled over. His voice was a roar when he demanded "Where's Bower's office?"

"Mr. Stone, you look ready to murder the man. Let me send for him."

"I want him here now and I'm not promising what I'll do when he arrives."

"Yes, sir." Lyman hurried to the door and motioned for one of the tellers. "Please ask Mr. Bower to come to my office immediately. It's very important."

The teller hurried away.

In only minutes the teller returned. "I'm sorry, Mr. Colbert, but Mr. Bower left, sir. Nobody seems to know where he went."

"When did he leave?"

"Someone said he left right after he came back from your office."

"I think I know where he went." Nathan grabbed his hat and put it on.

"Where, Mr. Stone?"

He turned and looked at Lyman. "Tilley's Place down on the docks. That man's been after Valissa and I'm going to stop him permanently."

"Please, Mr. Stone." Lyman's eyes widened.

"Nobody's going to stop me."

Lyman came around his desk and put his hand on Nathan's arm. "What good would you do Valissa if you were put in jail for killing a man?"

Nathan paused.

"It's true. I know you care for the woman and you want to kill any man who wants to cause her harm, but that would be the wrong thing to do. Now's the time to keep your head."

Nathan stared at him. "Maybe you're right, but I've got to go there. I'm sure Bower or Tilley, one or the other, knows where Valissa is."

"I think I should come with you."

Nathan started to tell him no, but thought maybe it would be a good idea. He knew Bower and Lyman were coworkers and it was possible he could get the man to talk. "All right, come on, but hurry."

~ * ~

"You told the bank manager what?" Glenn Tilley almost screamed at Milton Bower.

"I didn't mean to, but he had me cornered. I had to tell him that we planned to make Valissa Prescott one of your girls."

"I don't see why."

"I wanted him to know that the loan I made you was safe. I felt sure he'd like the idea. After all, he knows Valissa well. His daughter and she have been friends since childhood." Milton grinned. "I'm sure he realizes what a lovely girl Valissa is. My guess is he'll want to be a customer whenever we… "

"In the few times Colbert has been to my place, he's never asked for one of the women. The only time he's come is to have a drink or two and to play cards occasionally. Then he's usually with some other men."

"But when Valissa works here…"

"Bower, don't you understand? You may have messed the whole idea up. Colbert could tell that brute Stone our plans and if he comes back here, he'll probably tear this place apart looking for the woman." He looked at Milton as if he wanted to kill him, but thought better of it.

"But you said he'd already checked the place."

"He has. Three times. I don't think that was the last time he'll come in either." Glenn shook his head and looked disgusted. "I ought to shoot you right now. I could swear you were the one to kidnap Valissa Prescott and I knew nothing about it."

"Her brother would never let you…"

"Forget about her brother. He's no longer in the picture."

A frown crossed Milton Bower's face. "Where is he?"

"Hell, I don't know. I gave him some money and he took off. Said something about Dallas. I figure he's off to greener pastures."

The frown was still on Bower's face. "But I thought he'd stay here until his sister was settled in that hostess job you said you'd start her out on."

"That's your problem, Milton. You think too much and most of the time what you think is wrong." Glenn got up from the table they were sitting at and moved to the bar. "Give me a drink, Sid."

"Yes, sir." Sid reached under the bar and brought out a bottle of whisky. He poured a drink in a clean glass. "How about Bower? He want a drink, too?"

"Yeah. We'll start out with the good stuff and go from there." Tilley grinned and an evil glint entered his eyes

"Who knows? He may get so drunk he'll stumble in front of a carriage and get killed on his way back to the bank or home or wherever he plans to go from here."

"Wouldn't surprise me one bit, sir."

"Me neither, Sid. Me neither."

~ * ~

Flo knocked on the door of Kyle's room. When Rowena's soft voice told her to come in, she pushed the door open with her hip and entered. She had a tray with a pot of tea, a bowl of steaming chicken broth and a few sugar biscuits.

"I brought you some tea and I was hoping we might be able to get some of the broth down Mr. Kyle's throat."

"You're so thoughtful, but I don't think Kyle is awake enough to eat anything." Rowena smiled at her. "I could sure use some of that tea, though."

"Yes, Miss Rowena." Flo put the tray down and poured a cup. "Do you put anything in your tea?"

"A little sugar, please."

"Just like Miss Valissa."

"We began drinking it with sugar at school." Rowena's face turned to one of sadness. "Oh, Flo, I feel so guilty for letting Valissa borrow my buggy. Where could she have gone?"

"I don't know, but I sure wish Mr. Kyle could wake up enough to give us a clue." Flo handed her the tea. "Don't you fret yourself about the buggy, Miss Rowena. You were only trying to help a friend."

"I know, but I should have questioned her. I should have made her tell me why she was running away."

"She didn't tell you?"

"No. She said she'd write me the next day and explain. Of course, I doubt that she'll be able to do that now."

"If you don't mind me asking, why, Miss Rowena?"

"I think Valissa is in some kind of bad trouble. Trouble she may not be able to get out of unless Nathan finds her soon." She looked at the housekeeper. "Do you know why she ran away, Flo?"

Flo hesitated then said, "I hope I'm not breaking a confidence when I tell you, but I think Miss Valissa would have told you eventually."

"As I said, she promised to write me."

"Then I think you have a right to know what happened." Flo went on and told Rowena how Nathan had asked them to go with the two of them to witness the marriage. Then how beautiful Valissa looked in her mother's wedding gown and how happy the two of them seemed until his stepmother and another woman came and interrupted everything.

When she finished, Rowena said, "Now I understand how Valissa could misconstrue Nathan's actions. I would have probably thought the same thing."

"And I thought that, too, but I didn't expect Miss Valissa to react the way she did. I assumed she'd wait and confront the man when he finished talking to the women in his study, but she didn't. She must have hurried and run out while Alvin and I were changing out of our Sunday clothes." Flo sighed. "Of course, we were mistaken about Mr. Nathan's actions. He had no intention of deserting Miss Valissa. He planned for the wedding to go on as planned."

"He told me he was in love with her, but he didn't tell me the circumstances of why she left."

"I hope I haven't spoken out of turn."

"You haven't, Flo. You've only convinced me to push harder to find my friend. She has to know the truth before it's too late." Rowena sipped her tea. "The only thing I'm confused about is how Kyle came into the picture."

"He must have been watching for a chance to see her. We knew he was back in town and we expected him to try to get Miss Valissa alone, but we didn't expect her to give him such a good opportunity to find her alone."

Rowena looked back at the bed. "I can't believe he'd hurt Valissa. He was always gentle and sweet with us when we were children."

"I know he loves Miss Valissa, but I can't get over the fact that he gambled away her home."

"I know." A tear came into Rowena's eye. "I guess when you get desperate, you'll do anything to anyone no matter how much it hurts them."

Kyle stirred.

Flo moved forward. "Maybe he's waking up."

Rowena sat her tea on the table beside the bed and leaned over the patient. "Are you waking, Kyle?"

He mumbled something, but his words were not clear.

"What did you say? Can you tell me again?" Rowena took his hand.

In a muddled voice, Kyle whispered, "Help Valissa." He then closed his eyes and was unconscious again.

"I wonder what he means by that." Rowena looked at Flo.

"I don't know, but I'm going to send Alvin to find Mr. Nathan. I have a feeling that Mr. Kyle is going to wake up soon. I'm sure he can tell us where Miss Valissa is then."

Nineteen

Nathan jumped out of the carriage as soon as Phillips stopped in front of Tilley's. Lyman followed. "Are you sure Milton would have come here, Mr. Stone?"

"Positive." He began to pound on the locked front door.

"The place is shut up tight. How could he get in?"

"You said he was a partner here. I'm sure they'd let him in." He pounded again, this time followed by the loud words, "Open up, Tilley. I know you're in there."

In a minute, the door opened and Glenn Tilley looked at Nathan. There was hate in his eyes. "So, you're back again?"

"Yes, I'm back. Where's Milton Bower?" He didn't wait for Tilley to invite him in. He pushed the saloon owner aside and walked in. Lyman followed.

"Who?"

"Milton Bower. Your partner."

"I don't know what you're talking about."

"Come off it, Tilley." Nathan's voice thundered. "Bower told Colbert here all about your little partnership. Now where is he?"

"I haven't seen him."

Nathan grabbed Glenn's collar and pulled the man's face close to his. "You have ten seconds to tell me where the man is or I'm going to start that shooting process I described before." Nathan's gun was in his hand before anyone saw him reach for it. "Now start talking or you've lost your left foot."

Glenn swallowed as the pistol cocked. In a shaky voice, he said, "He's gone."

"Keep talking. Gone where?"

"I have no idea."

Nathan pulled his collar a little tighter and aimed the gun at the gambler's foot. "You better get an idea."

"I'm telling you the truth. He came in here almost in tears saying all his beautiful plans had been taken away from him. He drank a few glasses of whiskey then stumbled out. I figured he'd gone home or back to the bank."

Nathan shoved Tilley backward and the man landed in a chair at one of the poker tables. "It's the truth, Stone."

Nathan looked around. "Where's your barkeep?"

There was an instant of fear in Glenn Tilley's eyes, but he said, "He hasn't come in yet. We had a busy night and I told him not to bother coming back until this afternoon. He was glad to get the rest."

Nathan narrowed his eyes. "What did Bower say while he was here?"

"I told you. He said his plans had been ruined and he didn't know what he was going to do."

Lyman broke into the conversation. "Did he tell you that he'd stolen money from the bank?"

"Of course not. Why would he steal money anyway? He's a rich man."

"What about the idea he had of making Valissa Prescott his mistress?"

"I don't know anything about that, Mr. Colbert. If he had something like that on his mind, the man must be crazy. Miss Prescott is a lady."

"And she'd better stay a lady," Nathan growled.

"I figure if she stays around you, she won't be a lady long," Tilley snapped.

Before he could stop himself, Nathan backhanded the man and he fell from the chair to the floor.

"Watch your mouth," Nathan hissed.

The door beside the bar that led to the kitchen opened and Sid walked in. "What's going on, boss?"

"Get over here," Nathan demanded.

"Look, Mister. I have no…" He stopped talking when he saw Nathan's gun pointed at his head. He walked to the group in the center of the room without another word.

Tilley got to his feet and stared at Nathan and the banker. Nathan knew if hate could drip from anyone's eyes, it would drip from Glenn Tilley's.

"Where have you been?" Nathan demanded when Sid stood by his boss.

"I had to run an errand for Mr. Tilley."

"Oh?" Nathan cocked an eye. "When did he ask you to run this errand?"

"When I came in this morning, why?"

Nathan led a slow grin cross his face. "So, Tilley, the barkeep wasn't coming in until afternoon?"

Tilley didn't answer.

"I think the Mr. Tilley may have lied to you, Mr. Stone," Lyman Colbert said in a calm voice.

"I agree." Nathan turned back to Sid. "What was this errand you were sent to do?"

"I think that's Mr. Tilley's business."

"You think so, huh?" Nathan grabbed the man by the shirt and jerked him forward.

Sid reacted. He swung a fist toward Nathan's head, but Nathan saw it coming and ducked. The blow landed on his shoulder.

Nathan reacted quickly. He landed a left on Sid's nose and blood spurted. The man cursed and went to his knees. He was ready to come up swinging, when he saw the pistol pointed between his eyes. He sank and muttered, "I'll get you for that, you bastard."

The door to the saloon kitchen opened again and the cook stuck his head out. "What's all the noise in here? Sounds like a Saturday night."

"Nothing to worry about, Cookie," Glenn managed to say. "Go on about your work. Fix the girls a good meal."

"Don't know how you expect me to cook anything decent when you keep giving my supplies away," the man mumbled and shut the door.

A sudden realization settled over Nathan. He turned toward the door where Phillips had been standing by waiting to see if his boss needed him. "Phillips, do you have your gun on you?"

"Yes, sir."

"Then please come here and guard these men. I'm going to have a little talk with the cook. If either one of them moves, shoot him."

"Yes, sir," Phillips said again.

"What are you going to talk to my cook about?" Glenn snapped.

Nathan didn't answer him. "Come along, Mr. Colbert. This should be interesting."

~ * ~

Valissa paced the floor. It was getting late. Glenn had said he'd be back by noon with Kyle, but it was past twelve-thirty and neither man had shown up. She'd been excited about her brother coming back and had cooked what she thought would be a good meal for him. Since Glenn told her Kyle was intoxicated last night, she didn't think he'd want anything heavy. She'd made a chicken stew and had fixed pan bread. The small stove didn't have an oven so she couldn't bake biscuits. Because of the lack of wood, she'd let the fire go out as soon as the food finished cooking. Now everything was cold.

Valissa moved to the door and looked up the road. There was no sign of anyone. She knew there was nothing she could do but wait, and waiting was one thing she didn't do well.

Turning around, she grabbed a ladderback chair that was not as rickety as the rest and moved to the porch facing the water. She might as well enjoy the sound of the waves, she decided. They might help her to relax until Kyle arrived.

Though she tried to keep them at bay, it wasn't long until her thoughts drifted to Nathan Stone. She felt a stinging in her eyes. Why had he done her the way he did? Was he somewhere with the pretty Maurine Tucker? Or were they at Heartsong having a good laugh at her expense?

Was his mother, no, stepmother, happy that he'd chosen to go with the woman she wanted him to marry? How could he let the woman manipulate him the way Ada Stone seemed able to do? Wasn't he man enough to stand up to them?

Of course, he'd tried at first. He'd told them he was going to marry Valissa, no matter what they thought or said. Then when his stepmother mentioned the ranch, he'd caved in. He'd looked at her as if he couldn't believe what she was saying. He'd dropped Valissa's hand and… Wait. Yes, he'd dropped her hand, but he'd squeezed it before he let it go. What did that mean? Was he saying good-bye as she'd thought at the time or was he telling her not to worry, that he would handle everything?

Valissa's eyes got big and she sat up straight. Had she done the wrong thing by slipping out of the house before he had a chance to tell her what was going on?

"No," she said aloud and shook her head. "I'm not wrong. Nathan decided his ranch was more important than our marriage."

But there was doubt. What if…?

Leaping from the chair, Valissa went inside. She looked around the cabin. Why was she here? What if Nathan Stone had dropped her as she thought? Did she have to hide from him? Would the man actually hurt her physically?

"Of course not," she muttered.

She sat on the bed for a few minutes then bolted up again. "If they're not here in the next thirty minutes…" She didn't finish her sentence because she wasn't sure what she'd do. She only knew she had to do something. She couldn't sit here in this shack on this lonely beach and wonder what was going on at Heartsong or with her brother at Tilley's Place.

~ * ~

The kitchen actually made Nathan feel hungry as he entered. The cook stood at the stove, turning ham in one pan and potatoes in another. "Smells good."

The cook jerked around. "What do you want? We ain't ready to start serving the customers."

"I didn't figure you were, but my friend here and I thought if we gave you some extra money you might make an exception."

"How much money?"

"Five dollars." When the cook said nothing, Nathan added, "Each."

The cook's eyebrow went up. "In that case, take a seat there at the table. I guess you want some eggs with the ham and 'taters."

"That'd be nice." Nathan nodded for Lyman to sit at the table with him.

Cookie grabbed six eggs, broke them in a bowl, whipped them quickly, then put them in a hot pan of grease. "Be done in a minute. Where's your money?"

Nathan took out two fives and laid them on the table. "Right here."

In less than two minutes, the old geezer had two steaming cups of coffee and the food sitting before the men. The money had disappeared into his pocket.

"You been cooking here long?" Nathan asked.

" 'Bout two months."

"Like it?"

"It's all right. The boss man gets testy sometimes."

"You're right about that. He's sure testy with me." Nathan chuckled.

"What's your business here?" The cook eyed Nathan. "You just passing through or are you gamblers?"

"Actually, we're businessmen. We're thinking of buying this place."

Lyman looked surprised at Nathan's words, but only kept eating.

"You got enough money to buy this place?"

"I think so, but in case I don't have, I brought my banker with me."

"I see. Well, somebody sure should buy it. Tilley is crazy."

"How do you mean?"

"I guess I'm speaking out of turn, but he's always yakking about some woman he wants to put upstairs. Then he turns around and lets a broken down gambler stay here and freeload for several days. Lo and behold, now he's started giving away my supplies. The women are complaining because he's giving away their good sheets and things, too. I don't think he's going to make much money if he keeps up business like this." The cook turned back to the stove.

Nathan eyed Lyman. "What do you think, Mr. Colbert? Would this place be a good investment?"

"It could be, but I'd like to see you run it more efficiently. I agree with this cook. Somebody needs to watch their spending."

"How do you fellows like the food?" the cook asked without turning around.

"It's very good, don't you think so, Mr. Stone?"

"Yes. I do."

"I'm glad you like it. I hope you fellows will still want me to do the cooking when you take over. I've got a wife and four young'uns to feed."

"If you continue to cook like this, I don't see a problem." Nathan took another bite. "Now let's do a little more talking about Mr. Tilley giving away your supplies. Who does he give them to?"

The cook turned around. "Well, the first time was in the middle of the night. He comes and wakes me up and makes me fill a box of food for his friends, he called them. I carry it out to his buggy and he puts it in the back. The bum who was staying here, the one I told you about was going to drive the buggy and there was a woman in it, but I didn't see her too good. She had on one of them capes with a hood. Tilley wouldn't let me get too close to them."

"So they took Tilley's buggy?"

"Yeah. They come in another one, but Tilley said he'd see that it got back to wherever it belonged. Sid took it away a little later."

"Do you know where they went? The woman and the bum, I mean." Nathan could feel his heart beat faster. Maybe he was going to be able to find Valissa today.

"No. I come back in and went to bed. I was tired."

"I see." Nathan felt his heart sink a little. "Did you see them again?"

"Saw the man yesterday. He come back and said the woman wanted some things. He went in the saloon to talk to Tilley and then got in a poker game with some drunk seamen. He managed to get himself drunk, too. There was a commotion and I peeped in and the bum was saying he'd never let Tilley make a whore out of his sister. I didn't figure it was any of my business so I come back in the kitchen."

"Was that all?"

"It was for a while."

Nathan looked at him. "What happened then?"

"After a while, Mr. Tilley came in here with a long list. He took near all my week's supplies and put them in his buggy. He climbed in it and rode off. Then it weren't long until Sid come through here dragging that bum by the neck of his shirt. I could see the man was beat up pretty good, but Sid said he was just drunk and had passed out. He drug him outside and left him, then he come back and went back to the bar."

"Was that all?" Nathan was trying to keep his voice calm, but he was seething inside.

"Yeah. Purty much so. Mr. Tilley seemed to be in a good mood since then." The cook laughed. "He was in a good mood today until you fellows showed up."

"How long was Mr. Tilley gone when he left with the supplies?" Lyman asked.

"Well, let's see. I'd say about two or three hours."

"I see." Lyman looked at Nathan. "It couldn't be too far from here."

"I agree."

There was the sound of giggles and the chatter of women's voices on the back stairs. "Here comes the women. I guess I better get to cooking some more eggs. You men want to meet the women who work here?"

"Not today," Nathan said and stood. "We'll come back later."

"Don't forget about my job, now."

"We won't."

The two men slipped out of the kitchen and back into the saloon before the women made their appearance.

Nathan went directly to Glenn Tilley and jerked him to his feet. "All right, you bastard, where is she?"

"I don't know what you're talking about."

"Don't lie to me. The cook already told us you took supplies to Miss Prescott. Now where is she?"

"I'll fire that damn cook."

Nathan grabbed his gun and held it between Glenn's eyes and cocked it. "I don't have time for games. Where do you have Miss Prescott stashed?"

Tilley shivered. "In a house I own."

"Keep talking."

Glenn tried to back away, but it was no use. Nathan had a firm grip on his shoulder. "It's on the road to Galveston."

"Where on the road to Galveston?"

"About five miles out of town." Glenn took a breath when Nathan took his hand away. "It's about a mile beyond a little church on the left. There's a farm road off to the left. Go down it about half a mile and you'll see a cabin there."

"You better be telling me the truth, Glenn Tilley. If not, you're a dead man." Nathan shoved him backward and holstered his gun. "Let's go, men."

Phillips and Colbert followed Nathan out of the saloon. They knew they were being watched when they climbed into the carriage and Phillips shook the reins to start the horses on their way.

~ * ~

Glenn Tilley turned to Sid. "Give them time to get on the road to Huston, and then hitch up my buggy."

"You're not going after the woman now, are you, Boss?"

"You damn right I am. I've had enough of that man. I'm going to the cabin and get Valissa Prescott. I'll know the pleasure of her body before this day is out and by the time we get where we're going, she'll be ready to delight any man I send around."

"Glenn, be sensible. If anything happens to the woman, Nathan Stone will kill you."

"Not if he can't find me."

"I got a feeling he won't give up until he does find you."

"Just do what I said." Glenn stomped away and up the stairs before Sid could question him further.

In his office, he opened the safe. He was glad they'd had a good week and, to sweeten the pot, he'd been hiding some of Milton Bower's ill-gotten gains. He put all of the money in a case and grabbed his carpetbag. He'd take enough clothes to make himself presentable, but he'd have to buy new outfits when he arrived at his destination. That wouldn't be a problem. With Valissa as the first of his new group of women, he'd soon be making more money than ever. And the best place he knew to do it was Mexico.

Twenty

"Why are we stopping, Nathan?" Lyman asked as Phillips pulled the carriage to a halt two streets over from Tilley's Place.

"Tilley was lying through his teeth to me. He doesn't have a place on the road to Houston."

Lyman frowned. "How do you know?"

"I know the man. He'd never tell me that easily where Valissa is. He plans for me to get out of town, then he's going to wherever he has her hidden."

"So we're going to sit here until he decides to leave to get her?"

"Not exactly."

"What then?"

"I'm going to unhitch one of my horses and saddle him. Phillips will take you back to the bank and I'll follow Tilley."

"I don't think that's a good plan, Mr. Stone."

"You called me Nathan earlier."

"I'm sorry. It must have been a slip of the tongue."

"Doesn't matter. I prefer you call me that anyway."

"Sure, but still…"

"I know what I'm doing, Lyman."

"Maybe you do, but you could need some backup. I think Phillips will agree with me."

"It'll be hard for one horse to pull this carriage any distance. Just do like I say." Nathan got out of the carriage.

In a matter of minutes, he had one of the horses unhitched, saddled and was riding down an alley.

The carriage started to move, but Lyman banged on the small window to let Phillips know he wanted him to stop. He did.

"Is something wrong, Mr. Colbert?" he asked as Lyman climbed out.

"I think Mr. Stone could use some help. Let's follow him at a safe distance."

"I'm sorry, sir, but Mr. Stone told me to take you back to the bank. That's what I plan to do."

"What if Mr. Stone gets hurt and we could have prevented it? You'd feel sorry about that wouldn't you, Phillips?"

"Sir…" A black buggy coming up the street toward them caught Phillips' attention. He frowned.

"Is something wrong?"

"That looks like the buggy I fixed up for Miss Prescott. Alvin's old nag is pulling it."

They watched until Alvin pulled up to them. "Where's Mr. Nathan?"

"He took a horse and went to find Miss Prescott." Phillips eyed him.

"I've been looking everywhere for him. Kyle is muttering and we think he could wake up any minute. We're sure he knows where Miss Valissa is and Mr. Nathan needs to be there when he regains consciousness."

The look on Phillips' face told Lyman he didn't know what to do. Lyman decided to take over. "Somebody needs to be there, but it's impossible for Nathan to go there now."

"But…" Alvin started.

"Here's what we're going to do." He looked at the two men. "Alvin, Phillips and I are going to switch horses with you and take the buggy to catch up with Mr. Stone. I think that old horse you're using will be able to pull this carriage back to Heartsong. We'll use the faster horse to pull the buggy so we can follow Nathan."

"Are you sure we should do this?" Phillips asked.

"Yes, I'm sure." He looked at the men. "Do either of you have any guns?"

"I have mine." Phillips patted his side, "and there's a rifle under the seat in the carriage. Mr. Stone insists I keep it for protection."

"I have a rifle with me," Alvin said.

"You keep your rifle, Alvin. You might need it." Lyman looked at Phillips. "Get the one under your seat and put it in the buggy, then let's get those hoses switched. It probably won't be long until Glenn Tilley heads out. We're going to stay a safe distance behind, but we'll be there if Nathan needs us."

Used to taking orders, both men complied. It wasn't long until Alvin was headed back to Heartsong in Nathan's carriage. Phillips eased the buggy over to a street where they were sure they would be able to see Glenn Tilley's buggy when it pulled away.

~ * ~

Glenn heard his office door open and then close. He figured it was Angela. He knew he'd have to explain to her that he had to take a quick trip, but he'd be back soon. The slut wouldn't question him. She'd stopped doing that soon after he'd put her to work in the upstairs rooms.

Bless her heart. She'd been a good whore and Glenn knew he'd always have a soft spot in his heart for her, if he had a soft spot for anybody. Fool that she was, she still had the hopes that he'd one day give up the business, marry her and they'd have a somewhat normal old age. Women were so gullible.

"That you, Angela darling?" He called from the bedroom. When there was no answer, he added, "I'll be there in a minute."

"I can wait."

Glenn snapped his head around and looked into the barrel of the shotgun that Sid kept under the bar. "What the hell?"

"I see you're taking a trip."

"I'm going to get Valissa Prescott." Glenn couldn't keep the fright from his voice.

"No you're not, boss. You're running out and you plan to leave me behind."

"That's ridiculous, Sid. I'm not running out."

"Then why'd you clean out the safe and why are you packing clothes?"

"I thought I might have to stay at the cabin for a few days. You know how it is. I need to break her in." He hoped Sid would believe him, because he knew what Sid was capable of.

"Do you need your money for that?"

He could tell by the voice the barkeep didn't accept the explanation. "I didn't want to leave it here. You know how the girls are, they…" His voice faded when he saw Sid cock the gun. "Wait a minute…"

"Why should I wait? You planned to run out and leave all this mess for me, didn't you?"

"Of course not."

"Looks to me like you did." His cold eyes stared at the saloon owner. "You've tried it before, but you know I'll never let you go it alone. You need me."

"Why do I need you, Sid?"

"I'm your muscle, you know. I've done most of your dirty work since we've been in this town, but I always thought since we was kin that you'd be there when I needed you."

"I will, Sid. I always will."

"Don't look like it to me."

"You're wrong. We've worked together ever since your mother and mine run off with them drummers and left us to fend for ourselves. We've always been partners as well as cousins."

"We was 'til you got your mind all screwed up with that Prescott woman."

"That's not so, Sid."

"Yes it is." His eyes bored into Tilley's. "I've even killed for you and you know unless you're here to say I was in the saloon, they'll find out about it. I could hang."

"I didn't ask you to kill anyone."

"The hell you didn't. I knowed what you wanted me to do when that Prescott woman's brother fell out cold on the floor downstairs. I done it, too. Today, when nobody was looking, I managed to shove your partner in front of a buggy. The law might not care about Prescott since he was a gambler and he left his sister without a home. But Bower was an important man. They'll come looking for who done it to him."

"Don't worry, Sid. I'll be back before they come looking for you or anybody else."

"Your lies ain't gonna to work this time, Glenn. I know you plan to pick up that gal and head for someplace else. Probably Dallas or New Orleans. But it ain't going to happen. I'm going to stop you."

"Look, Sid. If you don't trust what I'm saying, come with me. We can get out of town and nobody will ever know what happened to us or the Prescott woman."

"I don't trust you no more, Glenn. You've done me dirty too many times. I've made up my mind. I'm going to kill you, then I'm going to pick up that Prescott woman myself. This time I'm going to break her in and then put her in a room somewhere to make money for me."

Horror crossed Glenn's eyes. "No, Sid. You can't do that. I want that woman."

Sid let out an eerie laugh. "Not this time, Glenn. It's my turn to get one of the pretty ones before you do."

"I know you always wanted Angela. Well, cousin, you can have her. I'm sure she'd like to be your woman."

"She's in love with you. Has been since you brought her here. She ain't going to ever be any other man's woman. I want to start out fresh and train one to love me the way she does you."

"You idiot, what makes you think you could ever train…" Glenn didn't finish his sentence because Sid swung the shotgun and caught him across the temple. He fell to the floor.

"You've called me that for the last time." Sid smiled as he laid his gun aside and pulled a big hunting knife from his boot. He leaned over his cousin and whispered, "I told you what would happen if you ever called me an idiot again and you didn't listen."

Without waiting for Glenn to answer, Sid slit his throat. Standing up and looking down at his cousin, he said, "I've been wantin' to do that for a long time. You're a cheat and a liar, Glenn Tilley. I trusted you for too many years. Now I'm the one in charge." He laughed and added, "I figure the authorities would think one of the women did it. Probably Angela. Then she'll get hers for telling me I'm not good enough for her."

As the blood began to seep into the rug, Sid picked up the carpetbag Glenn had packed. He grinned. It was a good thing the men were about the same size. Now he'd be able to wear the nice clothes. He grabbed the case with the money and headed out the door.

He had his plan made. He'd go out the front door and down the alley to the stable. There he'd pick up the buggy and horse and slip away. Nobody would ever know he'd gone.

It was a good thing Glenn had told the Stone man where his cabin was. It was the one thing Sid hadn't known that his cousin owned.

~ * ~

Angela sat at the table and ate slowly. She was too busy thinking to join in with the other girls' chatter about who they'd entertained the previous night and who was good and who wasn't. She was remembering what she'd overheard only a short time ago.

She'd started downstairs earlier than the other girls and stopped midway when she heard male voices. She paused, took a seat on a step and listened. It had netted her some good information. Information she'd use if she had to. She knew Cookie didn't know what his food had been used for, but she did. Glenn had raided his pantry so he could take supplies to that damn Prescott woman. The sound of her name made Angela seethe. Though she liked the green dress she'd got from the woman, she knew they'd never be friends when Glenn brought her into the business. He might think she'd bring in the best customers, but Angela would show him. Her regulars wouldn't let her down.

Angela couldn't help the jealously that raked through her body. She'd been Glenn's number one girl for a long time. She remembered the week she'd spent in the secret beach shack with Glenn. She'd been innocent and scared, but he'd wiped all her fears away with his kind words and his gentle ways. It didn't take long until she was deeply in love with him and knew that someday he'd return that love, if he didn't already.

She'd been so alone until he came along. She'd been living with an aunt and uncle on one of Galveston's back streets. Things were all right until her aunt died and left them. She thought life would go on, but she didn't count on the fact that her uncle decided she was going to take her aunt's place, not only in the home, but in his bed as well.

The first night he'd tried to force himself on her, she'd managed to hit him in the head with the lamp beside the bed and run out of the house. She didn't notice until she was a street away that somehow the lamp had started a fire. The house was old and the wood easily caught fire. People came running, but it was too late. The house burned down with everything in it, including her uncle.

Barely eighteen and scared she'd be put in jail, she was ready to be rescued when Glenn found her stealing an apple from a vendor. The vendor grabbed her arm and threatened to call the police, then Glenn intervened. He paid for the apple and then took her into his buggy and into his heart. They went directly to the beach cabin and though it took a few days, she found love for the first time in her life.

Things had been perfect until that fancy Prescott woman came waltzing in the saloon selling her dresses. She knew instantly that Glenn was interested in the woman, but she tried to tell herself that she was mistaken. Now she knew she wasn't. Glenn had the woman at the beach place. The place he'd sworn was their secret hideaway. He said nobody knew he owned it or where it was. Now she realized he'd lied to her. He had the Prescott woman there and she knew in her heart that he planned to replace her with this woman. She also knew she couldn't let it happen.

Glenn meant too much to her. He was her lifeline. Without him, she'd never be able to survive. It didn't matter how many men she entertained, she only loved Glenn. This would never change and she knew as long as she did as he told her to do, she'd stay his woman. Why, they'd grow old together and someday look back on this brothel as something they both only did for the money.

But it looked like things could change. The Prescott woman was going to get in her way. If Glenn was as taken with her as Angela thought he was, she'd no longer be his number one girl. She, like the other women who worked there, would have to be satisfied with whatever leftover time and affection Glenn would give her.

"No," she vowed silently. "I won't do it. I'll never give Glenn up to another woman. He's mine and he'll always be mine. I don't care what I have to do to keep him, but I'll do it. No miss high-bred society raised dame is coming in here and taking my place. I'll kill her first."

"What you smiling about, Angela?" One of the women across the table asked.

Angela shook her head. "It was just a thought about somebody I've loved."

"I see," the woman said and laughed. "We've all had those now and again."

Angela didn't answer, but she thought, "Nobody has had a man like this one as their very own and I intend to keep him."

~ * ~

Nathan frowned when Tilley's buggy pulled away from the back of the building, driven by the barkeep. Why wasn't Glenn in it? Did he send this man on another errand? If so, what?

It entered his mind that Tilley could be sending the man to pick up Valissa and bring her back here. He'd follow it for a little while and see. No need to panic yet.

He'd only gone a few streets when he realized somebody was following him. He kept a safe distance in front of his pursuers until they were headed out of town. It didn't take him long to realize the buggy was headed for the road that led to Houston.

He frowned again. Could Tilley have been telling the truth? Is his cabin really in this direction?

"No," he muttered. "I know the man lied. The barkeeper is headed this way for another reason."

When he knew Tilley's carriage would continue on this road, he pulled his horse off to the side and hid in a grove of palmetto trees. He wanted to know who followed him and why.

It didn't take long until the black buggy came into view. It startled him to see his black horse pulling it. When it grew closer, he saw Phillips driving and Colbert sitting at his side. He almost smiled when he saw a rifle across Colbert's lap.

As they came almost in line with his hiding place, he kicked his horse and galloped out of the trees. The horse reared as he stopped in the road in front of them. "What the hell are you two doing following me?"

"It's my fault, Nathan," Lyman said. "I'm afraid of what you might do if you don't like what you found at Tilley's cabin."

Nathan snorted. "You know damn good and well what I'd do. I've have killed the man if he'd touched Valissa."

"I hoped to prevent that."

Nathan reined in his anger. "Anyway, I won't have the chance. Sid, Tilley's barkeep, is driving the buggy. I assume Glenn Tilley is still at the saloon."

Lyman looked confused. "Then why are we following him?"

"I wanted to see where he went. I thought maybe Glenn sent him to get Valissa instead of going himself." He eyed the two men. "Now tell me, where is my carriage and why are you driving this one."

Lyman quickly explained about meeting up with Alvin.

Nathan seemed to be in thought for a minute. He then dismounted. "Here's what we're going to do now. Phillips, I want you to take this horse I'm riding and continue to follow the barkeep. Don't confront him unless you find he has Miss Prescott with him."

"Yes, sir." Without question, Phillips climbed out of the buggy and took the reins of the horse.

"What are we going to do?" Lyman looked at Nathan.

"You and I are going back to Heartsong. I want to see if Kyle Prescott is awake. I'm sure he knows where Valissa is and it looks like he's willing to tell me." Nathan got in the buggy and took the reins. Looking back at Phillips, who was mounted, he said, "Whenever you find out what the bartender is up to, come back to the house."

With a nod, Phillips rode off.

"Oh my goodness." Lyman broke the silence. "I should have given him this rifle."

"He won't need it. I always keep one with the saddle. You never know when you're going to run up on a rattlesnake of one kind or another."

Lyman's eyes got big, but he didn't answer.

Twenty-one

Valissa's steps slowed as she grew tired. She knew the afternoon was passing by the way the sun was sinking in the western sky. Though the going had been slow, she had no intention of giving up her trek. But she decided there was no reason why she couldn't rest a little while. She figured she'd walked a couple of miles in the hot sun and she had no need to wear herself out.

She saw a thicket off to the left of the road and decided it would provide some shade for her rest. She eased across the small ditch that separated it from the lonely road, and found a place she thought would be comfortable to sit. She put the shawl she'd been carrying down and sat on it. She was glad she'd brought the small bucket of water and she wished she'd brought some of the food she'd cooked for Kyle. She'd skipped eating because after deciding to walk into town, she didn't have food on her mind. She had taken the time to look for a canteen in the cabin, but when she didn't find one, she settled for the bucket. It had been awkward to carry, but she refused to put it down and leave it behind.

Scooping water up with her hands, she drank. As the cool liquid slid down her throat, she began to breathe easier.

A noise on the road drew her attention. Maybe it was Glenn bringing Kyle, though it didn't sound like a buggy.

Being as careful as she could, she parted the brush in front of her and noticed a small wagon being pulled by one horse, driven by a lone driver.

Valissa frowned. This was the first living being she'd seen since leaving the cabin. Why would a woman be on this deserted road? She started to flag the woman down, but something about the way she was dressed and the way she was bent over the seat stopped her. Valissa couldn't see the woman's face, but instinct told her the woman was angry.

She watched until the little wagon was out of sight, then sat again. Maybe she'd made a mistake. The woman might have helped her. She shook her head, drank a little more water, closed her eyes and thought about home. She pictured Flo cooking supper. She could almost smell the roasting beef or baking ham mixed with the sweet scent of coconut to be put in a pie or a cake. Of course there were coffee and tea.

Before she dozed off, the last thing she thought was that she hoped Nathan didn't forget to thank Flo for her efforts on his behalf.

~ * ~

By the time Angela reached the cabin, her irritation had turned into fury. She'd been jostled and bumped all the way from town in the wagon she managed to borrow from Mrs. Hinton, the storekeeper on the docks. Of course she had to give the woman three dollars of her hard-earned money to be able to use the thing. She wished when she'd slipped out back at the saloon she'd gone into the stable and borrowed Glenn's horse and buggy, without his permission of course. She didn't want him to know she was coming here. He might just decide to stop her and she had decided she wouldn't be stopped. She had a mission to carry out and she intended to carry it out today.

Stomping up to the front door she was surprised to find it unlocked. She pushed it open and stepped inside, expecting to see the Prescott woman. Although she found the cabin empty, this didn't stop Angela from gasping as she looked around.

She'd never seen the place so clean. Though none of the shabby furnishings had been changed, the place looked livable. Two of the bunk beds were neatly made with clean sheets, the floor had been swept and mopped, the table had been scrubbed and the window that looked out on the Gulf was clean.

"I don't believe this, Glenn. You cleaned it up for her, but not for me. Anytime we've come here it's been messy and dirty and you never seemed to care."

Angela's eyes blazed as she walked over to the stove and noticed the food there. She lifted the pot lid and raised her eyebrows in surprise that the food was fresh and smelled wonderful. If she weren't so mad, she'd heat it up and eat some and maybe she'd do that very thing a little later.

Right then, she had to find the woman and get rid of her, so Glenn would stop his silly pining over her.

Angela walked to the porch and looked up and down the beach wondering if Valissa had taken a walk. If so, there was nothing she could do but wait. When she didn't see anyone, she returned to the cabin.

Then she spied the carpetbag on the floor beside one of the bunks. "Well, you haven't gone far. Your belongings are still here."

Walking to it, she picked it up and plopped it on the bed. Snapping it open, she grinned when she pulled out a pink dress, square-necked and trimmed in white lace. Holding it up to her, Angela twirled around. "I suppose this is what a lady wears in the daytime. I think I'll keep it. Glenn might like to see it on me. He doesn't always have to see me in revealing clothes."

Tossing the dress on the bed, she pulled out two more. They weren't as pretty, but one appeared to be some kind of an evening dress. Angela figured if she removed the sleeves and some of the trim on the neck, it would be pretty to wear in the saloon.

She came to the underclothes next. Here she had to laugh out loud. No way she'd ever wear such prim and proper things. Why the bloomers were thick silk material and the chemise thin silk, but still too pristine to wear in her job. She shook her head. If all wives wore such unattractive things, no wonder their husbands sought out the company of women in bordellos.

In the bottom of the case, Angela found a silver comb and brush. She smiled. "Now, this I can use. I bet she paid a pretty penny for it." She placed it on the bed and pulled out a picture.

Staring at it, she wondered who it was. The woman looked like prissy Miss Prescott, but there was something about her that made Angela think it must be her mother and father. She started to rip the picture to shreds, but changed her mind. She tossed it beside the comb and brush. She might just frame it and tell everybody they were her parents, though she had no idea what her parents looked like.

With nothing else in the bag to interest her, Angela went back to the porch and looked up and down the beach again. Still no sign of Valissa Prescott.

"Oh, well," she said aloud. "She'll come in before dark."

She then turned to the stove and built a fire. No need to let this good food go to waste. She was hungry and it was just the thing to satisfy her appetite for food. Her appetite for revenge would be satisfied when Valissa Prescott walked through the door. And if she didn't come back before Angela had to start work tonight, she'd go back to town and make another trip out there tomorrow before Glenn had a chance to come.

~ * ~

Nathan decided to drop Lyman at the bank. He rushed back to Heartsong. He pulled the buggy into the stable, unhitched the horse, gave him a quick rubdown, put him in a stall and gave him some oats. He hated to take the time because he was in a hurry to get to Kyle's bedside to see if he were talking yet, but he knew one rule of a cowboy was that if you take good care of your horse, it'll take care of you.

Entering the house through the back door, he found Flo and Alvin in the kitchen. His first question was, "Has he said anything?"

"He's still muttering, but not much of what he says makes sense. Miss Rowena said she'd call us the minute she knew what he was saying." Flo automatically handed Nathan a cup of coffee. "Here, drink this. You look as if you need it."

Nathan took the coffee. "Thank you, Flo."

"Mr. Nathan, as I was coming home, I came upon a commotion on the main street. It seems Mr. Milton Bower either darted or was pushed into the street in front of a large coach. The driver did everything he could to stop, but was unable to. By the time he got the horses calm and got out to help Mr. Bower, the man was dead."

Nathan frowned. "Did you say somebody may have pushed him?"

"That's what the driver of the coach said. He thought he got a glimpse of someone running away, but was too busy trying to stop and help to pay much attention. By the time he did what he had to do, the man was gone."

Nathan didn't have time to ask further questions because Rowena's voice called down the back stairs, "Flo, I think he's waking up."

Nathan took the steps two at a time. Flo and Alvin followed him.

Rowena looked surprised to see Nathan, but she only nodded.

"What has he said?"

"I've… got… to save…Valissa…" Kyle's weak voice came from the bed as he tried to sit up.

"Lie still, Prescott, and tell us about Valissa." Nathan put his hand on the man's shoulder.

"Who're… you?"

"That doesn't matter…"

"I don't…trust you…"

Rowena moved over the bed. "You know me, don't you, Kyle?"

"Rowena?"

"Yes. You know I've always been Valissa's best friend, don't you?"

He nodded.

"Then please tell Mr. Stone here about Valissa. He's the man in love with her and he wants to save her."

"Are you…sure?" His voice sounded weaker.

"I'm positive. Now let's hear what you know about Valissa's whereabouts."

"She's at…the…cabin." He seemed to be fading fast.

"Is that cabin on the way to Houston?" Nathan tried to keep his voice calm.

"At… beach."

"Are you sure?"

Kyle's eyes closed. "Save…her…."

"Where at the beach, Prescott?"

Kyle didn't answer. He'd slipped back into a deep sleep.

Nathan reached to shake him, but Rowena caught his arm. "It's no use, Nathan. He can't hear you now."

"But I must know which way to…"

"Think, Mr. Nathan," Alvin said. "Which way is the most likely place a man would put a cabin on the beach?"

Nathan looked lost. "I don't know."

Rowena touched his arm. "I think the most logical place would be on the road to Brownsville. If you headed in the other direction, you'd be stopped by water. Galveston is an island, you know."

Nathan shook his head. "Thank you, Rowena."

"Come, Mr. Nathan. I'll go get the horse ready while you have something to eat." Alvin started out the door.

"I'll take another cup of coffee, but I've already had food." Nathan put his arm around Flo's shoulder as they followed Alvin out. "Don't worry. I'll not give up until I find her for the both of us."

"Thank you, Mr. Nathan." Flo wiped her eyes and leaned a little closer to him without meaning to.

~ * ~

After her rest, Valissa moved back to the road. She'd only gone a short distance when she heard a wagon coming up behind her. Good, she thought. Maybe I can hitch a ride into town. It's going to be dark before I get there if I have to keep walking.

She turned as the wagon pulled up beside her. Something about the woman driving looked familiar, but she wasn't sure where she'd seen her before. She decided it didn't matter. She looked friendly enough.

"Hello, ma'am, are you headed into Galveston?" As soon as she said it, Valissa knew it was a foolish question. Where else would the woman be headed?

"Is that where you're going?" the red-headed woman asked in an unfriendly voice.

"Yes. I have to get back to town."

"Why?"

"I was told my brother was sick and I feel I should go into town and help him." Valissa smiled in spite of the fact that she was tired and worried.

"Where is your brother?"

"He's at a place called Tilley's. It's down on the docks. Do you know where that is?"

"Yes, I do." The woman nodded. "Climb in if you want a ride."

"Oh, thank you. You're very kind." Valissa sat her bucket in the back of the little wagon and climbed on the seat beside the driver. "It seems I've been walking for hours. It must be farther into town than I realized. I was afraid it was going to get dark on me before I got there."

"Is your brother the only reason you want to get back to Galveston?"

Valissa frowned. "Of course. I'm worried about him."

The woman changed the subject abruptly. "My name's Angela."

"It's nice to meet you, Angela. I'm Valissa."

"What were you doing out here on this lonely beach road by yourself, Valissa?"

"My brother and I were staying at a cabin on the beach for a while."

"Just the two of you?"

"Yes."

"Who told you your brother was sick?"

"Mr. Tilley. He said he'd bring Kyle back to the cabin this morning, but he never showed up. I waited and waited, but when they didn't come I got worried. I was afraid something might have happened to my brother."

"Why is this Mr. Tilley so concerned about you and your brother?"

"I'm not sure. Kyle tells me he only wants to help us because he and Glenn are friends. I think Mr. Tilley has a more sinister plan."

"Oh? What kind of plan?"

"Kyle says he probably wants to offer me a job as a hostess in his saloon, but another friend was sure he'd want me to work upstairs with his other fallen women." Valissa shook her head. "I could never do that."

"If you loved him you could."

"Well, I don't love him."

"You don't?"

"No. I love somebody else."

"Who?" Angela eyed her.

"It doesn't matter. I'm afraid he doesn't love me."

"The man you're talking about won't stand a chance if Glenn decides he wants you to love him. He can be awfully persuasive if he wants you to fall in love with him."

Valissa shook her head. "I don't find him all that charming."

"Some women do," Angela snapped. "In fact, I hear he has a special woman working in his bordello. A woman he loves and plans to marry someday."

Again Valissa shook her head. "A man would never make the woman he loves work in a brothel. Besides, I doubt he'd ever end up marrying one who worked there, even if he did like her."

"Why not?" Angela's voice was high and she almost yelled the question.

"That's just the way men are, Angela. They don't mind being with the kind of women who work in such places, but when it comes to marriage, they want a woman who hasn't given herself to other men."

Angela reined in the horse and came to a stop. "How do you know? Does Glenn Tilley plan to marry you?"

"Of course not. I hardly know the man. Besides, I told you I loved someone else." Valissa frowned. "Anyway, why do you care what a saloon owner wants to do?"

"If I thought Glenn was going to marry any woman besides me, I'd...." Her voice trailed off.

Valissa stared at her companion. Then it dawned on her where she'd seen this woman. She'd bought one of the dresses when Valissa went to the saloon to sell them. "I'm sure you know Mr. Tilley better than I do, so you'd be a better judge of what he'd do."

"Are you trying to take him away from me?"

"No. I don't want him. I told you, I love someone else."

Angela's eyes narrowed. "Why should I believe you?"

"Let me assure you, Angela, if you want Glenn Tilley, you can have him. Personally I think the man is creepy. I don't want to have anything to do with him."

"Then why were you at his cabin?"

"I told you. My brother and I…"

"I think you're lying. I sit on the back steps at the saloon and listen to what's going on. I know for a fact that your brother is nothing but a drunk and a gambler. Glenn threw him out of the saloon yesterday and told him never to come back. He'll never be back to that rundown cabin." Angela grabbed Valissa's arms and shook her. "Glenn, on the other hand, probably means to come back for you. He intends for you to take my place."

"No. He couldn't possibly think that."

"I know what I'm talking about. I've heard him say he can't wait to get you upstairs at Tilley's as one on his girls."

"I'll never become one of his girls."

"I know you won't. I'll see you dead before I see you with my man." Angela's shrill voice screamed the words.

Valissa started to say something else, but she didn't get a chance. Angela dropped her arms and grabbed the rifle at her feet. With one swift motion, she hit Valissa in the side of the face with the butt of the gun. Valissa crumpled to the floor of the wagon, then Angela turned the horse and wagon and headed back toward the cabin.

Twenty-two

Phillips could tell Sid was getting exasperated by the way the buggy was swaying from one side of the road to the other. They had passed a church a mile or so back, but they hadn't seen any sign of a road of any sort leading off to the left or right of the one on which they traveled. He had begun to believe that if Glenn Tilley had any sort of cabin in this area, it was so well hidden they'd never find it.

Then around the next curve a road actually appeared, though it went off to the right instead of the left as Tilley had said. Phillips slowed the horse and watched as Sid swung the buggy to the right so quickly it looked as if it might turn over.

Again they went some distance before a two-story ranch house, build of wood and with a sweeping front porch appeared. A large barn with a connected corral, and several other out-buildings were off to the left of the house. Behind the homestead, a big pasture held a large herd of grazing cattle. This was a large working ranch, not a cabin.

Phillips couldn't help noting that if someone held Miss Prescott here, she wasn't suffering from any lack of comfort. This place seemed to have all the luxury of Stone Ranch.

He waited until Sid parked his buggy beside the hitching post near the front door then, pulling his hat down almost over his eyes, he walked his horse forward. He didn't understand why Sid ignored him, but figured he thought of him as one of the ranch hands. As Sid approached, a rotund woman wearing a big white apron came out onto the porch and looked at Sid. Phillips paused when he was close enough to hear the conversation.

"What can I do for you, fellow?"

"I've come to pick up Miss Prescott."

"You've got the wrong place. Ain't no Miss Prescott here." The woman was neither friendly or unfriendly.

"I know you're probably supposed to say that, but Glenn said this is where he stashed her. Tell her to come out now."

The woman looked confused. "Mister, I told you there ain't nobody named Prescott here. I don't even know anybody named Prescott."

Sid seemed to get more agitated. "Glenn told Stone he had Miss Valissa Prescott holed up in his cabin and I know she's here."

"I don't know who this Glenn you're talking about is, but this is the Circle S Ranch. It's owned by Mr. Robert Stanton and his family."

"You're lying!" Sid screamed at her. "Glenn said this was his place and I know it is."

"Mister, I don't lie to nobody. When I tell you there's nobody by the names you're throwing out around here, they're not here."

The front door opened again and an obviously pregnant woman stepped out. "What's going on here, Millie?"

"This here man is asking for somebody that ain't here, Mrs. Stanton. I keep telling him that…"

Mrs. Stanton turned toward Sid. "Sir, who are you looking for? One of our ranch hands?"

"No, damn it. I'm looking for Miss Valissa Prescott and I don't aim to leave here without her." Sid reached back toward his buggy and took the rifle from the floor. "Now tell her to get out here if she knows what's good for her."

The pregnant woman let out a little scream and Millie moved in front of her. "It'll be all right, Mrs. Stanton. Go back inside."

"Don't move," Sid ordered and leveled the gun at them.

Phillips knew he couldn't let the situation get any more dangerous for the woman. Taking his gun from his side, he pulled his horse close enough to ram the pistol in Sid's shoulder. "Drop your gun."

Startled, Sid whirled around. "You! What are you doing here?"

"I followed you."

"I'll kill you for that." He turned the gun toward Phillips, but he was too slow.

Phillips fired and the gun fell. Sid grabbed his injured hand as he cursed.

Phillips dismounted, still looking directly at Sid and, holding the gun on him, he spoke to the women. "If one of you ladies will give me something to tie around this criminal's wound, I'll be happy to take him off your hands."

Millie jerked a dishtowel from her apron pocket and tossed it to Phillips. "Thank you for the help, sir. May I ask who you are?"

"Yes, ma'am. I'm Ryan Phillips and I've been following this man all the way from Galveston. He's wanted back there."

The pregnant woman spoke. "Well, I'm sure glad you came along. Would you like to tie this fellow up and wait here for my husband to come in off the range? I'm sure he'd like to thank you."

About that time a big grey gelding came rushing into the front yard followed by two other horses. The first rider had a gun pulled and was holding it toward Phillips. "Drop that gun and get your hands up, Mister."

"No, Robert," the woman shouted. "Mr. Phillips just saved Millie and me from the man with the injured hand. He pulled a gun on us."

Robert holstered his gun and got off his horse. "Sorry, I mistook you for the bad guy. I heard a shot when I was coming in and I just reacted."

"It was no problem. I expected trouble from this one, but I never dreamed he'd bully two women."

"I guess I'm beholding to you then." He walked toward Phillips.

After the excitement settled, Phillips agreed to let the cowhands tie Sid in the barn while he shared a meal with the Stanton family. He was glad he did when he learned what had been happening on this ranch.

~ * ~

When Valissa came to, she found she was tied to one of the bunks in the beach shack. Her head pounded and every bone in her body seemed to be aching. Glancing down, she realized she was naked and wondered why. Then she looked toward the other woman in the room. Angela was stirring something in a pot on the small potbellied stove.

Oh, Lord, what's she going to do to me?

Angela must have heard Valissa's movements because she turned around with an evil grin. "So you decided to wake up."

"What happened?"

"Damn, I hoped you'd remember, but I guess you city women aren't as smart as I thought you were."

"I don't understand." When Angela didn't answer, she asked, "Why am I naked and why do you have me tied here?"

"You fool. I have you here because you were going back to Galveston to be with my man. I couldn't let you do that." She laughed. "As for being naked, I figured you'd feel it better when I decided to give you some licks from the whip Mrs. Hinton had in the wagon to use on her stupid old horse."

Valissa groaned in pain. "Is that why my back hurts so?"

Angela shrugged and turned back to her cooking. "I wanted to try out the whip, but I guess I should've waited until you were awake. You'd feel them licks more then."

"Why are you doing this, Angela?"

Angela whirled around. "For heaven's sake, stop asking that question. I've told you over and over it's because you were trying to take Glenn away from me. I won't let you do that."

"And I've told you that I don't want Glenn Tilley. He's all yours."

Angela walked the short distance to the bed and slapped Valissa across the mouth. "I won't listen to any more of your lies. Now shut up. I'm making my supper and when I finish, I'm going to finish you."

Valissa got quiet, but her mind was working. *What can I say or do that would make Angela believe me? I have to come up with a plan or this woman is crazy enough to think killing me would solve all her problems. Oh, how I wish I'd never left Heartsong. That was probably my biggest mistake. I still can't help wondering if Nathan didn't mean that we'd be married after he had it out with his stepmother. It's too bad that it's too late now. Oh, Lord, I didn't know how much that man meant to me until I left him.*

Angela took up a bowl of whatever she was cooking and set it on the table. She gave Valissa a wicked grin. "I bet you'd like something to eat, too, wouldn't you?"

Valissa shook her head. "I'm not hungry."

"Let's see about that." She ladled another bowl and walked up to Valissa. "Open your mouth."

"I said I wasn't hungry."

Angela grabbed a handful of Valissa's raven hair which hung down her back. "I said open your mouth."

She obeyed and Angela poured some of the hot stew into her mouth. The remainder ran down her cheeks and onto her shoulders.

Valissa screamed as she felt the burns. Then she began to choke.

Angela tossed the bowl aside and pushed Valissa's head forward. "Don't you dare choke and die on me. I want you to suffer more before you leave this world."

Somehow Valissa managed to spit out the stew and began to cough.

"There. You're going to be all right." Angela slapped her back and walked back to the table where she sat down to her supper.

Valissa was in agony from the burns, but she managed to cry silently. She wouldn't give the woman the satisfaction of knowing how much she was suffering.

~ * ~

Nathan knew he pushed his horse too hard, but he couldn't help it. He assumed Tilley planned to grab Valissa and run away with her and he knew he had to get to Valissa before Glenn Tilley did. He figured that Sid heading for Houston had been a trick to draw him in that direction. Thank heavens he didn't fall for it. If he could just find the beach cabin in time.

Within minutes of these thoughts, the small shack came into view. Slowing the horse as a precaution, he walked toward the shanty as quietly as possible. He didn't want to alert Tilley if he were inside.

Seeing the small wagon and horse standing beside the shack, he shook his head. Did the man actually think he could get away from Galveston in that rig? It looked like something somebody would use to deliver hay to the cows in the fields, not a wagon to travel in.

Stopping his horse several yards from the cabin, Nathan decided to slip in as quietly as possible. Wrapping the reins around a small palm, he eased up to the one front window on foot. When he looked inside, his blood ran cold.

He saw Valissa tied to the bed and a woman getting ready to hit her naked body with a whip. Without giving her any warning, he rammed the door with his shoulder and it fell away. He came into the room with his gun in his hand.

Angela screamed. "Get out of here."

Nathan grabbed her wrist, and holstering his gun, he jerked the whip from her hand. Though he tried never to be rough with a woman, he shoved her against the wall and turned toward Valissa.

Angela didn't stay against the wall. She leaped at his back and began screaming and biting at his neck.

Nathan knew he didn't have time for her tactics. He slung her off his back, grabbed her arms and in minutes she was tied to one of the chairs. Though she still screamed and cursed at him, Nathan turned again to Valissa.

The woman was barely conscious, but he saw her try to smile at him.

He smiled back as he untied her and laid her on the bed as gently as he could. He spread a sheet on her naked body. "I'm going to try to help you as much as I can, sweetheart. Then we'll find you a doctor."

She gave him another faint smile.

By the time Nathan had washed Valissa's wounds, there was the sound of a buggy outside. He stood.

"That'll be Glenn. He'll kill you for trying me up," Angela said.

Nathan ignored her and went to the door with his gun in his hand. He frowned with confusion when he saw Lyman Colbert get out of the buggy.

"What are you doing here?"

"Thought you might need some help."

"Come in." Nathan went back to Valissa. "She's in pretty bad shape and I've got to get her to the doctor."

Lyman glanced at Angela, who looked disappointed at seeing him. "I thought you'd be Glenn."

"Glenn Tilley, you mean?"

"Yes."

Lyman shook his head. "No need to keep looking for him, ma'am. He's dead."

"No."

"What happened?" Nathan was surprised.

"I'll explain everything later. What do you need me to do, Nathan?"

"Let me use your buggy to get Valissa to the doctor." He gave Lyman a lopsided grin. "I hate to do this to you, but there's a rundown wagon outside. Could you use it to escort that woman to the sheriff? She's been torturing Valissa and I fully intend to press charges."

"I certainly will."

"Nobody's taking me anywhere. I'm waiting for Glenn."

"I told you he's dead." Lyman looked at her. "Maybe you killed him."

"No. I love him."

"Sorry to leave you with her, but I think time is of the essence, Lyman."

"I agree. I'll see you back at Heartsong and explain everything."

Nathan nodded and wrapped the sheet tighter around Valissa. He scooped her up in his arms and headed out the door.

"Come on, little girl," Lyman said to Angela. "Let's head to town."

"I'm not going."

"I promise to tell you all about Glenn Tilley."

"Oh," she mumbled. "Then I guess I'll go."

The buggy with Nathan's horse tied behind headed up the road and the small wagon followed.

Twenty-three

Five weeks later, Valissa sat before the dressing table in the beautifully designed gown she had thought was for another woman. She put the finishing touches on her upswept hairdo. "Are you sure you want to go to Mrs. Maxmillion's party after we have dinner, Nathan?"

"Of course, I do. In fact, I can't wait." He put on the jacket to his evening suit.

"I didn't think you liked parties."

"That was before I had a beautiful wife to escort." He leaned down and kissed her neck. "After two weeks of wedded bliss, I'm more anxious than ever to tell the world she belongs to me and only me."

"Forever?" Valissa's aqua eyes looked at him from the mirror."

"For infinity, my love."

"Oh, Nathan, you're so sweet." She reached for the earrings lying on the dressing table, but Nathan put his hand on hers and stopped her.

"I don't think you should wear those."

"And why not?"

"Because you should wear the ones I chose." He pulled a box from his pocket. "I've been waiting for the right time to give you these."

Valissa gasped. "Grandmother's earrings. You didn't sell them. But I thought…"

"How could I sell something that would break the heart of the woman I love?" He handed her the earrings.

She slipped them on, stood and turned to him. "They're the perfect finishing touch to this outfit. How can I ever thank you?"

He pulled her into his arms. "I'll think of a way."

"My dear husband," she said with a playful smile. "You can be so naughty at times."

"Of course I can."

She giggled. "Well, now is not the time. I think we should go down and face our dinner guests."

"I need a kiss first."

"Oh, Nathan, you're more romantic than I ever dreamed you'd be."

He tightened his arms around her. "Do you mind?"

"I'm thrilled." She turned her face toward his. "Just don't get carried away. We have guests, you know."

"They can wait." His mouth covered hers and it awakened every nerve in her healed body, a body that got well quicker than anyone ever dreamed it would.

The doctor had told them it was because she had a strong constitution. She knew differently. It was because she couldn't wait to get married. Nathan had told her he'd wait as long as he needed to for the nuptials, but she decided three weeks were long enough. She vowed she'd be well in that length of time and she was.

The wedding went on as first was planned, with a few exceptions. She wore her mother's wedding dress and they were married in the beautiful parlor of Heartsong with Alvin and Flo as their special attendants. Also attending were Rowena and Kyle. Though Kyle had to be brought down and put in a wheelchair, it didn't mar the festivities. The doctor had assured them he'd be walking soon.

Finally, Valissa pulled back from the kiss. "If we don't get downstairs soon, you know what will happen."

"I know. I'll rip that gown off you and have you in our bed within minutes."

"I don't want my beautiful gown ripped, though I thought you were having it made for a friend of yours."

"Had I told you it was for you all along, you'd have never accepted it, would you?"

"Of course not."

"Then I did the right thing when I told you it was for a friend."

"You hardly knew me at the time, so what possessed you to have this dress and all those you ordered made for me in the first place?"

"When I heard you were bent on selling your gowns at the docks, I couldn't help myself. I was cad enough to take your home, but I knew I couldn't take your clothes, too."

She kissed his chin. "I love you, Mr. Stone."

"I love you, too, Mrs. Stone."

"Now, let's go greet our guests." She slipped her arm into his.

He sighed and said, "I guess we must."

As they entered the dining room, the women gasped and began telling Valissa how beautiful she looked. The men stood with approving smiles on their faces.

It was a small gathering. Kyle's place was at the end of the table with Rowena to his right. Lyman and Beverly Colbert were beside Valissa's place on Nathan's right. Beside Rowena were Wilbur Colbert and Candice Maxmillion.

Nathan ushered Valissa to her place and pulled out her chair. "Welcome friends. Please, be seated."

When they were all in their chairs, Flo entered with a huge roasted turkey and set it before Nathan. Alvin followed, carrying a tray loaded with all kinds of vegetables. Phillips came in and served wine. He paused and smiled at Candice. She looked a little flustered, but returned his smile.

Valissa noticed the actions between them and wondered what was going on. She didn't say anything, though, because a subdued Beverly drew her attention by saying, "Mrs. Stone, that's the most beautiful dress I think I've ever seen. Mrs. Dupree-Fontaine outdid herself."

"Thank you, Mrs. Colbert, and please call me Valissa as you always have."

"Thank you, dear."

As he stood and began carving the turkey, Nathan said, "Well, Lyman, I guess you wondered why I insisted on having this little party before we head to the festivities at the Maxmillion mansion."

"I must say, it crossed my mind."

"As you all know, we've had a lot of large and small occurrences happen at Heartsong in the last couple of months." They nodded their heads and he went on. "Of course, the fact that the Prescott home changed hands was one of the most talked about."

Again nods.

"Now that that is settled," he winked at Valissa and continued, "I have a few announcements to make. First, I want you to know that I've bought a ranch between here and Houston. My driver, Phillips, found out it was for sale when he followed Milton Bower's killer there and captured him. Valissa and I intend to live there part-time, but for the present, most of our time will be spent here in Galveston. My wife loves her home here and I've come to love it, too."

He handed a plate of turkey to Valissa, who passed it to Mrs. Colbert. After the women were all served, he began making plates for the men and continued his announcements. "We received a wire the other day. It seems the charges against Kyle in California have been dropped. The witness finally admitted it was in self-defense when Kyle had to shoot the man who was about to kill him."

"That's good news," Lyman said.

"I was happy about it." Valissa smiled at her brother.

Nathan nodded and went on. "I've had a long talk with Kyle. He's decided that gambling is not what he wants to do for the rest of his life. To get away from it and all the talk about him, Kyle has asked if he could live at the ranch I bought and learn to be a cowboy. With the right training, I think he'll make a good one. I'm bringing several of the hands from my ranch near Fort Worth so there'll be plenty of experienced men to work with him. Thanks to you, Lyman, we now know Bower didn't steal all the Prescott money, so if he does well and likes the job, Kyle has enough of his inheritance left to buy a place of his own."

"I'm sure he plans to do that," Rowena said, then dropped her head when her mother gave her a sharp look.

Valissa smiled at her and said, "I'm sure about it, too, Rowena."

Kyle smiled at both of them.

"Wilbur." Nathan looked at the young man.

"Yes, sir." Wilbur's eyes got big.

Having finished everyone's plate, Nathan put down his carving knife and sat. He began filling his plate with the vegetables as they came by him. "I'm not pleased with the job you're doing at the bank."

Beverly started to say something, but Lyman's hand on her arm stopped her.

"I'm leaving it up to your uncle about whether or not you remain with the bank, but I want you to understand that if you don't learn the business and start doing your job correctly, you are going to have to look for employment elsewhere. And when I say elsewhere, that means you will not be offered another job in any of my companies."

"What do you want me to do?" Wilbur sounded whiney.

"For heaven's sake, Wilbur. Mr. Stone wants you to be a man and accept responsibility for doing your work. Even I know all you want to do is marry a rich woman and live a life of ease." Candice looked down at the man beside her.

"I might favor rich people, but I'd make a good husband." Wilbur stuck out his stubborn chin.

"Well, don't look at me as your meal ticket. I may be as homely as they come, but I have no intention of marrying you just because you think I'm flattered with your attention. If and when I ever get married, it'll be because the man appreciates me and doesn't care what I look like." Candice took the bowl Rowena passed her and ladled green beans almandine onto her plate.

Valissa couldn't help saying, "Candice, I have a feeling you're going to find that right man soon."

"I think so too, Valissa." Candice passed on the beans and smiled.

Nathan spoke again. "As you all know, Sid, the barkeep at Tilley's, was found guilty and is sentenced to hang for the deaths of Milton Bower and Glenn Tilley. Angela, the woman who held Valissa prisoner, is now in a mental institution. The poor woman won't accept the fact that Tilley is dead."

"She kept muttering about what she was going to tell him when I took her to the sheriff's office. She was still waiting for him to come get her."

Beverly glanced at her husband. "I wish you hadn't taken such a chance on your life, dear. You know you don't know a thing about facing criminals and it doesn't matter if they're male or female."

"I was never in danger, Beverly."

"He's right, Mrs. Colbert." Nathan grinned. "He was always safe and that brings me to why I insisted on this dinner with you people."

All eyes turned to him.

Valissa knew what he was about to say, but she couldn't help the excitement that began to build inside. She was proud of Nathan and wanted to shout it to everyone, but she managed to stay quiet.

Nathan cleared his throat. "Lyman, I came to Galveston because I knew someone was taking money at the bank. When Valissa went over the books, she confirmed my suspicions. The only problem was I didn't know who in the bank I could trust. I even thought you were the guilty party for a while. Then you came to me and told me all about Milton Bower's schemes. I knew then you were an honest man. Then you went to Tilley's with me and later followed me to the cabin where I found Valissa. It was at this time that I realized what a brave man you are."

"Thank you, Nathan. I don't think I did anything special. Most any man would do the same in my position."

"No, he wouldn't, Lyman. It takes a special man to do what you did. That's why I've decided to remove you as the president of my bank here."

Beverly and Rowena gasped. Lyman looked stunned, but only stared at Nathan.

Nathan went on "Now, instead of working at the bank, I want you to come into my business as a partner. I will give you ten percent of every business I own in Galveston, which will, of course, more than double your responsibilities as well as your salary."

The women gasped again. This time with delight.

"Nathan, I'm overwhelmed." Lyman looked as if he couldn't believe what was being said.

"You're not going to refuse, are you?"

"Of course not. I'm just trying to take it all in."

"Good. Now at the Maxmillion party, I want to introduce you as my new partner."

"This is going to cause a stir, sir," Candice said with a laugh. "I can't wait to hear all the gossip."

"How do you mean?" Nathan looked at her.

"Well, not many people know you own more than fifty percent of Daddy's business. Does this mean that Mr. Colbert will be in business with Daddy, too?"

"It sure does."

She grinned. "Good. That's going to take some pressure off me."

Nathan frowned and Candice laughed again.

"It's just that since mother is considered the top woman in society here, I'm a big embarrassment to her because I'm single. She thinks because she's rich, some man will eventually want to marry me."

"Why, Candice…" Wilbur started.

"Don't even say it, Wilbur Colbert. I wouldn't marry a mouse like you if you were the last man on earth. Don't you realize I know your aunt and my mother arranged for you to be my date tonight?"

Beverly looked at Candice and spoke. "I'm sorry, dear. I guess I was wrong to think you'd be embarrassed by not having a date."

"Humph." Candice stuck up her nose. "And you thought I'd be proud to walk into the ballroom with a man who barely comes to my shoulders?"

Wilbur stood and threw his napkin on the table. "Well, if that's the way everyone feels about me, I'm leaving."

Lyman's voice was harsh when he said, "Sit down and shut up, Wilbur. It doesn't matter the circumstances, you've asked Miss Maxmillion to this party and you will escort her."

"And if I don't?"

"Then return to my house and pack your bags. You may as well head back to St. Louis to work in the general store with my brother."

"But he sent me here to better myself."

"Then take advantage of it. It's your decision."

Wilbur meekly sat.

Nathan looked at Beverly as if nothing had happened. "This is for you, Mrs. Colbert. Next to my wife, you're going to become the person all of Galveston society is going to look up to. I want to be sure you're up to the job."

"What do you mean?" Beverly stared at him.

"It means that when next fall rolls around, people will be saying that you're a nobody if you aren't invited to Mrs. Colbert's soirée."

"I…You mean…I…"

"For heaven's sake, Mother, calm down. You've always wanted to be in the prime of things, and now you are, thanks to Nathan and Daddy." Rowena reached over and took Kyle's hand. "While we're at it, I want you to know that Kyle and I are going to marry as soon as he's able to start his new job on the ranch. I'll be moving there with him."

"Oh, my." Beverly looked as if she might faint.

"Don't you dare pass out, Beverly," Lyman demanded. "We've got a lot to celebrate tonight."

"That's true." Nathan pushed back his plate as Flo and Alvin brought in dessert. "I only have one more thing to say."

Again all eyes turned to him. "Lyman, I think your first job is to find me a driver I can trust. You know the people and this town and I think I'm going to need one right away."

"Why's that, Nathan?"

"Ryan Phillips has been with me for a long time. He's allowed me to invest a lot of his money and in so doing, he's quite a wealthy man.

I think he's ready to settle down, take another job and share that wealth with a special woman."

"Really, honey?" Valissa looked at him. This was something Nathan hadn't told her. "Who? Do we know her?"

"Oh, yes, we know her." He dipped into his creamy parfait. "I may have done myself a disservice by letting the help know I can make them rich."

"How?" Valissa asked again.

"Flo and Alvin asked me to invest some of their money. Lord, I hate the thoughts of losing her as my cook. She will be impossible to replace."

~ * ~

It was after midnight when the big black carriage pulled away from the Maxmillion mansion with only Nathan and Valissa inside. He pulled her into his arms and laughed. "I think we made quite a splash, don't you, darling?"

"I'm not sure I like making splashes." She laughed.

"Oh, I thought when I first came to Heartsong, you were upset because you weren't invited to this party."

"At the time, I was. I guess it had never dawned on me how tiring they could be."

"Oh? Did I dance you too much?"

"No. I could have danced with you all night. It was those women who shunned me a few weeks ago, then tonight kept coming up to me and gushing such sweet things about our marriage and about the clothes I had on. Even about how wonderful it is that Kyle is out of trouble."

"So, being in the limelight of society isn't really your cup of tea?"

"No, it's not. I think we may spend the fall season on that new ranch of yours."

He chuckled and pulled her tighter. "Or maybe the old one?"

"I don't think I want to spend a season with your stepmother."

"There's not much danger of that. One of the hands coming to the Circle S told me that she's about ready to sell out. I'm sending Lyman to Fort Worth next week to buy it. She won't know until it's all over who the new owner is."

"Then what will you do with the Circle S?"

"Who says I can't own two ranches? Besides, I think I'll have an offer to buy that one soon. Maybe two."

"Oh?"

"Kyle wants to live away from Galveston and I think Rowena does, too. Wouldn't it be nice to have them only a few miles from here?"

"Yes, but you said two offers."

"Phillips is a good rancher. I think he intends to settle on a ranch with his bride as soon as they're hitched."

"Who in the world is he going to marry?"

"Candice Maxmillion, of course."

Valissa starred at him.

"Get that look off your face and let's quit talking about other people. I want to make love to my wife."

Valissa gasped. "Not here in the carriage."

"Why not? We're married."

"But Nathan. Can't you wait until we get home?"

He frowned. "I guess I can, but why should I?"

"Because…Well, just because."

"My dear, are you always going to make me wait until we get to Valissa's home at Heartsong when I want to make love to you?" He kissed her ear and let his lips trickle down her neck.

She snuggled closer to him. "I think love should always be made at home, and just to let you know, I'll always think of Heartsong as one of my homes."

"One of your homes?" His hands began to rove over her body.

"Nathan, my love, anywhere I am with you becomes Valissa's home." She gave him a seductive look and added, "Even this carriage."

He grinned and yelled in a booming voice, "Take the long way back to Heartsong, Phillips."

"Yes, sir," came the faint reply.

Nathan then turned all his attention to Valissa as she surrendered in his arms.

Meet

Agnes Alexander

Agnes Alexander, author of six western historical romances, is the pen name of mystery and romantic suspense author Lynette Hall Hampton. She lives in her home state of North Carolina, but loves to travel, especially in the western states. She loves to hear from her fans and she can be contacted though her website AgnesAlexander.com.

www.ingramcontent.com/pod-product-compliance
Lightning Source LLC
Chambersburg PA
CBHW072256130726
47910CB00012B/2029